"Audacious … witty and fun." ALASTAIR MABBOTT, *Herald*

"Effortless … Smart, funny and all-round good company, wherever Shona goes, readers will eagerly follow." *Scotsman*

"I couldn't wait to be reunited with this character. I utterly love her … More, more, more, please!" LYNNE TRUSS

"A delightful addition to the ranks of comic crime, mixing sharp observation with a lightness of touch." LAURA WILSON, *Guardian*

"Jane Austen stylings and Stella Gibbons satirical wit." *Scotsman*

"Every bit as light-hearted, level-headed, inventive, hilarious, and altogether enchanting as its heroine." *Kirkus,* STARRED REVIEW

"Marvellous… Readers will appreciate the skill with which Wojtas mirrors Spark's style." *Publishers Weekly,* STARRED REVIEW

"I loved this book. Shona is a unique sleuth whose mission made for most entertaining reading." ALEX GRAY

"Knowing, original and very funny." SIMON BRETT

"A carefully and delightfully constructed romp in the tradition of Gogol and of Wodehouse." NORTHWORDS NOW

"*Anna Karenina* written by P.G. Wodehouse." LINDA CRACKNELL

"A thrilling and fast-paced tale … written with verve, lightness of touch and joie de vivre … unadulterated fun." SCOTS WHAY HAE

"The crème de la crème of crime fiction debuts." ALLAN GUTHRIE

"Clever, witty, and brain-tickling." RAVEN CRIME READS

"Laugh-out-loud funny … a real charmer." LIVE AND DEADLY

Also by Olga Wojtas:

Miss Blaine's Prefect and the Golden Samovar
Miss Blaine's Prefect and the Vampire Menace

To Gina,
with warmest wishes

MISS BLAINE'S
PREFECT
and the
WEIRD
SISTERS

Olga Wojtas

Olga Wojtas

CONTRABAND 🔒

Published by Contraband
An imprint of Saraband,
3 Clairmont Gardens
Glasgow, G3 7LW

ISBN: 9781913393380

10 9 8 7 6 5 4 3 2 1

Printed and bound in Great Britain by Clays Ltd, Elcograf S.p.A

For Kate

One

I like stories where people get turned into things. Gregor Samsa, turned into a gigantic insect. Daphne, turned into a tree. Zeus, turned into a cuckoo. Echo, turned into an echo.

You're immediately intrigued, imagining what it must be like to find yourself transformed, reading on to find out what happens. That's because it's a story. I can tell you, it's a lot less intriguing and a lot more alarming when it actually happens to you.

A moment before, I had been Shona McMonagle, former pupil of the Marcia Blaine School for Girls in Edinburgh, proudly getting on with my time-travelling mission arranged by Miss Blaine herself. It's true there had been some confusion about my identity thanks to eleventh-century Gaelic, but that's not relevant right now. The point is that I was here, all five foot six of me, maybe slightly heavier than expected for my height, but it's mainly muscle since I work out a lot. Being fifty-something is no excuse to take it easy.

So there I was, me, Shona, and the next moment I was still me, Shona, except I was now a mouse. Mice are small. And vulnerable. A huge owl was wheeling round in the night sky and heading straight towards me. It was moving fast, and I was in open country. There was no chance of outrunning it. My only hope was to try to explain things.

As a human, I have a good rapport with dogs and wolves, but that's a very different dynamic. Could mice and owls communicate? The predator was about two feet away now, its talons spread to strike, its beak opening to crush the back of my neck. I had to give it a try.

"Don't eat me!" I squeaked. "I'm not a mouse, I'm a librarian."

The owl skidded to a halt and eyeballed me before demanding, "What's a librarian when it's at home?"

I drew myself up to my full three inches. "Librarianship is a vocation. I am a librarian whether I'm at home, in Morningside Library, at the gym or here."

"That's all very well," said the owl, "but I don't see why it should stop me eating you."

"Because I do an extremely important job," I said.

It looked sceptical. I realised it was going to be difficult to explain the importance of reading to an owl. I wondered if I should tell it about my tireless efforts to prevent anyone from borrowing a copy of *The Prime of Miss Jean Brodie*. Strictly speaking, that's not part of my job description, but Muriel Spark's oeuvre is such a foul calumny against my alma mater that I will not allow the public to have access to it. That's the trouble with fiction: too many people believe it's true.

I was just about to start explaining how the school had been misrepresented when I saw the owl had backed up and was preparing to launch another attack. I wondered whether Miss Blaine would accept my being eaten by an owl as an excuse for failing in my mission. From what I knew of her, the answer was no. I only had little legs, but I was going to have to make a dash for it.

And then there was a sudden sound behind me and the owl veered away and disappeared into the night sky. I looked round. When you're a mouse, there's one thing worse than an owl, and that's a cat. This was a cat.

But I really must stop flashing forward. That's exactly the sort of tricksy thing Mrs Spark does in her writing, and when you're in the future one moment, then in the present, which of course now seems to be the past, you've no idea where you are. And I find things quite challenging enough since our school's founder,

Marcia Blaine herself, started sending me on time-travelling missions. Since my transformation into a mouse stemmed from a series of events beginning with a visit from Miss Blaine, that's where I should begin as well.

I was at my desk in Morningside Library when a figure appeared in front of me, clutching a heavy volume.

"William Shakespeare!" she declaimed as she let it go. It thudded on to the desk, scattering my book reservation notes and sending a box of paper clips flying.

Everyone looked round, glaring. The library is no longer the temple of silence it was in my young day, but the noise is more usually small children singing "The Wheels on the Bus" rather than adults shouting the odds about the Swan of Avon. I had to remove Miss Blaine before there were complaints.

"Let's go upstairs for a wee cup of tea," I said.

"I don't want a cup of tea, I want a disclaimer," she snapped.

"Nevertheless," I said, this being one of the Founder's favourite words, "the seats are comfier upstairs." This wasn't entirely true, but our Morningside regulars, sensing an impending row, were edging closer like ravening tigers.

"Very well. But bring that thing with you." She gestured towards the book on my desk and marched off in the direction of the stairs, the ravening tigers suddenly pretending to be engrossed in the shelves nearest to them. I picked up *The Complete Works of William Shakespeare* and followed her upstairs. Usually she was sounding off about *The Prime of Miss Jean Brodie*. Not that I blamed her for a second – I sound off about it myself. I'm not afraid to say that Mrs Spark did a very wrong thing in writing such a scandalously lewd book about our irreproachable school. But Miss Blaine being aggrieved by Shakespeare, that was new. I organised a cup of tea and some Bourbon biscuits in the hope of calming her down.

She took a sip and then said, "I understand there is a series on the televisual device entitled *The Crown*, a historical drama that purports to be about the royal family."

"I understand that as well," I said cautiously.

"And there have been calls for this series to have a disclaimer explaining that it is a work of fiction."

"I don't think they're going to do that," I said even more cautiously.

"What they do or do not do is of no interest to me," she said. "I never watch the televisual device. What I wish for is a disclaimer *here*." She thumped her hand down on the book, which I had laid on the table. Tea spilled over into the saucer.

"You want the complete works of William Shakespeare to have a disclaimer?" I asked.

"Are you mad, girl? Why on earth should I want the complete works of William Shakespeare to have a disclaimer?"

Miss Blaine was normally very sharp. But she was also very old – at least two hundred by my reckoning – and perhaps a little bit of confusion was only to be expected.

"Help yourself to a Bourbon," I said sympathetically.

"Kindly focus on the matter before you, the disclaimer," she snapped. "This is no time to be distracted by biscuits."

I wondered whether the time travelling was getting to Miss Blaine so that she couldn't remember what she had said from one moment to the next.

She grabbed the book and began flicking through it. "I have no objection to this ... or this. *The Taming of the Shrew*, a comedy, forsooth! But let it pass. No, here..." Her finger jabbed at a page. "This is where we must have a disclaimer."

"*Macbeth*?" I said. "But why?"

"Because," she said, picking up a Bourbon with such force that it crumbled between her fingers, "it is arrant nonsense. Macbeth and Lady Macbeth conspiring to murder King Duncan so that Macbeth can take over the throne – complete fabrication. It was Duncan who started a fight with Macbeth, who killed him perfectly properly in battle."

"I know that," I said. "Macbeth was one of the best kings the Scots have had, and Lady Macbeth was a devout, pragmatic

4

woman who was instrumental in organising a pilgrimage to Rome to see the Pope."

Miss Blaine made a phlegmy choking sound, "Grrrch." Some of the Bourbon crumbs must have got into her airways. I sprang up to thump her on the back.

She fixed me with a look and made the noise again. "Not Lady Macbeth," she said.

"Ah," I said, working out that she was not choking but speaking. "The real Macbeth's real wife, Gruoch."

"Calling them Macbeth and Lady Macbeth is itself a travesty. It was not the practice of Scotswomen to take their husband's surname until the nineteenth century. And the area was Gaelic-speaking. Macbeth's name was Mac Bethad in his own time, meaning 'son of life', now modernised to MacBheatha." She fixed me with a gimlet stare. "Do you have the Gaelic?"

"Of course," I said.

Her look changed to one of faint approval, and I decided to chance disagreeing with her.

"Miss Blaine, Shakespeare's plays are works of fiction. You might as well complain about his portrayal of Antony and Cleopatra, or Hamlet, or Henry IV Part One."

"I leave that to the Romans, the Egyptians, the Danes and the English," she said. "What concerns me is the misrepresentation of our Scottish heritage. You, having had the finest education in the world in the school I founded, may understand the difference between fact and fiction. But not everyone is so fortunate. There are others who went to lesser academies who will take *Macbeth* for fact. That is why a disclaimer is required."

She produced a fountain pen, grabbed a spare sheet of blank paper and proceeded to write in elegant copperplate, "The story, characters and incidents portrayed herein are fictitious. No identification with actual persons (living or deceased), places and buildings is intended or should be inferred."

She wafted the paper around for a while to let the ink dry, and then shoved it across the table to me.

5

"There. Get this printed up and inserted in every copy of Shakespeare containing the so-called Scottish play," she said.

I didn't like the sound of that. But I also didn't like to refuse a direct order from the Founder, so I just smiled in an agreeable sort of way.

"William Shakespeare, forsooth!" she said. "He has the occasional clever turn of phrase, but he's not a patch on our Scottish playwrights." She gave a reminiscent sigh. "I remember a gentleman friend taking me to the Playhouse in Edinburgh to see the premiere of *Douglas* by the Reverend John Home."

When she started the sentence, I thought she meant the Edinburgh Playhouse where I once won the Sing-a-Long-a-the-Sound-of-Music fancy dress competition dressed as a brown paper package tied up with strings. But by the end of the sentence, I realised she was talking about Edinburgh's first public theatre beside the Royal Mile, which premiered *Douglas* in 1757. And if she had been with a gentleman friend, she must be closer to three hundred than two hundred. I looked on her with new respect.

"A truly transcendent experience," she said. "In the middle of the performance, I was so moved that I leaped to my feet and cried, 'Whaur's yer Wullie Shakespeare noo?'"

She must have been very moved indeed to lapse into the demotic.

"When Mr Shakespeare wrote *Macbeth*, he was being nothing more than a great big sook," she added. "One moment, he was sucking up to Queen Elizabeth, murderer of our own dear Mary, Queen of Scots. The next, he was sucking up to Elizabeth's successor, James VI and I."

"James was Mary, Queen of Scots' son," I offered. "It served Elizabeth right that he got to succeed her."

"Heavens, girl, James was a dreadful, dreadful man."

"Did you know him?" I asked with interest, and was nearly carbonised by the blazing look she turned on me.

"Just how old do you think I am?" she demanded.

"You're obviously in your prime, Miss Blaine, but I'm sorry,

I've never been that good with ages," I said.

She harrumphed a bit, but seemed mollified. "I know he was a dreadful man because of my historical studies," she said. "He was King of Scots in Edinburgh, but when he became King of England as well, he moved to London. Is that appropriate behaviour?"

She looked meaningfully at the cupboard where I keep all of the copies of *The Prime of Miss Jean Brodie* under lock and key to stop borrowers finding them.

"Mrs Spark also moved from Edinburgh to London," she said.

"Incomprehensible," I said.

"And," she went on, "King James didn't like witches. Never trust a man who doesn't like witches."

"I won't," I promised.

"Witches are wise women," she said. "They are our sisters. We must resist patriarchal oppression wherever it is found." She picked up another Bourbon biscuit and crunched into it. "Mr Shakespeare pandered to the king's prejudices by presenting the witches as dark and evil creatures. Were I as old as you seem to think, I would have brought a class action against him."

"But you're not a witch," I objected.

"I," she said, "am a wise woman."

I could scarcely argue with that.

"And I could do with another cup of tea," she added. That was scarcely surprising, given the amount that had ended up in the saucer.

I went back to the kitchenette and switched on the kettle, pondering my strategy about the disclaimer. I could scarcely stick the note in the books with something sticky: no librarian could bring her or himself to deface any of our stock. Paperclips were a no-no for the same reason. I could put a loose slip of paper in each book, but it would inevitably fall out. I was afraid of Miss Blaine's reaction if she found any of the books on the shelves without a disclaimer, so there seemed only one solution. Remove the books from the shelves.

They could be available on special request, at which point I could give the borrower a verbal rundown of the true history of Macbeth. The problem was where to hold them. My locked cupboard, keeping *The Prime of Miss Jean Brodie* from the reading public for their own good, was already bulging at the seams. Perhaps the storeroom on the ground floor where we kept our coats, although I would have to put my coat over the books to hide them from my colleagues. Dorothy in particular would simply put them back on the shelves – I suspect she's the one who keeps re-ordering *The Prime of Miss Jean Brodie*.

I rinsed Miss Blaine's cup and saucer, feeling much more cheerful. But before the kettle had boiled, I began to feel the initial abdominal twinges that meant I was about to time travel.

Miss Blaine was going to have to wait a wee while for her refill.

Two

I was lying on rough ground in the dark, and I was very itchy.
I patted myself down and found I was wearing a coarsely spun
long-sleeved jerkin and a pair of breeks. Despite the discomfort, I
was pleased about the breeks. My missions often involve running,
jumping and martial arts, and that can be very tricky if you're
wearing a fancy frock.

A wiggle of my toes confirmed that I still had on my trusty Doc
Martens. I was well prepared for whatever my mission might be.
It was an honour to have been chosen by Miss Blaine to be a time
traveller, not confining the Blaine ethos of making the world a
better place to the twenty-first century. But right now, I had no
idea where I was and why, and I really felt that advance instructions, written or verbal, would be a help. I didn't dwell on this
thought for long, however. The last time I had done so, I felt a
sharp pain in my foot, despite the DMs, as though someone had
trodden on it very hard. I suspect Miss Blaine considers working
out what the mission is to be part of the mission itself.

The ghastly abdominal pains were beginning to ease up. I was
now able to stand, but I stayed where I was, gathering information about my whereabouts. I was indoors, but I was pretty sure I
wasn't in a house. I ran my hand across the ground. Uneven rock.
I was in a cave. Some way away, I could see burning logs, with a
large black cauldron placed on top of them. The mingled smoke
and steam gave me the impression of looking through one of the
net curtains so popular in Morningside windows.

And I could hear a strangely discordant chanting: it began

in catalectic trochaic tetrameter, DUM-da, DUM-da, DUM-da, DUM, then DUM-da, DUM-da, DUM-da, DUM, but then there was a rhythm that I couldn't work out at all, perhaps something to do with contemporary jazz.

The voices sounded female. It was time to find out more. I commando-crawled towards the cauldron, using my arms to pull myself forward while keeping my tummy and legs on the ground.

As I got closer, I could hear better.

"Round about the cauldron go," chanted a voice.

"See the poisoned entrails glow," chanted a second.

"I'm not touching any entrails," came a third. "Especially if they're glowing."

"Then chuck in the toe of frog," the first voice chanted.

"Go and get it, off you jog," chanted the second.

"This is a wind-up, isn't it?" came the third voice. "Do frogs even have toes?"

"Eight toes front, and ten toes back," chanted the first voice.

"Frogs go ribbit, ducks go quack," chanted the second.

"You just won't let it go, will you?" said the third voice. "So I made a mistake. It was a momentary lapse. I do actually know the difference between a frog and a duck."

I had crawled close enough to see the three figures who were slowly circling the cauldron. They were all wearing black cloaks, they all had button noses, and they all had Cupid's bow lips. The first had hair as black as her cloak, plaited in a circlet on top of her head. The second had silver hair brushed upwards from her forehead in a stylish quiff. The third had straggly fair hair that looked as though it hadn't been combed for a month. I warmed to her. Not only did she not talk in trochaic tetrameter, but she obviously had better things to do than care about her appearance. A large black cat rubbed itself against her ankles.

What puzzled me was that they sounded very like the three witches in Shakespeare's *Macbeth*, or at least two of them did. But as Miss Blaine had rightly said, the play wasn't an accurate representation of what had happened. The bit about the witches was pure sensationalism. Although Miss Blaine had also said that witches were wise women, and I wasn't entirely sure this lot merited that description.

The black cat suddenly arched its back and hissed, looking straight at me.

The three witches stopped their circling.

"By the pricking of my thumbs, something freakish this way comes," said the black-haired first one.

I got to my feet. "I'm not remotely freakish," I said. "I'm from Edinburgh."

Now that I was close to the light of the fire, I could see that my jerkin and breeks were made of hodden grey, and that my DMs were clarted in mud, masking their twenty-first-century origins.

The silver-haired second witch gave the fair-haired third witch a shove. "One more spell gone wrong for Mo? Did you bring this, yes, or no?"

"Don't blame me," the third protested. "I didn't do a thing."

"That's right, just deny it flat," snorted the first one. "Like when you called up the cat."

The third one suddenly looked shifty, and glanced down at the black cat, which glanced back up at her. An instant later, she recovered herself. "I told you, I didn't call up the cat. It just appeared one day when you were out. The same thing must have happened here. Probably something to do with atmospheric pressure."

I wasn't going to get very far if they thought I was something that had been conjured up by mistake. I needed them to think of me as an equal.

"How can you possibly think any of you could be capable of summoning me," I scoffed. "I was sent here by an all-powerful sorceress."

The three witches clutched each other in alarm.

"Hecate's sent this thing here?" said the first one.

Hecate, ruler of all witches, so presumably in charge of this coven.

"Not Hecate," I interrupted before the second witch could complete the first one's rhyme. "Much more powerful than her. The crème de la crème of sorceresses, Marcia Blaine."

They exchanged confused glances.

"Never heard of her," said the third one.

"Exactly," I said. "Being the crème de la crème, she deals only with the crème de la crème. She wouldn't bother with the likes of you. Speaking of which, who are you?"

"I'm in charge here – my name's Ina," said the first one. She pointed to the second one. "This one is my sister Mina."

"And I'm Mo," said the third one. "I don't rhyme."

Ina, Mina and Mo. Ina with the black plaits crowning her head. Mina with the silver quiff. Mo who didn't care about her appearance or trochaic tetrameter.

Ina went on, "As I'm sure you must have guessed, I'm the eldest and the best."

She indicated Mina with a disparaging nod. "*She* says, if you can believe her, that she'd like to be a scriever." That fine Scots word for a writer. Under my editorship, the school magazine referred to all of the writers as scrievers, so I was immediately on Mina's side.

"And why shouldn't you?" I said encouragingly to the disparaged one.

"Witching doesn't give me time for writing sci-fi, romps or crime. No one ever gets to switch, if they're picked out as a witch."

I could understand that being a witch was a vocation, like librarianship, but this sounded much too constricting. There always has to be room for other things.

"You really should try to write every day," I told Mina. I was about to advise her to stay up late and write at night when everyone was asleep, but then I reflected that witches probably did most of their work at night. "There's no right or wrong. Just get into a routine that suits you," I said.

She gave me a thoughtful nod.

I turned to Ina. "What about you? Finding the witchcraft

fulfilling without the need to try something different?"

"Being a witch is just sublime. Every day I get to rhyme," she said.

I was going to tell her that Robert Burns didn't have to be a witch in order to rhyme, but if she thought the first was necessary for the second, who was I to interfere?

"And Mo? Happy in your work?"

This time, both Ina and Mina laughed rather unkindly.

"Little sis? You must be kidding," said Ina. "There's no spell would do her bidding."

"That's true. She's a total prat," said Mina. "Thinks a newt's eye's ear of bat."

"That is not true!" shouted Mo. "I keep telling you, I knew what I was doing, I just sneezed, and that's why it went wrong. Anyway, the duck seemed quite happy."

So they really were sisters. Family dynamics can be very awkward, and I felt quite sorry for Mo, having her two older siblings ganging up on her. I also felt quite thirsty after the time travelling, especially being in such a smoky atmosphere.

"I wonder, could I have something to drink?" I asked.

They seemed quite abashed that they hadn't offered me refreshments, and turned to the cauldron, which was bubbling away. I didn't like the look of it and I didn't like the smell of it.

For the first time, I noticed that I had a belt round my waist, with a pouch hanging from it. Miss Blaine had explained to me that my time-travelling missions were pro bono, but she had always ensured that I had somewhere to stay, and adequate provisions. I opened the pouch and a vastly more pleasant smell wafted up to my nostrils.

"Thank you, Miss Blaine," I murmured. It was a bag of tea leaves, my own special blend of Darjeeling and Earl Grey.

Tea. Miss Blaine. I had been making tea for Miss Blaine. When I suddenly found myself transported, the kettle hadn't yet boiled. What if it had now come to the boil but failed to switch itself off? It was a pretty old kettle, and the switch could be a bit dodgy.

13

What if it boiled dry and set the kitchenette on fire? And the entire library went up in flames before the fire brigade could save it, because it was full of combustible material, i.e. books?

"Do any of you have a spell that would stop a library from burning down in the twenty-first century?" I asked.

They looked at me blankly.

"What's a library?" asked Mo.

"It's a place where they keep books – the things that scrievers write," I said.

Mina perked up at this, but didn't volunteer any spells.

"And what's the twenty-first century?" Mo continued.

"It's a long way in the future," I said.

I was going to lose whatever superiority I had if they thought I needed their help.

"I was testing you," I said imperiously. "I see you're not very good."

Ina and Mina shuffled their feet and looked at the ground, but Mo was proving tougher than I thought.

"What can you do?" she demanded.

"I can make a potion, a magical draught," I said, producing the bag of tea leaves.

They wrinkled their noses at the scent.

"I need a fresh cauldron, full of boiling water," I went on.

They disappeared into a darkened recess in the cave, and I took advantage of their absence to send a thought to Miss Blaine, just in case the kettle had malfunctioned – *follow the nearest escape route to the assembly point* – but there was no indication that I'd succeeded. Perhaps there was no signal because I was in a cave. I would try again when I was outside.

There was a clanking sound of metal against rock, and Ina, Mina and Mo reappeared, followed by a large cauldron walking along like something out of a Disney cartoon. It settled on the ground in front of me, looking mercifully free of eyes of newts or anything else unsavoury. Ina snapped her fingers, and the cauldron filled with water. Mina snapped hers, and flaming logs appeared underneath it.

I could see Mo felt left out but was trying not to show it, studying her fingernails and singing tunelessly under her breath. The black cat wandered up to her and rubbed itself against her legs.

"This is a complicated spell," I said. "I'll need assistance. Mo, would you help?"

Ina and Mina looked set to argue, and I added, "The last thing we need is poetry. That could ruin everything." Mo smiled gratefully.

The water was bubbling away now. I was uncomfortably aware that it might be doing exactly the same in the Morningside Library kitchenette, but I tried to put that out of my mind.

"The water has to be just below boiling point," I told Mo. "Switch the heat off."

She snapped her fingers and the logs stopped flaming.

I passed the bag of tea leaves to Mo so that she could take a handful, and took a handful myself. I waited for the bubbling to die down before saying, "On the count of three – one, two, three."

We both hurled the tea into the cauldron at the same time. Ina and Mina screwed up their faces and stuck their fingers in their ears. After a while, they took their fingers out of their ears and opened their eyes.

Ina said, "Nothing's happened, what a blow. That's what comes of asking Mo."

"Mo did exactly what was required of her," I said. "It may look as though nothing is happening, but the potion is steeping. That is how it reaches its strength. Look – it's changing colour already."

They peered through the smoke into the cauldron to see that the clear water was turning brown.

"We need to leave it for a couple of minutes longer, and in the meantime, I want one more ingredient," I said.

Ina grabbed Mina's arm. "Adder's fork? Or blindworm's sting?"

Mina shook her head. "Lizard's leg. Or howlet's wing."

"None of the above," I said. "Milk."

"Sow's milk? Hedgehog's? Tiger's? Whale's? Porcupine's? Alpaca's? Snail's?" asked Ina.

Before Mina could start, I said firmly, "Cow's."

But she still had something to say. "Cow's milk? That's a tough old test. Don't be scared, Mo – do your best."

From Mo's reaction, I deduced that conjuring up cow's milk was one of the easier spells. A second later, a jug of milk was in my hand.

"And some goblets," I commanded. I didn't bother asking for china teacups. If these really were the three witches who accosted Macbeth, then we were in the first half of the eleventh century, when porcelain was in its infancy in China, and completely unknown in Europe.

Mo snapped her fingers again, and four gold goblets floated in front of me. I poured a little milk into each.

"Now I need to add the potion," I said. "Is there a ladle I could use?"

A ladle materialised from nowhere, plunged itself into the cauldron, emerged dripping, and delivered just the right amount of tea to each goblet. I can do magic tricks, but at this moment, I really wanted to learn witchcraft.

Ina, Mina and Mo clicked their fingers, and three goblets sped in their direction. I grabbed the fourth from mid-air.

"Drink it," I said, and they began gulping it down.

"Not in a oner," I said severely. "Sniff it first. Savour it. Experience it."

I demonstrated, inhaling the wonderful floral notes of the Darjeeling, mingling with the bracing citrus sharpness of the Earl Grey. Then I tasted the refreshing combination of tangy bergamot and sweet muskiness. The abdominal pain had virtually disappeared, and the tea made me feel very much better.

Ina sniffed at the goblet, took another sip, and looked about her.

"Tell me, this peculiar brew, what is it supposed to do?" she asked.

"It's full of antioxidants, so it's great for your immune system, it reduces blood pressure, and it may well combat heart disease," I said.

They looked seriously unimpressed, so I tried again. "It makes you more alert, and better able to concentrate. That in turn improves the efficacy of your spells, which enhances your reputation."

Ina nudged Mina. "This could help us with the boss."

"It might stop her getting cross," said Mina.

"Hecate?" I said. "What's she cross about?"

"She's always cross," said Mo. "She's horrible to us. She's horrible to everybody. But if we could show her some really great spells, she might ease up on us a bit."

"You, a spell that's really great? Making frogs disintegrate?" scoffed Ina.

"It didn't disintegrate – it just turned into a duck," objected Mo. She turned to me. "Does your sorceress drink this stuff?"

"All the time," I said. "That's why she's all-powerful." Once again I imagined the kettle boiling dry in the library kitchenette, which wasn't a good thing to think about.

Mo turned to the black cat at her heels "Here, Hemlock," she said, "come and try it."

She put her goblet down on the rough ground. The black cat sniffed at it without enthusiasm but then prowled over to the jug I had laid down, and began lapping up the milk.

Ina suddenly put down her goblet as well and said, "By the pricking of my ear, someone new will soon appear."

The three of them gazed through the smoke towards the entrance of the cave. The cat took the opportunity to reconsider and began slurping their abandoned tea. I kept on drinking mine, grateful for the refreshing brew after my journey, and hoping it would make me more alert and better able to concentrate.

Mina, raising her arm dramatically, said, "Now the countdown has begun – show yourself, in three – two – one."

A big hairy Highlander appeared at the entrance to the cave, stooping to get in. He was a terrifying figure, muscular and bearded. He wore a dark woollen tunic and trousers, and what looked worryingly like a complete bearskin as a cloak. I could imagine he'd killed the bear himself with his bare, as it were, hands. He wasn't the sort of bloke you'd want to meet on a dark night, and from the glimpse of the outside world beyond his vast bulk, I could see the sun was already setting.

Better to find out more about him before he found out about me. I slipped back into a darker part of the cave.

"Hello, ladies. How are you today?" he said in a meek, respectful voice that didn't go at all with his appearance.

Ina stepped forward. "Hail to thee, the Thane of Glamis. Come and have a few wee drams."

Mina was behind her. "Hail to thee, the Thane of Cawdor. Umm…" As she looked round for inspiration, her gaze fell on the second-best cauldron, and she ended triumphantly, "We've got flavoured boiling water."

Mo peeped round the pair of them and waved. "Hello, Macbeth. Hail to thee, that shalt be king hereafter."

"Oh dear," said Macbeth. "Has she been talking to you about it as well?"

This was interesting for several reasons. First, Macbeth, as expected, was speaking in Gaelic. The witches were continuing to speak in English, but he and they all understood one another perfectly well. I wondered whether I was hearing them in English because it was my first language. The witches must be equipped with some sort of simultaneous translation system. And to think we call this the Dark Ages.

Second, the "Thane of Glamis, Thane of Cawdor" business was highly dubious. The eleventh-century *Orygynale Cronykil* says that Macbeth was Thane of Cromarty and then Thane of Moray. Of course, it's questionable how good a source it is when the title's so badly spelled. And I could see that it would be tricky even for someone as poetic as Ina to find a rhyme for "Cromarty".

Third, who was "she"? When "she" was mentioned, the witches had all exchanged uneasy glances.

Macbeth sighed. "So fair and foul a day I have not seen."

I snorted. I couldn't help it. "Come off it," I said. "This is Scotland. Four seasons in one day." I spoke Gaelic so that Macbeth would understand me, since the witches had their interpreting skills.

Macbeth had taken a step backwards at the sound of my voice and was clutching the bearskin cloak round him in a protective way.

"Is this your familiar?" he asked the witches.

"Scarcely familiar, since we've only just met," I said, stepping forward. "I'm Shona McMonagle."

I said my name without thinking, and realised too late that in speaking to a Gael, I should have made my first name more recognisable as "Shonnet". And I had given the masculine "mac" form of my surname rather than the feminine "nic". In the eleventh century, it would confuse him to find a woman with a man's name.

He didn't look confused. "Seonaidh MacMhonaidhghil," he repeated, which sounded very much like "Shona McMonagle" but meant "Johnny, son of the white moor". And then he said, "Are you a fool?"

It was a very rude remark, but he made it quite politely, as though he was genuinely seeking information. I still thought that making an issue of my elementary mistake deserved a sharp reply. And one from Shakespeare came to mind. Miss Blaine might not be a fan of the bard, but even she conceded that he could come up with a good turn of phrase.

I fixed Macbeth with a stare. "Better a witty fool than a foolish wit."

"Very good," said Macbeth with a shy smile, which I accepted as an apology. "May I ask who your master is?"

I took this to mean my employer, which is the City of Edinburgh Council, but right now I wasn't employed in the library.

Miss Blaine doesn't pay, so I wasn't employed by her either.

"I work on my own head," I said.

"Sorry?" said Macbeth.

"It's a Gaelic expression," I explained. "It means freelance."

"Really? Would you like to come and work for me as my fool?"

I had thought he was being rude when he called me a fool. But he meant a jester, an entertainer. I could scarcely contain my excitement. Our historians all believe that jesters weren't a thing until the thirteenth century, and here we were in Scotland leading the way two hundred years earlier. When I got back to the library, I would have to write a monograph about it.

And since, so far, there was no indication of what my mission might be, working for Macbeth would be a good opportunity to assess the situation further. But I couldn't imagine Miss Blaine taking kindly to my making money on her time.

"What would the remuneration be?" I asked.

"You'd be fed, and allowed to sleep indoors," said Macbeth.

"Done," I said. I thought it would be no bad thing to show that I appreciated the appointment.

"I am as happy as a shoe," I said.

"What?" said Macbeth.

"It's a Gaelic expression," I explained.

"Really? How happy is a shoe?" he asked.

"Very happy," I said. "Obviously. Otherwise I would just have said 'I'm happy.'"

"Then I'm as happy as a shoe as well," he said. "Go up to the castle, and announce yourself to my wife."

After he said "wife" he made a vomiting sound. Under other circumstances, I would have called him out on it, but remembering my conversation with Miss Blaine, I understood that he wasn't disrespecting his better half.

"Gruoch," I repeated.

"She'll be thrilled. The king's coming to stay, and with you, she'll be able to provide him with some top-class entertainment. Tell her to fix you up with a pig's bladder; you can hit the king over the head with it, and that'll be really funny."

"The king," I said cautiously. "I've forgotten his name just for the moment. Remind me."

"Duncan," said Macbeth. "He's actually been king for six years now." He was still speaking with his customary politeness, but I felt there was an implied rebuke that I didn't know the king's name after all this time.

"I've only just arrived in these parts," I said curtly.

"Of course, of course. Being a freelance fool must keep you on the move."

The significance of what he had said suddenly struck me. Duncan had been on the throne for six years. And in the sixth year of his reign, in 1040, he was killed by Macbeth.

"All the travelling makes me lose track of time," I said. "Just checking, is this the year of Our Lord one thousand and two twenties?" I might have inadvertently misspoken my name, but at least I had remembered that the Gaels counted in a way that was all their own.

"That's right," said Macbeth with his shy smile. "Well done."

"And when you say the king's coming to stay with you, that's Duncan, then?"

He frowned slightly. "Yes, King Duncan, the king. That's what I've been saying." Then his expression cleared. "Ah, I see – you're being a fool. I didn't realise for a moment."

"So I had you fooled," I said.

"Oh, that's very good," he said. "Very clever wordplay. If you keep up that standard tonight, the king will be tremendously impressed. Anyway, I'd better go and catch a few goats or stags or something for the banquet. You go and introduce yourself to what the Sassenachs call the trouble and strife." He looked guiltily at the witches. "Sorry, ladies, that was a joke, obviously."

Ina replied, "Don't say sorry, bro – it's cool. We like it when you play the fool."

Mina said, "Joke away, we know you're kidding. Ever seen us look forbidding?"

Mo had her hands tightly clasped and seemed to be seeking inspiration from the bubbles in the cauldron. "What you say here goes no further. After all, we're all in this together," she intoned clunkily.

Ina turned on her. "Scansion rubbish, rhyme pathetic. Just back off from things poetic."

Crestfallen, Mo looked round to busy herself with something else. She caught sight of the black cat, which now had its head inside the milk jug. When she retrieved the animal, it had a white head and front paw, and a splodge of milk on its chest. Mo spat on the hem of her black cloak and set about cleaning it up. I was surprised that it didn't protest, but I supposed if you were a witch's familiar, you put up with a lot.

"Right, I'd better get off hunting," said Macbeth. "Lovely to see you, ladies. See you later, fool."

It was like being spoken to by B. A. Baracus.

Once he had disappeared to roam in the gloaming, I finished off my goblet of lukewarm tea, and felt ready for almost anything.

"How do I get to the castle?" I asked the witches.

They looked at me doubtfully.

"Every time that we go there, we hover through the fog and filthy air," said Ina.

I was about to say that if she thought the eleventh-century air was filthy, she should try the post-industrial revolution stuff, when Mina chimed in, "You won't be giving that a try – you don't look light enough to fly."

"This is solid muscle," I said with dignity. "Which means I'm perfectly happy to walk. Can you give me directions?"

Ina and Mina rolled their eyes.

"We don't walk, it takes too long," said Ina.

"No good, we'd just tell you wrong," said Mina.

"I'll take you," said Mo unexpectedly. "I know the way on the ground."

"Can't rhyme, can't spell, now she's walking," said Ina to Mina with a shrug.

"Young witches nowadays, it's shocking," Mina replied.

Mo ignored them, and led the way out of the cave, the black cat padding along by her side. She hadn't cleaned it very well, since it still had a spot of milk on its chest.

"The cat's coming with us?" I asked. "I didn't realise you could take cats for a walk."

"We're not taking Hemlock for a walk, he's chosen to accompany us," said Mo. "Cats are autonomous. Isn't that right, Hemlock?"

The cat gave a miaow of agreement.

"Hemlock, that's quite an unusual name for a cat," I said.

"Do you reckon? I wondered if it was too ordinary, but I couldn't think of anything else."

I supposed it depended on what you were used to. She was dealing with spells and potions all day (or possibly all night), and had picked a name from there. But I worked in a library all day, and would never dream of calling a cat Reference, Bibliography or Interlibrary Loan.

I'm wary of cats. Dogs are transparent. You know what they're thinking, and you can tell them who's boss. Cats are inscrutable and, as one philosopher put it, "Dogs have owners; cats have staff."

"It's good to get away from my sisters for a while," said Mo. "They're always putting me down because I can't do spells, and I don't know how to rhyme. And they say I treat Hemlock like a pet instead of a familiar, but how can I treat him any other way when…"

I was vaguely aware she had stopped talking, but I wasn't really listening. I had expected the cave to give out on to a blasted heath. Instead, despite the gathering gloom, I could see we were in pleasant countryside with rolling hills. So much for William Shakespeare.

As we negotiated our way across the heather, Mo suddenly stared towards the north-west.

"Funny that wood being there," she said. "I don't remember it."

"It's the half-light," I told her. "It makes things look different. You're probably used to seeing things in the pitch-black, or rather not seeing them."

"I suppose," she said hesitantly, then changed the subject. "Thanks for letting me help you with your potion spell. I was worried at first that I would do it wrong, and then I realised you were in charge of the spell, so I wasn't really doing anything. But Ina and Mina didn't know that."

"Hold it right there," I said. "You've got it completely wrong."

"Yes, I usually have," she muttered.

I get very distressed by women's lack of confidence due to patriarchal oppression. But I thought witches would be more self-assured. Now I saw poor Mo's diffidence was nothing to do with sexist warlocks, but the result of her own sisters' criticisms. Despite what Miss Blaine said, I was coming to the conclusion that although these witches were women, they weren't that wise. It was down to me to invoke the true spirit of sisterhood and give Mo a pep talk.

"Let's have a seat," I said.

Sitting on the heather was quite scratchy, but given how itchy my hodden grey tunic and breeks were, it didn't make much difference. Mo sat down opposite me and the black cat jumped on to her lap. I saw that it still had a white spot on its chest. I began to think I had done Mo an injustice – maybe it wasn't milk, maybe it was permanent.

"You," I said, "are a very talented, capable witch. I wouldn't have asked for your help otherwise, or the brew would have gone wrong. I absolutely didn't do the spell for you. We both contributed equally."

I looked at her keenly. "Do you want to be a witch?"

"Oh yes," she said with sudden vehemence. "But I want to be a good witch."

"Do you mean you want to be good at being a witch, or you want to be a witch who does good?" I asked.

She looked slightly puzzled. "Isn't that the same thing?"

The black cat nudged its way under her arm, indicating that it wanted to be stroked. Sure enough, this had no effect on the remaining milk stain. The cat actually had a spot of white fur on its chest.

"I like to think I'm quite a good witch already," she said in a low voice. "I do Ina and Mina's hair, although I never seem to get round to doing my own." This was presumably the witch equivalent of cobbler's bairns being the poorest shod.

"You've seen me in action, Hemlock. What do you think?" she asked.

The cat licked her fingers.

"There, you've got a fan," I said, joining in the pretence that the cat could understand her and was demonstrating its approval.

Mo gazed down at the cat. "I could do more if you like, Hemlock."

The cat stopped licking her fingers and began to lick its paws.

"All right," she said. "You've made yourself clear."

Not to me, I thought, but I freely admit I'm not a cat person, so wouldn't pick up on the meaning of paw-licking.

"That's a great start, that you think you're quite a good witch," I said encouragingly. "Have faith in yourself. Don't pay attention to what Ina and Mina say."

"But they're my big sisters. They're much more experienced than me."

"Experience isn't everything," I said. "I had no experience at all when I went on my first time-travelling mission, and now here I am on my third."

She shot me an awestruck look. "Your sorceress must be very happy with you. Hecate's never happy with us. I told my sisters I did the spell wrong because I sneezed, but that's not true. Hecate comes out of nowhere when you least expect it and criticises. I was just thinking, what if she turns up right now, and I got all tense and tongue-tied, and instead of turning the tadpole into a frog, I turned it into a duck."

"You were turning a tadpole into a frog? Doesn't it do that by itself?"

25

"Not as quickly," she said.

"You need to stop worrying about Hecate," I said. "Work to the best of your ability, and pay attention only to justified criticism."

Mo seemed to shrink into herself. "You haven't met her," she whispered. "She's scary. She wouldn't like you."

I was taken aback. Not to blow my own trumpet, but I have a good sense of humour and well-developed social skills, I've had the finest education in the world, and I make an excellent cauldron of tea. What's not to like? Unless—

"Is she from Glasgow?" I asked.

"I think she comes from the underworld," said Mo.

There was certainly a lot of that in Glasgow.

"She wouldn't like you because you're a man," Mo went on. "She doesn't like men."

It was one thing Macbeth thinking I was a man, but it was troubling that a witch could be so ignorant.

"I'm not a man," I said.

"Oh, I know that. You're the familiar of your great sorceress. I've no idea what your real shape is, but right now you appear in the form of a man, and that's enough for Hecate not to like you."

I was appalled that Hecate could be guilty of such a gross generalisation.

"A lot of men are perfectly fine," I said sharply. I thought back to some of the men I'd met on my travels who were not only perfectly fine but also rather gorgeous.

"I know," said Mo dolefully as she stroked the cat. "But don't let Hecate hear you say that."

"I'll tell her she's being ridiculous," I said. "The only ones she should be objecting to are the male chauvinist pigs."

"I don't think she's got a problem with pigs, just with men," said Mo. "And please don't tell her she's being ridiculous. That'll make her angry, and you wouldn't like her when she's angry."

"I don't much like her now," I said. But I started thinking about my own unconscious bias. I had been startled by Macbeth, because he didn't fit my stereotypical view of a mediaeval king.

Obviously, at some level, I was influenced by Shakespeare's portrayal of him as ambitious, ruthless and murderous. But leaving that aside, even though I knew Macbeth had been a well-respected, benevolent ruler for seventeen years, the guy I'd met just didn't seem macho enough. I scolded myself for being so narrow-minded. Surely a monarch's best qualities should be humility, compassion and consensus-building. If that was appropriate in the twenty-first century, why should it be less so in the eleventh? I resolved to sign up for a diversity-awareness training course as soon as I got back to Morningside Library. And I could include my new insights into kingship in my monograph. I would have my own observations once I got to the castle, but Mo could also be a useful source of information.

"You seem to know Macbeth quite well," I said.

"Obviously. He's family," she said.

This was a surprise, a thane related to witches. Ina had called him "bro", but I hadn't realised it was intended to be taken literally. I thought she was just trying to liven up the trochaic tetrameter with a bit of gangsta rap.

"Is he a warlock?" I asked.

"Oh no," she said, sounding a bit shocked. "He'd be useless."

I was delighted with her response. Building up her self-confidence wasn't going to be as difficult as I thought. "Listen to yourself," I said. "You say he'd be useless, which means you know the qualities necessary for being a practitioner in the black arts, and you know he hasn't got them."

"Ina and Mina say *I'm* useless," she muttered.

I had no idea how they'd managed that, given the rhyming difficulties. The only full rhymes I could think of were "truceless" and "juiceless", and I couldn't see how a trochaic tetrameter couplet could encapsulate either of these along with Mo's supposed inadequacy. Time for another pep talk.

"But why are they saying it? It's because they're scared you're so much better than them. Keep telling yourself that."

The illusory truth effect, proven in numerous research studies:

you believe something's true when you've heard it enough times, although it's not entirely clear how many times is enough.

"I bet he's really jealous of you being a witch when he's not good enough," I went on.

"But he's not interested in witchcraft," she said, looking puzzled, and then her face cleared. "When I said he was family, I didn't mean he was our brother. He's our brother-in-law. Gruoch's our big sister. She's not a witch either."

This was another brilliant opportunity for my monograph. Shakespeare had also horribly misrepresented Lady Macbeth. Now I could get some charming childhood anecdotes to put the record straight.

"We don't like her," Mo announced.

"Because she's not a witch?"

"It's nothing to do with that," said Mo with dignity. "We're not bigots. We don't like her because she's a murderer."

Three

"A murderer?" I echoed.

The real Gruoch was supposed to be a paragon of virtue, making donations to the church. And not even Shakespeare claimed she was a murderer. He had her considering murdering Duncan, but then she couldn't bring herself to do it because the king looked like her old dad. That showed rather a sweet side to her personality. And now Mo was telling me she was a thoroughly dodgy piece of work.

"Who did she murder?" I asked.

"Her first husband. She says it was an accident, but me and Ina and Mina don't believe it."

I was beginning to get the impression that this was quite a dysfunctional family with a lot of sibling rivalry. Perhaps Ina and Mina's lack of self-esteem sprang from an unfavourable comparison with their elder sister. I felt it was a bit harsh that when poor Gruoch was widowed, they couldn't even be sympathetic, and actively maligned her. I would get Mo to tell me the facts of the case, and gently guide her towards an understanding of how unfair they were being.

"How did he die?" I asked.

Even in the twilight, I could see Mo's colour rise. "They were doing what married couples do," she said in a low voice.

I wondered for a moment whether Mo wished she was part of a married couple.

"That's very sad to lose a spouse under those circumstances, but at least there's the consolation of knowing he died happy,"

29

I said. "She can scarcely be blamed for her husband having a coronary through over-exertion."

The look she gave me wouldn't have gone amiss in a Presbyterian congregation whose minister started giving a reading from *Fifty Shades of Grey* instead of Mark's Gospel.

"They weren't doing *that*," she said. "And it wasn't a coronary."

"So what happened?"

"He came home and went over to give her a kiss. She was busy gralloching a deer for tea, and she says she forgot she was still holding the knife, and accidentally disembowelled him."

"Ah," I said. This put a different complexion on it. But there might still be extenuating circumstances. I remembered the wife of the Gucci heir putting out a contract on him because she found him irritating.

"Was he irritating?" I asked.

"No, he was lovely. A really nice, gentle guy. Like Macbeth. I've no idea why either of them married her. Maybe she didn't give them a choice."

This was before the days of a proper legal system, but I didn't like to think you could go around murdering people with impunity.

"Was there any sort of trial? Any sort of inquiry?" I asked.

"Of course not," said Mo. "Who wants to get on the wrong side of someone with a disembowelling knife?"

I still wasn't entirely convinced. Mina had admitted she wanted to be a scriever and this sounded like exactly the sort of story a scriever would make up. I could imagine Mo listening to it and accepting it all as fact. I'm a very good judge of character: I would wait until I met Gruoch and make my mind up then.

"Let's get on our way," I said, standing up.

Mo eased the cat off her lap and then something caught her attention.

"That wood's got closer," she said. "It's as though it's following us."

I peered in the same direction. The trees did indeed look as though they were several hilltops nearer, an interesting optical illusion. I was going to tell her about the Electric Brae in Ayrshire, where a car in neutral will appear to roll uphill. But that was going to involve explaining electricity, with reference to Benjamin Franklin, Michael Faraday, Thomas Edison and Nikola Tesla, and I wanted to get to the castle before it got much darker. So I just said, "Yes."

We set off again, the black cat barely visible in the heather, and eventually I saw a big barn on a summit in the distance.

"There it is," said Mo. "Glamis Castle, Sabhal Mòr Glamis."

I had been thinking of a castle as something high and turreted, or at least a motte-and-bailey construction with ditches and palisades, but this was an earlier period, before we'd adopted cutting-edge developments from continental Europe. I was going to be able to include architecture in my monograph.

"I'll leave you here," said Mo.

"You're not going to say hello to your big sister?"

Mo shook her head. "I'd get into trouble with the others. We're upset with her for being a murderer, although I'd like to hear her explain to us why she did it, in case she had a good reason. But she doesn't talk to us any more, so we don't talk to her. Good luck with being a fool – you're a natural."

And with a mermaid-like flip of her feet, she soared upwards and away. It looked a good way of travelling. Since it worked by magic, it presumably wasn't bound by the laws of physics, which meant Mina's wisecrack about me being too heavy to fly was just plain rude.

I set off in the direction of the castle, and saw a white spot in front of my eyes.

"You've forgotten your cat," I called, but by this time Mo was too far away to hear.

"Come on, then," I said to the cat.

It gave me a haughty look and stalked off, its tail high, as though this was its territory. It seemed to be going in the right direction, so I followed and ended up climbing the steep hill to the big barn, which was part wood, part drystone dyke. It had an impressively solid wooden door. I knocked three times.

"Knock, knock, knock! Who's there?" came a querulous voice.

"Me," I said, and the door was heaved open by a small, wild-haired man who peered out short-sightedly.

"Fat lot of use that is, saying 'me'," he grumbled. "How am I supposed to know who 'me' is?"

"Sorry," I said. "Force of habit. I know who I am. Who are you?"

"Who am I? Isn't it obvious? I'm the porter."

"Hello, Mr Porter," I said. I was going to tell him that there was a music hall song about him, involving getting on the wrong train. But I knew better than to try to explain rail travel, with reference to Richard Trevithick, James Watt, George Stephenson and Crewe Junction.

So I just said, "I've come to see Gruoch." And in order to convince him I was there on legitimate business, I added, "I'm a fool."

"You certainly are if you've come to see Grumpychops," he said. "She's in one of her moods. His thaneship is late home, and she wants to know why."

"He's hunting stags and goats," I said.

"Off enjoying himself? That'll go down well. I'm glad you're the one to tell her, not me."

He stood back to let me come in, slammed the door behind me, and pushed the drawbar back through the brackets. Beyond the entrance was a large hall with long wooden tables and benches, presumably where the feast would be. It was lit by torches on the walls and shallow stone dishes hanging from the ceiling, filled with oil. At the back of the hall I could see two narrow corridors – servants were scuttling in and out with firewood and provisions, but I couldn't see anybody who might qualify as the lady of the house.

"Gruoch?" I asked.

"Down there, second on the left. And be careful." With that, the porter sat down on the ground by the door, no doubt waiting for Macbeth.

I crossed the great hall and went along the corridor to the second door, which was partially open, so I tapped at it out of politeness and went straight in.

It was a bedchamber, containing a big wooden-framed bed covered in deerskin. A large carved oak chest was by the wall, with a bench and small table under the window, which was a hole in the wall with wooden shutters over it.

The room had only one occupant, standing in the centre, and there was absolutely no doubt that this was Gruoch. Her hair wasn't black or silver or fair, but reddish-brown, hanging in two long braids, and, like her sisters, she had a button nose and Cupid's bow lips.

She was wearing a heavy woollen gown, useful in a draughty big barn, dyed a deep dark green, which set off her Titian hair. She had on a bearskin cloak that matched Macbeth's. Round her waist was an embroidered girdle, and tucked in the girdle was a dagger. It looked sinister, but I remembered that at this point in history, it was a useful piece of cutlery.

The porter had prepared me for a hostile encounter, but he couldn't have been more wrong. She was smiling broadly.

"Hello," she said in the friendliest way imaginable, as though I was her favourite person in the whole world.

"Hello," I said.

Her demeanour changed in an instant. She drew herself up, scowling, her hand clutching the pommel of the dagger.

I was bewildered by this transformation until I saw the black cat with a white spot cross the room to rub itself against her ankles. It must have sneaked into the big barn behind me, and Gruoch had been talking to it, not me.

She bent down to stroke it. "Hello, my darling Spot," she purred, then turned to me again with her scowl back in place.

"Who are you? And why are you wearing men's clothing?" she demanded. "That's completely inappropriate for a female." She was the first person in this era to recognise me for what I was.

"I'm a fool," I said, hoping this would be sufficient explanation.

"But it's men who are fools," she said, giving a bark of laughter.

It sounded to me like another unacceptable generalisation, and I shot her a disapproving look. Even if she was only saying that men had the monopoly of being professional fools, that was incorrect as well. I was going to tell her about Jane the Foole, a female jester in the Tudor court. But that would be five hundred years in the future, and since I had a verbal contract, I decided that I wasn't going to waste my time debating the matter.

"Your husband hired me as a fool to entertain the king," I said curtly. "And just to let you know, he thinks I'm a man, as does everyone else I've met."

She looked me over. "I suppose you are quite … stocky. They just haven't bothered to give you a second glance."

This was what it was like to be fifty-something, I thought bleakly. Everyone says middle-aged women become invisible.

"If you've seen my husband, can you tell me if it's true – has the king really made him Thane of Cawdor?" she asked.

"I think so," I said. "That's certainly what the…" I stopped abruptly. I had been about to say that was what the witches had said. But if Mo wasn't even prepared to come to the castle, there were frictions there that I probably shouldn't get involved with. It was probably also best not to mention the "king hereafter" reference. "That's certainly what the talk is, and I haven't heard your husband contradict it," I concluded.

She clenched her fists, her expression fiercely triumphant. "It's happening," she whispered. "Now they'll all see what a great man he is."

She seemed to have forgotten that I was there. I gave a small cough.

"The great man told me to come and ask you for a pig's bladder," I added.

She looked heavenward. "And where am I supposed to get a pig's bladder?" she asked.

"From a pig, I imagine," I said.

Another bark of laughter. "Oh, that's very good. I can see why he hired you. I don't suppose you happen to know where he is?"

"He's off getting the tea. For the king's banquet tonight."

The colour visibly drained from her face. "Please tell me you're still joking," she said, sinking on to a small wooden stool. I could see the cat preparing to jump up on to her lap, and then it sensed the change of mood and slank under the wooden-framed bed.

"I'm not joking in the slightest," I told her. "That's why he's late home. He's out hunting."

At that very moment, the door opened once again and Macbeth strode in.

"Hello, my darling," he said, going over to Gruoch and plonking a kiss on her cheek. He didn't seem to notice that she had gone into a complete decline. He gave me a cheerful smile. "Hello, fool."

"Hello," I said.

"The fool says the banquet's tonight," hissed Gruoch.

"That's right," said Macbeth. "I've just delivered the needful to the kitchens."

"But… but…" She clutched at his tunic and pulled herself upright. "That's impossible. He can't come here, not yet. Your brother hasn't arrived."

I could understand that if royalty was coming to stay, you would want the whole family to be there. But it was very odd that she was so worried about her brother-in-law when she didn't seem to have invited her sisters. Perhaps she had, and Mo hadn't liked to tell me. Perhaps she had, and Ina and Mina hadn't liked to tell Mo. I was a fool – I was licensed to ask the questions other people couldn't.

"And what about your sisters?" I asked.

Gruoch stared at me. "What do you know of my sisters?"

"I know you haven't mentioned them. Have you invited them?"

"How could I do that when we're not in touch?" she said acidly. "My husband and I have nothing to do with my sisters. They're weird."

I looked at Macbeth, who was the picture of innocence, giving not the slightest indication that he'd just been chatting to them earlier. That was interesting.

"Speaking of invitations," he said, "I didn't mention a particular time to Duncan. I just said I would see him soon."

Gruoch sank down on the stool again, letting out a long breath. "In that case, we may be able to retrieve the situation. Your brother will definitely be here tomorrow?"

"Definitely," agreed Macbeth.

She crossed to the door and bellowed down the corridor, "Vellum, quill and ink for the Thane of Cawdor!"

Moments later, a servant rushed in and laid the objects on a small wooden table by the window.

"Close the door behind you when you leave," Gruoch ordered. "The Thane of Cawdor mustn't get caught in a draught."

As the servant passed me, I saw him roll his eyes, but he duly closed the door behind him.

"You, fool!" snapped Gruoch. "Can you write?"

This time, I was the one to roll my eyes. Perhaps that was a little unfair, since Gruoch didn't yet know that I had had the finest education in the world.

"No problem," I said.

"And you can take dictation?"

"Dictate away," I said, settling myself at the table and dipping the quill into the ink pot. The contents were intriguing – it looked to me like carbon ink, made up of a mixture of charcoal and gum arabic.

"My Liege Lord," she began.

It was amazing how smoothly the inked quill moved over the vellum, my writing strong black against the soft yellow. I resolved to spend more time on calligraphy when I got back home.

"We are preparing our humble dwelling for the honour of your visit," Gruoch went on. "These things take time, so we would be deeply grateful if you could delay your arrival until tomorrow evening. Your trusty liegeman." She turned to Macbeth. "Then you sign it." She turned back to me. "That's not part of the dictation."

"Do you think I'm stupid?" I asked.

"No, I think you're a fool."

Macbeth laughed heartily. "Very good, darling! Keep that up and Duncan won't know the difference between my fool and my wife."

Belatedly, he realised that didn't sound great. He rushed over to the table, grabbed the quill and signed his name with a flourish.

"Nice penmanship, by the way," he said as he handed the quill back to me.

Gruoch came over to have a look and cleared her throat noisily the way our teachers did when they couldn't find anything to complain about.

"And write 'Thane of Glamis' underneath," she ordered me.

"Duncan's just made me Thane of Cawdor as well, remember," said Macbeth.

"Of course he has, my darling, and very well deserved it is too," she said. "Fool, add 'and Cawdor' after Glamis."

This was all wrong. This was Shakespearean, not Scottish history. But perhaps I was supposed to go along with it.

"Anything else you want to add after that?" I asked, thinking of "King Hereafter".

"Like what?" asked Gruoch in a brittle tone.

"No, nothing. Just checking," I said. I went to lay the quill down carefully on top of the ink pot so it wouldn't mark the table, just as Gruoch snatched at the vellum to check it over. Somehow the ink pot got upended and she got splashed.

Macbeth gasped. "You fool! All of the gum arabic is over her little hand!"

In a way, it was nice that he was so protective of her, but it was also completely excessive.

"Not all of it," I said. "And it'll wash off. If you don't need me for any more writing, I'll go and practise my routine for tomorrow night."

Gruoch, who seemed a lot less worried about the ink than her husband, rolled up the vellum. "Forget your routine. Go and deliver this to Duncan."

I was going to argue that this wasn't part of my job description when I realised I didn't actually have a job description. And since I was still in the dark as to my mission, an outing might help to clarify things.

"Right away," I said. "Where will I find him?"

Macbeth waved a vague hand at the shuttered window. "Out there somewhere."

"You're really going to have to be a bit more specific, or he'll be here before I've had time to tell him not to come," I said.

Macbeth concentrated. "Last time I saw him, he was west south-west."

It looked as though this was the most I was going to get out of him. I took the rolled parchment from Gruoch and left on my mission. The porter refused to let me take one of the torches off the wall, claiming that there was a fine moon, and sent me out, closing the drawbar after me.

The moon wasn't that fine, but fortunately as well as having a good sense of humour, I also have a good sense of direction. I headed west south-west and, after walking for around three miles, found myself on the edge of a dark, dense wood, the trees packed close together. I was quite surprised, since I had had a pretty good look at the landscape during my trek with Mo, and I didn't remember any wood in this direction. I couldn't see any way round it, so I was just going to have to go through it.

But as I reached the nearest tree, I noticed something odd. The branches were fine, but instead of a trunk, it had two legs, dressed in woollen hose with criss-cross bindings.

"You're not a tree," I said.

"Yes I am," said the tree.

"Stop talking, you idiot," said the tree next to it. "Trees can't talk."

"And yet," I said, "here you both are, talking. Which rather confirms that you aren't trees."

"We are," insisted the first.

"We're Birnam Wood," said the second. "Which is made of trees."

"And is also in Birnam," I said. "Which is nowhere near here."

"Tell me about it," grumbled a tree in the row behind. "We're about thirty miles east north-east of there. That's some route march."

"What are you doing here?" I asked.

"Like anyone tells us anything," scoffed another tree. "All we know is we have to march, and as if that wasn't bad enough, we have to keep holding these branches when we set up camp. They're not light, you know."

"We're the poor bloody infantry," said its neighbour. "You don't catch the king or the top brass carrying branches."

"King Duncan?" I said. "I'm heading west south-west trying to find him. Do you have any idea where he is?"

A sudden wind soughed through the branches, a wind I couldn't feel but could only hear. Eventually I realised it was the trees sucking in their breath and then having a whispered conversation.

"He could be a spy."

"Or an assassin."

"That beardless youth? Don't be daft."

"You only have to look at him to know he's not a threat to anyone."

I had mixed feelings about this. I have considerable expertise in martial arts and unarmed combat, but it was quite nice to be thought a beardless youth.

The trees continued whispering.

"I'm surprised you can see a thing. There's not much of a moon."

"Even if he is a spy or an assassin, that's nothing to do with us."

"I think it is. We're supposed to protect the king, aren't we?"

"Are we?"

"Poor bloody infantry, we're supposed to do everything. Well, I'm sick of it."

There was the sound of a tree clearing its throat. "We're camouflage for the king. If you go about twelve rows in, you'll find a glade. He should be there."

"That's very kind of you," I said. "I've got a message for him. I don't mean that in any sinister way. I really have got a message for him, written on vellum. And you all make a very convincing wood. I was right up against you before I realised you had feet."

The two trees nearest to me touched branches in a high-five sort of way.

Getting through to the twelfth row wasn't easy because the trees were so densely packed. I kept up a litany of *sorry, excuse me, don't want to disturb you, could I just squeeze through*, but I still managed to step on a good few toes, and got a good few smacks on the head from the branches.

Eventually I reached the glade, which was lit by torches held nervously at branch's length by a circle of trees. A dozen or so men were sitting around on wooden stools, quaffing from drinking horns and gnawing on chunks of meat. One man sat on a stool that was higher than the others, wearing a long saffron-coloured tunic and a pair of trews, a sheepskin round his shoulders, and a gold circlet round his head.

I could understand why not even Shakespeare's Lady Macbeth could bring herself to murder King Duncan. Although I knew he was only about forty, he looked like everyone's favourite grandpa, the kind of grandpa you remember when you're three years old and every adult seems uniformly ancient. He had white hair and twinkly eyes.

I stepped into the glade and bowed low. As a rule, being an egalitarian, I don't hold with the upper classes, but in this instance, I wasn't acting on my own behalf. And then I realised I had no idea how to address a mediaeval monarch. It was an understandable gap in my education, my egalitarian views having been fostered by the school, but right now it was a bit awkward. I knew England's Henry VIII had adopted the title "Your Majesty", but that was never the Scottish form until Miss Blaine's least favourite sovereign, James VI, turned into James I as well. I took a gamble.

"Your Grace," I said, "I bring a message from Macbeth, the Thane of Glamis and Thane of Cawdor."

"What, all three of them?" asked Duncan, and the others collapsed in paroxysms of mirth, slapping their thighs.

"Most amusing, your Grace," I said, kneeling in front of him and handing over the roll of vellum.

He read it through and then called, "We're on, lads. At last."

There was a general murmur of approval.

"Very good," he said to me. "Tell Macbeth, or failing him, the Thane of Glamis, or failing him, the Thane of Cawdor, that I'll be delighted to come for tea tomorrow night."

Loud chortles broke out again among his companions.

I stood up and bowed again. "Still most amusing, your Grace," I said, turning to go.

"Wait," he said, "have some refreshment before your return journey."

He signalled to one of the thanes to bring me a drinking horn, confirming my view that he was a thoroughly nice chap. But I never touch alcohol on a mission.

"Thanks, but I've brought my own," I said. "Do you happen to have a clean cooking pot and some water? And do you by any chance have some milk?"

Some trees were brought into service to fetch the cooking pot, and before long, I was chucking more of Miss Blaine's tea leaves into simmering water, then filling the drinking horns with milk and tea.

Duncan took a large draught.

"A wonder!" he said. "What is it?"

It was no good telling him about China or India, since Europeans didn't yet know they existed.

"It's called tea. A herbal concoction from my home in Dunedin," I said.

He looked at me keenly. "You're no ordinary messenger. Tell me who you really are."

"I'm a fool," I said.

His expression changed to one of dismay.

"I'm most terribly sorry," he said. "You must excuse my feeble attempts at humour. I would never have dared to try making a joke had I known I was in the company of a professional."

"That's all right," I said, sipping my tea. "It was really quite good for an amateur. It made that lot laugh, didn't it?"

He beamed.

"By the way," I said, "you'll find that tea is a bit too wet without…" – I was going to say "a wee biscuit," and then realised I was again ahead of my time – "… a wee bannock."

Duncan signalled to a tree. "Bannocks all round," he said. "And take one for yourself."

"Much obliged, my liege," said the tree.

If you had to have a king, this was exactly the sort of king you would want to have.

The bannock came drizzled with honey, and I dunked it in the drinking horn, a move that everyone else copied.

"It must be wonderful to be a fool," said the king, sounding slightly wistful. "Do you have a pig's bladder?"

"No, and I don't have frog's legs either," I said.

Duncan looked momentarily mystified and then he guffawed. At this, all of the thanes guffawed as well.

Emboldened by this, I decided to bring up the issue that was bothering me. Normally you're not supposed to ask royalty questions, but just answer theirs, including "And what do you do?" and "Have you come far?". But I reckoned my status as a fool gave me a certain latitude.

"Your Grace," I said, "why are you in the middle of Birnam Wood, especially when this isn't Birnam?"

"Forward planning," he said, tapping his nose confidentially.

"Of course," I said. "That makes perfect sense. But I wonder why you're in the middle of Birnam Wood, especially when this isn't Birnam."

He began chuckling, as did the thanes, and then suddenly stopped. "Oh," he said, "that wasn't a joke, was it?"

"If it was, it wasn't intentional," I said. "Probably best not to treat it as one."

"Macbeth invited me to come and stay," he said. "He told me

he would see me soon, but he didn't say exactly when. It's a real palaver making a royal progress, and I didn't want to end up being late, so I thought I would start moving closer to his castle. But I didn't want Macbeth to know in case he was embarrassed about keeping me waiting, so I decided to travel incognito."

"And there's nothing more incognito than a moving grove," I said.

He looked at me anxiously to see whether this was a joke or not. I kept a poker face and he relaxed.

"That's what I thought," he said. "You see a forest three miles from your castle, you think nothing of it. So now I'm all set. I'll arrive in good time, and my army can encircle the castle with their branches while I'm there, which should look quite picturesque."

I was getting increasingly excited about my monograph. The popular view of mediaeval monarchs is that if they weren't completely useless, they were despotic tyrants. And here was someone who not only cared about his subjects, but also cared about aesthetics.

"Very strategic," I said. "Thank you for your gracious message to Macbeth, not to mention the Thane of Glamis and the Thane of Cawdor."

"The Thane of Glamis and the Thane of Cawdor!" gurgled one of the entourage.

"I said not to mention them," I snapped.

There were a few intakes of breath, and then the thanes burst into applause, led by the king. For an instant, I wondered whether I had made the wrong career choice, and whether I should have been a stand-up comedian. But no – librarianship is my *raison d'être*. I could always do a few gigs in the libraries' outreach programme.

I bowed again to Duncan. "I'll be on my way, your Grace, and I look forward to seeing you at the feast."

As I started battling my way between the trees again, he called after me, "Remember to get a pig's bladder. You can hit Macbeth over the head with it, and that'll be really funny." I could hear the thanes laughing at the very thought.

Eventually I found my way back out to the moor and set off for the castle. But I couldn't have gone more than two miles when there was a whooshing sound, and a tall, black-cloaked figure was silhouetted against the moon as it soared downwards to land right in front of me.

"Hello, Mo," I said, but when the tall figure threw back the hood of its cloak, it wasn't Mo at all. It was a hideous old woman with a sharp nose and jagged teeth, teeth that I could see only too well, since her mouth was open in a rictus grin.

"Kneel, mortal!" she commanded, her voice as unprepossessing as her looks.

I had been prepared to kneel in front of Duncan in my role as messenger, but I certainly wasn't going to obey an abrupt order from someone I didn't even know.

"Sorry, who are you?" I asked.

She took a step closer. "I am Hecate," she rasped.

"Ah, the witches' line manager." I said it perfectly neutrally, so as not to give away that I knew they didn't like her at all.

"You've been consorting with one of my girls," she spat.

I could imagine Marcia Blaine teachers saying exactly the same thing to quivering youths from Heriot's or the Royal High. But I had nothing to quiver about.

"Scarcely consorting," I said. "More chatting."

"You were alone on the moors with her."

"No, I wasn't. She had her cat with her."

"Don't presume to bandy words with me, mortal. I do not permit men to consort with my girls."

"I'm just going to stop you there so that I can contradict you again," I said. "You're straying into personal areas that are off-limits for managerial interference. And more to the point, I'm not a man."

She gave a raucous cackle. "Oh, really? You mortals have an expression: Are you a man or a mouse? If you're not a man, that leaves only one option."

She raised her hand and pointed a bony forefinger at me.

An instant later, I was a mouse.

Four

Which is where we began. The cat had seen off the owl, which was a good thing, but it was now creeping towards me, which wasn't.

It was time to repeat my entreaty. "Please don't eat me. I'm—"

"I know," said the cat. "You're a librarian."

It said it with familiarity, as though it wasn't a strange, unknown word.

"You know what a librarian is?" I asked.

"Of course I do. I have a very fine library at home."

I sighed inwardly. I had thought for a moment that the cat really understood the word, but it had obviously just ascribed a meaning to it that matched with something it knew. "Librarian" probably meant something like "dead mouse". And then I remembered that I looked like a mouse.

"I may look like a mouse, but I'm actually a person," I clarified.

"You said." The cat sounded slightly weary. "We have met, you know." It sat upright and in the moonlight I saw the white spot on its chest.

"I'm terribly sorry – I didn't realise it was you. Did you follow me all the way from the castle?"

"I did. It's a pleasant evening for a stroll, and I was interested in your destination. After all, a cat may look at a king."

That startled me. I knew it was an old English proverb, but I thought it dated from the sixteenth century. Now I knew it was much earlier. This monograph was going to cover a lot of material.

"I'm very grateful to you for chasing the owl away," I said. "Thank you."

45

"Not at all," said the cat. "We're acquaintances. It's the least I could do."

It was one thing being acquaintances when I was Shona. It was quite another when I was a mouse.

"Well, thanks again," I said. "I'm just off to hide somewhere for the moment. You can't be too careful – there might be another owl around."

I had barely got into scampering position when I found myself going backwards instead of forwards. I scrabbled at the ground with my little paws, to absolutely no effect. I was being pulled by my tail. And the cat was doing the pulling.

"Don't go," it said. "I was enjoying chatting."

"Glad I wasn't boring you," I said, making a virtue of necessity, since the paw was still clamped firmly over my tail. I'm usually very cool-headed in a crisis, but I'm generally not a mouse that's being pinned to the ground by a cat. The cat wanted to chat, so I had better chat. I felt like Scheherazade, having to keep talking to avoid being killed. But while she managed to come up with a thousand and one stories, my mind had gone blank. I gazed up to the heavens for inspiration and the only thing I could think of was, "It's a braw bricht moonlicht nicht the nicht."

"What?" said the cat.

I had no idea how the simultaneous translation was working between two different species of animal, but this suggested that the Highland cat didn't understand Lowland Scots.

"It's a fine bright moonlight night," I said. "Tonight. Not too cold, either."

"No," it agreed.

I was going to have to do better than that. Rather than doing all the talking myself, I needed to draw the cat into the conversation.

"Have you known Gruoch for long?" I asked.

"No," it said.

Thanks to my mouse panic, I was making basic mistakes, asking closed questions, which could be answered with a brief yes or no, rather than an open question that called for detail.

"Tell me what you think of Glamis Castle," I said.

"No," it said.

"Speaking of the castle," I said, "I'm sure you'd prefer to be back there. It's not that mild a night, and it'll be lovely and warm indoors. And I'm sure they have milk."

"Will you come too?" asked the cat.

"Of course," I said heartily. "Let's go." The second my tail was free, I was going to scarper.

"But it's miles," said the cat. "You'll never manage to keep up."

"That's okay," I said. "You go on and get your milk, and I'll see you when I see you."

"I could carry you in my mouth," said the cat.

My little mouse heart thudded. "That's a very kind offer, but I really wouldn't want to put you to any trouble," I hedged.

"It's no trouble. You're very light."

It was a change from the witches having a go about my weight, but I still wasn't keen on the idea.

"I keep thinking of the fable," I said.

"Which particular one?" it asked. "Belling the cat? That's a good one. The mice are in such fear of their lives that they hold a conference to decide what to do about the cat. One mouse says they should hang a bell round the cat's neck so that they know when it's coming. An old mouse says it's a brilliant idea, but he has just one question – who's going to hang the bell round the cat's neck? And the moral of the fable is that there's no point coming up with ideas that are completely impractical."

The moral as far as I was concerned was that cats were a real and present danger to mice.

"That's an interesting fable," I said. "But the one I have in mind is about the scorpion and the frog."

"I don't know that one," said the cat, looking intrigued.

"A scorpion wants to get to the other side of a river, and asks a frog to carry it across," I said. "The frog refuses, because it's scared the scorpion will sting it. The scorpion says it wouldn't do that, because then they would both drown, so the frog lets

47

the scorpion climb on its back, and starts swimming across the river. But halfway across, the scorpion stings it. With its last gasp, the frog asks the scorpion what it wanted to do that for, and the scorpion says it can't help it, it's just what it does."

"What a very interesting story," said the cat. "I must remember that." Then it gave a low menacing growl. "You're applying that to us, aren't you? You're suggesting that if I carry you back to the castle in my mouth, I'm going to eat you. I very much resent that. Let me tell you something. I have eaten boar's head, roasted swan, peacocks, herons, porpoise and conger eel, larks and rabbits. But I have never eaten a mouse, and I don't intend to start now."

Obviously I knew that an eleventh-century cat wouldn't have the benefit of Whiskas, but I had no idea it would have such a varied diet, or that it would reject mice. My monograph would have an entire section on the eating habits of mediaeval cats.

Then I hesitated. "You're not saying all this just to lull me into a false sense of security? So that I agree to let you carry me back to the castle and then you eat me? After all, you're a cat. You might not be able to help it."

The cat closed its eyes and opened them again, in a way that suggested it was being long-suffering.

"Are you a mouse?" it asked.

"I think we've been through this already," I said. "I look like a mouse. But I'm a person."

"And I look like a cat," it said. "But I'm a person as well." With that, it released my tail.

This cast a different light on things. "Hecate turned you into a cat?" I asked.

"Not Hecate. Mo."

"Oh dear," I said. She claimed she had inadvertently turned the tadpole into a duck because she had sneezed, but her sisters' poor opinion of her witching skills now sounded justified. "Had you gone to her for a cure? What was she trying to do? Sort out a migraine? Ingrown toenails?"

I stopped myself quickly. I had no right to ask intrusive questions

48

about its medical complaints. I wasn't a doctor's receptionist.

"She was trying to save me," it said simply.

"Save you from what?"

"From Hecate," it said. "I was there in the cave as me, and then Hecate turned up, and in that very second, Mo turned me into a cat. I didn't understand at the time, but later I realised that Hecate hated men and if she'd seen me, a man, in the cave, she would have done something much worse to me."

Like turn him into a mouse, I thought. Or a tadpole. That was impressively quick thinking on Mo's part.

"Hecate didn't seem to think there was anything odd about a black cat being around," he said. "But Ina and Mina gave Mo a really hard time about it. They said she must have called me up by accident when she was trying to do something else, and that she couldn't get anything right. They said it in trochaic tetrameter, of course."

I was impressed. Most people I meet don't know their trochaic tetrameter from their dactylic hexameter.

"Mo told them it was nothing to do with her, and that I'd just turned up out of the blue, which was true as far as it went," he said. "But she hasn't told them I'm not a cat."

Perhaps Hecate's suspicion of me and Mo was because the youngest witch had previous.

"Were you and Mo ... consorting?" I asked.

"Chance would be a fine thing," he sighed. "But no, a lovely-looking woman like that could do much better than me. And even if she had been inclined to give me the time of day, time is what we didn't have. I arrived, I saw her, she saw me, and I was a cat. I'm able to understand people when they talk. Unfortunately, people can't understand cat – they just hear me miaowing and purring. But I think Mo knows I'm happy."

"Happy?" I burst out. "How can you possibly be happy when you're a person who's been turned into a cat?"

He stretched out languorously and batted a playful paw at a passing beetle.

"It's a good life here. Two homes and no responsibilities."

Typical cat, dividing its time between two families, both of whom thought it belonged to them. But I could see a problem.

"Doesn't Macbeth object to you turning up at his castle when you live in the witches' cave?" I asked.

"He's got no idea. He thinks I'm two different cats: Mo's cat Hemlock, and his wife's cat Spot."

I was beginning to think the Thane of Glamis and Cawdor wasn't the brightest.

"What do you think of Gruoch?" I asked.

"She's lovely," he said promptly. "Feeds me the best of everything from the kitchens. I get some pretty dodgy leftovers from the witches."

I had been hoping for something a bit more insightful, but no, still a typical cat, equating food with goodness.

A new thought struck me. "I know people can't understand you, but can you understand what people say?"

"Not always. I've never worked out what they mean when they say they're feeling a little middle-y."

I stared at the cat in surprise. Perhaps we were talking in cat and mouse, but it sounded like English to me.

"Feeling a little middle-y is a Gaelic expression," I said. "It means not feeling well."

"Really?" said the cat. "Yes, that makes sense now."

"I have to say, I'm impressed by your language skills," I told him.

"They're reasonable, I suppose," he said. "I studied in Latin, obviously, and I picked up French, Italian and Spanish during my travels."

"And when did you learn Gaelic?" I asked.

"I've never learned Gaelic," he said. "Why would I? I'd have no use for it."

This was mystifying. "Do you understand Gruoch? And Macbeth? And all of the people who say they're feeling a little middle-y?"

"Obviously," he said, with one of these contemptuous looks

that cats are so good at.

I felt a bit miffed. Here I was, using abilities that came from having had the finest education in the world, while this cat had been automatically equipped with the witches' simultaneous translation system.

"Where are you from originally?" I asked.

"London," he said.

Now his decision to stay in his present form made sense. I could well understand how being a cat in Scotland was far preferable to being a person in London.

"And you told us you're from Edinburgh," he said. "That's where the king comes from."

Could it be?

"Not James VI and I?"

"James I, that's right."

He wasn't from the eleventh century; he was from the seventeenth. I was so keen on putting my next question that I let his metropolitan bias go.

"Are you William Shakespeare?"

He sprang up, hissing, the indication of quite a cross cat. "That strutting player, whose conceit lies in his hamstring? I most certainly am not."

I'd obviously touched a nerve, although I thought it was a bit rich to use Shakespeare's own words to be rude about Shakespeare. But conscious that I was still a mouse, and he was still a cat, I decided not to make an issue of it.

"Sorry," I said. "How do you come to be here?"

His ears were flat against his head now, and the tip of his tail was twitching slightly. If he hadn't been a cat, I would have said he was embarrassed.

"An experiment that went wrong," he muttered.

"Were you trying to go somewhere else?" I asked.

"I wasn't trying to go anywhere. I was trying to turn base metal into gold."

Ah, so the cat was an alchemist. Some people sneer at alchemists, but they were pioneers. Scientists now have all the advantages of knowing about atoms and isotopes and neutrons and protons, but they can still make only tiny amounts of gold out of mercury and lead. The cat was hampered by having none of the modern scientific know-how, so could be forgiven for turning to the occult. He had probably been summoning the devil when it all went horribly wrong.

"I had a lot of money worries, and I didn't fancy being arrested for debt again," he muttered. "Now do you understand why I don't want to go back? Although I miss my books. Reading maketh a full man."

"Indeed it doth," I said. "So it's just as well you're a cat."

I gave him the benefit of the doubt that by Man, he meant human being. The seventeenth century wasn't noted for its gender-neutral language. And discrimination was fuelled by the King James Bible, which cavalierly translated everything as male when the original texts were much more gender inclusive. I could see why James VI and I wasn't Miss Blaine's favourite person.

My jocular remark to the cat was an attempt to cheer him up, since his financial situation militated against him going home, but I should have known better than to be flippant about books. He turned such a woebegone expression on me that I patted his big cat paw with my little mouse paw.

"There, there," I said. "Mo will probably accidentally conjure up some books at any moment now."

But he refused to be consoled. "I loved my books," he said. "I even set up a cataloguing system. I had three key areas – philosophy, history and poetry – and then they could be subdivided, and subdivided again."

I had been sceptical about his understanding of the word "librarian", but that was when I thought he was a cat. Now I knew he not only understood the word, he embodied it.

"Just before you turned up, I was explaining to the owl that librarianship is a vocation," I said sternly. "This is sheer self-indulgence on your part to hide yourself away in the eleventh century when you've got a seventeenth-century cataloguing system to sort out."

"I can't catalogue from a debtors' prison," he objected. "You take my life when you do take the means whereby I live." And then, quite brazenly changing the subject, he said, "What about you? Why has your sorceress sent you here?"

"I'm not entirely sure," I admitted. "She's sent me on a mission, which means I'm here to put something right, probably to save someone. But I don't know who yet."

"Perhaps you're here to save me," he mused.

I was pretty sure Miss Blaine wasn't concerned with saving Londoners. She would undoubtedly argue that they had their own education system to look after them. And I didn't feel motivated to save a librarian who had abandoned his books. But I still felt at a disadvantage being a mouse to his cat, so I decided not to say any of this.

"We've been chatting all this time, and we haven't really introduced ourselves properly," I said. "Mo calls you Hemlock, but Gruoch calls you Spot. Which would you prefer me to call you?"

"I'd prefer you to call me by my real name, Frank," he said.

"Frank. That's a nice name. And please call me Shona. That's a female name. Despite the way I dress, I'm a woman. It's a bit irritating that people just look at the clothes and then make assumptions."

"I'm hardly likely to do that," he said. "On the stage, we see men dressed as women often enough. I don't see why women shouldn't dress as men."

Considering he came from the seventeenth century, this was remarkably broad-minded, although a bit disappointing that he hadn't concluded that there should be equal opportunities when it came to acting roles.

The quiet of the night was suddenly broken by the hooting of an owl.

"Too-wit, too-woo, a merry note," said Frank.

"Not that merry when you're a mouse," I reminded him. "Now that I'm fairly sure you're not going to eat me, could you take me back to the castle?"

I felt a moment's dread as he padded towards me and opened his jaws wide. But the next thing, my head was sticking out of one side of his mouth, my tail was sticking out of the other, and we were hurtling across the moor. I remembered reading that cats could run at thirty miles an hour. I suspected Frank was going a lot faster. I was thoroughly travel sick by the time we reached Glamis and he spat me out on the ground. I lay where I had fallen, head reeling, stomach churning.

"Get up," said Frank dispassionately. "This is still owl territory. You need to get inside."

I staggered to my feet and found we were at the door of the big barn. It was massive and close fitting, with only a tiny gap, which couldn't have been more than a quarter of an inch. I paused for a moment, baffled. But as I investigated it with my supersensitive whiskers, I was fascinated to find that I could flatten my rib-cage, which would let me squeeze through the tiniest aperture. I concentrated hard on how I was doing it, in the hope that I could replicate it when I got back to human form.

My head poked through the gap, and I realised that if it could get through, the rest of me could as well. A quick wriggle and I was on the other side. And then I found I was halfway up the sleeve of the small, wild-haired porter, who was lying behind the door, somewhat the worse for wear.

He gave a yell. "Mouse! I'm being attacked by a mouse! Spot! Spot! Where's that damned cat?"

There was a pitiful mewing and scratching on the other side of the front door. The porter lurched to open it, tugging at the drawbar, and I clung on to his homespun sleeve with all four paws.

"What are you doing out there, you stupid animal?" he demanded as Frank scurried in. "You're needed in here."

He waved his arm around in a bid to dislodge me. I might have managed to keep my grip if I hadn't just had that nightmare journey, but I was already feeling quite giddy, and tumbled off the sleeve straight into Frank's mouth.

"That's more like it," said the porter. "And this time, eat the whole lot. Don't leave bits of it around for us to step on."

"He must be confusing me with another cat," said Frank a little indistinctly, since he had his mouth full. With me. "I told you, I don't eat mice."

He trotted into the dining hall, to be warmly congratulated on his hunting skills by passing servants. Had I been a real mouse, I could imagine getting a complex.

When we got to the safety of the corridor, he dropped me on the ground and said, "I'm off to the kitchens. It's better if you stay here." I was touched that he was concerned about my safety until he added, "They'll only want me to chase you, which will take up valuable eating time."

He sauntered off, tail high.

I glared after him for a while, and then made my way to the Macbeths' bedroom, the only room whose location I knew. The door was closed, but I did my rib-cage-flattening trick again, and as I mouse-limboed underneath, I heard Macbeth say nervously, "I really don't think I'm up to it."

If they were discussing something personal, I would just go back out again.

"Of course you are, my darling," said Gruoch. "All it takes is a bit of oomph."

I was relieved to find them both fully clothed, Macbeth shuffling uncertainly up and down the room, Lady Macbeth sitting by the window, casually removing a stray piece of food from between her teeth with her dagger. I chided myself for my mistake. Not Lady Macbeth, an offensive and inaccurate construct by William Shakespeare, but Gruoch, the pious wife of a benign leader. It was seeing the dagger before me that led me astray.

The large, carved oak chest by the wall had a mouse-sized space underneath. I reached it without being seen, and peeped out.

"Honestly, I wouldn't know where to start," said Macbeth.

Lady Macbeth went over to the wooden-framed bed. "It couldn't be easier. I'll show you," she said. I wondered if it was time to go back out. But instead of getting on to the bed, she held the dagger above her head in both hands, then drove it downwards with a huge exhalation of breath, tearing through several layers of fur into the straw-filled mattress. The bed frame juddered with the force of the attack, and I began to feel a little apprehensive.

"There," she said.

Macbeth looked distinctly queasy. "There's obviously a knack to it, and I don't think I've got it," he said.

"Of course you have, sweetheart," she purred, sashaying back to him and running her hand over his bicep. "It's a matter of strength, and you're my big strong hero."

Macbeth beamed shyly at this, but then she muttered, "Not that you need much strength. He's an old man, after all, forty if he's a day."

Being fifty-something, under other circumstances I would have been very offended by this. But right now, my apprehension was turning to horror. Surely not? King Duncan was born in 1001, and I'd already established that this was the year one thousand and two twenties.

"Come on, my darling," she said. "You'll be doing him a favour. Put Duncan out of his misery."

Sure enough. Despite the fact that it was all wrong, they were following the outline of Shakespeare's plot. And now I understood what my mission was. It was to stop Macbeth murdering Duncan. As Miss Blaine had said, the real Macbeth killed the real Duncan in a fair fight. If they followed the wrong history, then the time would be out of joint. It was up to me to set it right. I had to make sure Duncan wasn't murdered.

Macbeth was looking as distressed as I felt.

"I'm not sure," he said.

"Look, do you want to be king?" demanded Gruoch sharply.

"No I don't," said Macbeth.

"Yes you do," said Gruoch.

"Yes I do," said Macbeth.

She twined her arms round him and nuzzled his neck. "My hero," she breathed. "My great big soppy hero who's going to be king. You'll be wonderful. You'll get to wear a crown, and sit at the head of the table at feasts."

Using her womanly wiles to manipulate a defenceless man. I was disgusted.

"What about ruling?" Macbeth asked uncertainly.

"Don't you worry your precious head about that," she cooed. "I'll take care of that for you, along with making sure you have clean shirts."

"My angel," he said. "I don't deserve you."

No, you don't, I thought, even though you've been stupid enough to judge her on her looks rather than her personality.

Gruoch was stroking his hair now. "All you have to do," she said, "is go into his bedroom with the dagger. That's all."

Not quite all, I thought bitterly. There was the small matter of plunging it into a sleeping old – not old at all, a not-even-forty-year-old – king. Shakespeare had got Lady Macbeth taped: ruthless, ambitious, goading her perfectly nice husband into committing murder. But perhaps there was hope. Macbeth was still full of the milk of human kindness and wasn't yet at the stage where it had curdled.

He was looking extremely unhappy. In among his beard, I could see his bottom lip quiver slightly.

"I know it's for the best," he said. "But I'm sure I'll get it wrong. Can't you do it?"

"Now you're being silly, my darling. You know it has to be you."

"But you know how. Your first husband—"

"Darling, that was completely different. I made it look like an accident."

I should never have doubted the witches. They were right – their sister had murdered her first husband. And now she was persuading her second husband to become a murderer as well. But what could I do? I was only a mouse. Were I back in human form, it would be no problem. Macbeth might be a big muscular bloke, but I have speed, stamina and strength, and I know some really good judo throws. And as for Gruoch, she might be a murderer, but I could snap her like a twig.

There was no doubt in my mind that she would goad Macbeth into performing the fatal deed. He wasn't tough enough to stand up to her, and in any case, it must have crossed his mind that if she could murder her first husband, she could murder her second as well.

There was a mewing and scratching at the door. Gruoch opened it, and Frank immediately rushed over to twirl himself round her ankles.

"Hello, Spot. Where have you been?" she scolded affectionately, leaning down to scratch him behind his ears. "Sometimes I think you only come here when you're hungry."

Frank yowled in protest and rubbed his head against her.

"I'm just joking, Spot. I know you love us really."

Don't kid yourself, I thought. This is pure cupboard love. Then my nose started to twitch involuntarily. It was almost as though I could smell cheese, obviously a reaction to the knowledge that Frank had been stuffing his face in the kitchen while excluding me.

Frank was peeking at me from behind Gruoch's skirts in what was presumably a triumphalist manner. Except he didn't look triumphalist, he looked intense, and he was tossing his head in a way he seemed to think was significant.

I gave him my best prefect's stare, the kind that even the fourth years found daunting, but its effect was rather undermined by my being a tiny rodent. I didn't dare make a sound in case the Macbeths heard me. If Gruoch was gearing her husband up to commit regicide, she wouldn't think twice about telling him to tread on a mouse. But I mouthed, "What?" at the cat.

He answered out loud, and I remembered that I was the only one who could hear the words: to Macbeth and Gruoch, it sounded like miaows.

"I've brought you some bannock and cheese." He nodded towards the end of the chest I was hiding under. As he came in, he must have managed to drop off a few crumbs. They were very small, but then, so was I, and they would provide a very adequate tea. I put my front paws together in a gesture of thanks and nodded back at him. I was just wondering how I could snaffle the crumbs without being seen when I discovered that Frank talking to me had created the necessary diversion.

Gruoch scooped him up, crooning, "What's the matter, poppet? Are you still cross with me?"

Frank gave a low rumbling purr as I nipped out to retrieve my bannock and cheese.

"You're a sleepy boy," said Gruoch. "You curl up on the nice warm sheepskin and dream about catching big, fat mice."

At least that left me out of the equation. I was a small, scrawny mouse. Munching on a fragment of cheese, I watched Gruoch gently put Frank down on a sheepskin by the table, where his purr changed into what sounded very much like a snore. Cats can sleep for twenty hours out of twenty-four.

"This is perfect," Gruoch said in an undertone to Macbeth. "We don't want to alert anyone with any yelling, so you're going to practise without wakening the cat."

She held the dagger out to him.

"Can you show me again?" he pleaded. "I've forgotten what you did."

It was probably the sleeping cat that saved him from a reply as sharp as the dagger. She went back over to the bed and duplicated her earlier two-handed onslaught on the fur bedspreads and the straw mattress. What was particularly sinister this time was her utter silence, not a hint of heavy breathing or any exertion. It was as though it was a move she had made so many times, she didn't even need to think about it.

"You try," she whispered, handing over the dagger.

He clutched it, but didn't move.

"Stop staring at it as though you don't know what it is," she hissed. "Look, do it one-handed if that makes it easier. Just lift your arm up and bring it down fast."

He had his back to me now, but I could see him lift his arm up and bring it down fast. He ended the move with a shuddering groan.

Gruoch, her hand clamped over her mouth in horror, rushed over to him.

"Oh, my darling, you mustn't do it like that," she gasped. "Are you all right?"

Macbeth sat down heavily on the bed, sending bits of straw drifting to the floor.

"I told you I'd get it wrong," he said hoarsely.

"You did very well," she said in a shaky voice. "In future, just remember that when you bring your arm down, it's important to keep the dagger pointing forward, not pointing at yourself."

She hurried over to the oak chest I was hiding under. I darted further back to avoid detection, but that meant I could no longer see anything. I heard the creak of the chest being opened, and then the sound of ripping cloth.

"Don't worry," she was saying. "'Tis but a scratch. We'll get it sorted in next to no time."

There was another groan from Macbeth and bustling noises from Gruoch.

"There," she said, her voice still wavering, "that's the tourniquet sorted. The blood will wash out of your trousers, I'll darn them and they'll be as good as new."

I dared to crawl back to my vantage point at the front of the oak chest, and could see Gruoch with her arms round Macbeth, her hands covered in blood. She was a murderess, and she was trying to turn her husband into a murderer, but she really did care about him. That was something in her favour, I supposed. And then I thought: the Krays and Al Capone were always really good to their old mums, but that didn't stop them being a thoroughly bad lot.

"Let's do a bit more practising," she said, pulling Macbeth to his feet. He took a few tentative steps, limping heavily. He glanced down at his trouser leg, which was splattered red below the tourniquet, and subsided back on to the bed.

"Feel sick," he announced faintly. "Can't stand the sight of blood."

"There, there," said Gruoch soothingly. "I'll wash my hands. And we'll leave the dagger until we've done some more work on that downward move."

That sounded wise. Next time, he might sever his femoral artery.

She crossed to the door and bellowed down the corridor, "A spurtle for the Thane of Cawdor!"

This was exciting. At home, I always start the day with a bowl of porridge, and I wouldn't dream of stirring it with anything other than a spurtle. The top of it's carved to look a bit like a thistle, but I couldn't wait to see what an authentic eleventh-century spurtle in an aristocratic household was like. It would be something else to address in my monograph.

Moments later, a servant rushed in with what was unmistakably a stick. Not a trace of carving to be seen. It looked like something that had just been hauled off one of the branches in Birnam Wood. That brought me to my senses. In the middle of Birnam Wood was Duncan, King of Scots, who had accepted an invitation to come to Glamis Castle the following night, when he was going to be murdered by Macbeth. Already Lady Macbeth – for I could no longer bring myself to think of her as the saintly Gruoch – was coaching her husband in how to attack the bed with the spurtle-stick. And I had to stop them.

But how? As a mouse, my capacities were limited, mainly consisting of being able to flatten my rib-cage. Had I realised the dreadful implications of delivering the invitation to Duncan, as a mouse I could have dragged it into the bushes and hidden it. As myself, I could simply not have delivered it. What I had to do now was get back into human form, go to Duncan and explain that Macbeth had written him a second letter saying that due to unforeseen circumstances, it was no longer possible to invite him to stay, and would he mind leaving it until another time. I would have to find an excuse for not having the letter. I thought for a while. It would sound slightly implausible to say a mouse had eaten it, since a mouse would take quite a long time to eat a piece of vellum, and as protector of the vellum, I should have been able to shoo the mouse away before it had done too much damage. And then the solution presented itself. I could say that when I was en route with the letter, a golden eagle had swooped down and flown off with it.

It was an excellent plan, apart from the getting back into human form bit. I had no idea how to achieve that. But perhaps I knew someone who did. First, I needed to get out from under the oak chest. And then I needed to go somewhere where I would be alone and unobserved. If I was suddenly transformed from a mouse into myself, it would be more than obvious. And that wasn't advisable when Lady Macbeth was in the same room, with a dagger to hand.

She was currently preoccupied.

"No, my darling," she was saying. "You're still stabbing your leg with the spurtle. You have to lean forward, over and down. Forward, over and down. Not quite, darling, but very much better. Well, very slightly better."

I took the opportunity to scurry from the oak chest to the door, which the departing servant had closed behind him, flattening my rib-cage and emerging into the corridor. The easiest place would be outside, I decided – I would be able to get a good, clear signal.

Instead of going back through the dining hall to the front door, having to evade servants and the porter, I aimed for the nearest window. Climbing a vertical wall felt like the easiest thing I had ever done. Again, I attempted to log the technique so that I could duplicate it when I got back to my human life. I shimmied round the wooden shutter on to the open window ledge. It was a long way down, particularly given my own length of less than three inches. And then I was descending, unhurriedly and capably, my tiny claws latching on to the clay-coated wall.

I wondered whether any producers would be interested in a remake of *Escape from Alcatraz*, starring mice. But I needed to focus on the present. It was still a relatively braw bricht moonlicht nicht, and I prayed the colour of my fur was blending in with the colour of the clay to camouflage me from passing owls.

Eventually, I reached the ground unscathed, and scampered into the safety of a crowberry patch. From there, I concentrated really, really hard. *Miss Blaine*, I transmitted, *this is Shona McMonagle, except now I'm a mouse, which wasn't my fault, and I wonder if you could turn me back into me so that I can complete my mission.*

I kept concentrating, and while I didn't exactly hear a voice, my fur and whiskers were ruffled by a gust of wind, which seemed to grumble, *Well might you wonder, girl.*

I waited for a while, but nothing happened. I was on my own. And then I wasn't. Something was creeping through the crowberry patch towards me. I focused on my tiny claws and my tiny teeth and wondered how big the something's claws and teeth might be.

"So this is where you've got to," said Frank. "I didn't even know you'd gone. You could have wakened me."

Relief made me forthright. "Yes, that would have worked, a mouse trotting over to the Macbeths' cat and squeaking in its ear. You'd have been superannuated before you got your eyes open."

"Perhaps," he conceded. "But why did you leave?"

I tried to use words he would understand. "I wanted to send a message up into the heavens for my sorceress, but it's not been as successful as I hoped. I really need to be a person again."

"Mo can sort that out for you," he said.

"That'll be right," I said.

"Good. Do you want to go now?"

I wasn't sure whether he didn't understand because he was a cat or because he was English.

"When I say, 'That'll be right', it's meant ironically," I explained.

He considered this. "So when you say, 'That'll be right', you mean, 'That'll be wrong'?"

"That's about right," I said.

His fur bristled. "What you're really saying is that you don't believe me."

"I wouldn't put it quite like that. It's more that I think you may be mistaken. She wouldn't be my go-to witch, not after the problem with the tadpole, and turning you into a cat."

He was standing rigidly now, his tail stiff and straight. "The tadpole problem was because she sneezed. And turning me into a cat certainly saved my life. She's the most talented and proficient witch I know."

I forbore to ask how many witches he knew. "That's not what her sisters say," I reminded him.

"You don't want to listen to a word they say. She may be their little sister, but she's well in advance of what they can do. I think they're conscious of their own limitations, and they put her down to mask their own lack of confidence."

"That's very insightful," I said, although I thought all he was doing was building on what I had said to Mo in a bid to boost her confidence.

"I consider myself something of a student of human nature," he murmured, not giving me any credit. "It's a skill that informs my writing."

He was so defensive about Mo that I wondered if he might have a wee bit of a crush on her. So much so that he was missing the obvious evidence that she was a pretty useless witch.

"If she's able to turn me back, why hasn't she turned you back?" I demanded.

"She's tried a few times when she was sure Ina, Mina and Hecate were out of the way. It's quite a complex spell, involving a bell, a book and a candle."

"Isn't that for excommunicating people?" I asked.

"I'm an Anglican so it wouldn't work on me. In any case, Mo does it differently; she uses a pentangle too. I've deduced that it's effective only if the subject wants to be turned back."

"You don't want that?" I said. "Why on earth not?"

"I've already told you. My financial difficulties."

"But you don't need to go back to the seventeenth century. You can stay here, but as a person, not a cat."

"I wouldn't like that. Who could I talk to? The people round here aren't exactly sophisticated."

"How dare you!" I burst out. "I'm sick and tired of you Londoners thinking you're superior to everyone else, and treating us Scots as though we're ignorant teuchters."

His wee cat face frowned. "That's not what I think at all. It's not a geographical issue. But I'm a man of letters, a lawyer, a statesman, a natural philosopher. I can see you're very sophisticated, but you're not likely to be here for long if your sorceress needs you for other business. There's nobody else here I could have a serious conversation with. No, being a cat is much better."

"Being a mouse isn't better for me," I said. "I've got things to do and people to see."

"Nice rhyming," he said. "Although I have to admit that iambic pentameter is my default rhythm."

"It's the same with Shakespeare's plays," I said, remembering too late how rude he had been about his contemporary.

But he merely looked surprised. "Is it? So he's taking to play-wrighting as well as acting and directing? He must have a lot of time on his hands."

At least Shakespeare was sticking to one thing. Being a man of letters, a lawyer, a statesman and a natural philosopher suggested a bit of a grasshopper mind.

"If Mo's my best bet, I should get on my way," I said a little stiffly. "You enjoy your time in the castle with the well-stocked kitchens."

"Don't be silly," he said. "It would take you days to get back, supposing an owl didn't get you first. I'll take you."

I was about to thank him for the bannock and cheese by way of apology when his jaws clamped round me, and we were off. It wasn't any easier this time, and I was feeling positively nauseous by the time we reached the witches' cave, especially as Frank didn't let me down, but trotted inside with me in his teeth like a trophy.

"Hemlock!" Mo greeted him. "Welcome home. You must be starving. Oh, you've brought your tea with you. I'm not blaming you – you've got to live. But this time, could you eat the whole lot? Ina and Mina get upset when you leave bits of it around for us to step on."

"She's confusing me with another cat," mumbled Frank, and I could feel his teeth scratching my back. "I definitely do not eat mice."

I was beginning to suspect he protested too much, and that his non-mouse eating was confined to when he was a man of letters, lawyer, statesman and natural philosopher. He opened his mouth wide and I fell out, trying to stop my head spinning.

"The poor thing's gone catatonic with fear," said Mo. She reached down and very gently picked me up, putting me in the pouch round her waist, which was full of pungent herbs. I managed to haul myself up so that I could peep over the top. "I'm sorry to take away your tea, Hemlock, but I couldn't bear to see you eat the helpless little thing."

Frank put out a delicate paw, extended his claws and scored the earth floor.

"Don't be cross," said Mo. "I can give you some nice smoked salmon instead. Would you like that? Listen to me, chattering away to a cat as though it can understand me."

Frank scored another line. And another. And another. And another.

Mo laughed. "Goodness, Hemlock, you really are a witch's cat now. There you are, scratching at the ground because you're in a temper, and it almost looks as though you've drawn a pentangle."

"Almost?" snorted Frank. "It couldn't be more perfect if it was drawn with a ruler."

He had told me Mo couldn't understand him, but I was still startled when she responded light-heartedly, "Are you miaowing for food?" You would think that if a witch turned you into something, she would still be able to work out what you were saying. Was this another indication that she really was pretty useless?

"Let me find that smoked salmon," Mo went on.

As she turned, Frank clamped his clawed paws on the hem of her black cloak, detaining her.

"That's enough now," she said severely. "You silly thing, if only you could understand people talk instead of just cat – I'm not abandoning you, I'm going to get you something to eat." She pulled the cloak hard, dislodging Frank.

He stalked past her and jumped lithely up on to a protrusion in the cave's stone wall, which the witches used as a shelf. He walked along it, and with a flick of his paw, he dislodged a bell, a book and a candle, sending them crashing to the ground.

Mo stared at the trio of objects. "Oh, Hemlock," she said sorrowfully. "You must be desperate to turn into a man again. But I've tried so hard to get the spell to work, over and over, and it's no good."

She dabbed her eyes with the edge of her cloak. "Honestly, Hemlock, there's nothing I'd like more than to turn you back, although it would never work out between us, would it? Those few instants before Hecate appeared – I'd never seen anyone so handsome. I was actually relieved when I had to transform you to stop Hecate seeing you. I knew if you'd stayed in your human form, you wouldn't have given me a second glance. You'd have been off with Ina or Mina, and I really wouldn't have been able to bear that."

She sat down on a stool by the bubbling cauldron and Frank made a balletic leap from the shelf to land beside her. She stroked his head.

"Part of me's glad that you're staying a cat, and I can keep you here with me," she said. "But I wish I could meet you as a person and find out all about you. I'm sorry I'm such a rubbish witch and I can't do the spell properly. I'd better put these things back. I know you want me to try again, but I thought I was doing it right all the other times, and nothing happened."

"Shona, can you jump out of the pouch?" Frank called to me.

"I think so," I said. "As far as I know, my terminal velocity's low enough to let me fall quite a long distance without injuring myself."

I scrambled over the edge of the pouch and let myself drop. It was a wonderful sensation, as though I was floating gently like thistledown. I landed on the ground with absolutely no jarring.

I was lying there, calculating what else I could fall off, when Frank pounced, snatching me up in his jaws.

"No, Hemlock!" shrieked Mo. "You mustn't kill the poor mouse. I told you, you can have some salmon instead."

She lunged at Frank, but he easily evaded her and took me over to the pentangle he had drawn, carefully depositing me right in the centre. Then he sat back and looked at Mo, his tail swishing backwards and forwards.

"Oh, Hemlock," she said in wonderment. "Is this what you've been trying to tell me all along? I've never met such a clever cat."

"I'm not a cat, as you very well know," said Frank sourly. "I'm a man of letters, a lawyer, a statesman and a natural philosopher in the shape of a cat. You'd think a witch would know better than to judge by appearances."

"Don't yowl, Hemlock dear," said Mo. "Now I understand. I'll get on with it right away. You don't need to worry, we won't be disturbed. Hecate's off being horrible to witches further north, and Ina and Mina are out flying."

She lit the candle, rang the bell and began reading from the book. I had expected an incantation in Latin, but as my ear became attuned to Mo's rhythmical chanting, I realised it must be much older Celtic magic.

"*Brochan lom, tana lom, brochan lom na sùghain,*" she intoned, an almost sing-song quality to her voice. "*Brochan tana, tana, tana, brochan lom na sùghain.*"

Meagre and thin porridge, thin, thin, thin, meagre porridge.

As I crouched in the pentangle, the English words made no sense; and yet they must have had a mystical significance, because as the incantation went on, I became aware of my limbs elongating, my torso, my neck – and suddenly there I was, Shona McMonagle, person, lying on a pentangle on very rough ground, wearing my hodden grey and my clarty DMs.

I hardly had time to adjust to not being tiny, or to check whether I still had a collapsible rib-cage and prehensile phalanges, when I heard Mo's voice.

"Oh," said Mo. "It's you."

She sounded disappointed.

"Who were you expecting?" I asked.

She looked round at Frank.

I decided it best not to mention that I knew all about the *tendresse* she had for him. She had, after all, thought she was speaking to herself.

"Why were you expecting the cat to turn into someone when I was the one in the pentangle?" I asked.

She looked a wee bit uncomfortable. "I thought you were some sort of sacrifice. Something bad would happen to you, and then Hemlock would be a person again. I mean, I didn't know it was you, obviously."

"Obviously," I agreed, leaving it up to her to decide whether or not I was being sarcastic.

She picked up Frank, cradled him in her arms, and kissed him on his wee black nose.

"I probably wasn't confident enough when I tried it before," she said. "Now I know what I'm doing, I'll have you back to your old self in no time."

She attempted to put Frank in the middle of the pentangle. Despite myself, I was impressed. All four of his legs shot out at right angles, he hissed, spat, scratched and clawed.

"Ow!" Mo dropped him (he landed with weightless elegance) and sucked at a badly scratched finger. "What's that all about?"

"He doesn't want to go back to his old self," I said. "Obviously."

Mo scowled at me. "It's not obvious at all. He's just a wee bit skittish about being picked up."

"Trust me," I said. "He and I have talked about it."

"Mice and cats have conversations, do they?" She made it sound absurd. I thought that was a bit much from someone whose relatives threw frogs' toes into cauldrons.

"How else would I know he wants to stay a cat?" I pointed out.

"That doesn't make any sense. Why would he want to stay a cat?"

69

"Well," I began. I was swithering between telling her about his money troubles in the seventeenth century, or explaining that apart from me, there was nobody sophisticated enough for him to talk to in the eleventh century, when a lump of black fur cannonballed into me, practically knocking me over. I guessed this meant he didn't want me repeating our conversation.

"It's a matter of personal choice," I concluded. "Anyway, aren't you going to ask why I was a mouse?"

She shrugged. "Hecate?"

"That's right," I said. "And she turned me into a mouse because she thought I was consorting with you."

Mo gasped. "I do not consort! And certainly not with the likes of you."

I took this to mean people from Edinburgh, which confirmed Frank's view of the lack of local sophistication.

"Anyway, I can't hang about chatting," I said. "I'm on a mission. I have to get back to the castle."

"What sort of a mission?" asked Mo.

I considered telling her that her sister was pressurising Macbeth into committing a murder. But that might create more family tensions. The witches were obviously fond of their brother-in-law, and it wouldn't do to have them forming a bad opinion of him when I was going to stop him before any harm was done.

"I'm a fool," I reminded her. "I'm the after-dinner entertainment. I have to work out my routine and, most important of all, I have to source a pig's bladder."

Mo giggled. "You can hit Gruoch over the head with it, and that'll be really funny. She won't think it's funny, which will make it funnier for everyone else."

"Good to know," I said. "I'll remember to incorporate that."

"I wish I could be there to see it," said Mo longingly. "But she never invites us to the castle, and even if she did, Ina and Mina would refuse to go."

"It's awkward when you've got a relative who's a murderer," I said. "I can understand you'd want to keep your distance in case it looked as though you were condoning her behaviour."

"That and her snootiness," said Mo. "She thinks she's better than us, always has done. But Ina, Mina and me, we treat everyone the same, no matter who they are, witch, non-witch, Highlander, Lowlander."

"Ask her about the English," muttered Frank.

"Poor Hemlock, that was a heartfelt miaow. Have we been ignoring you?" said Mo, bending down to stroke him. "We may treat everyone the same, but we love cats best of all."

"How do you feel about the English?" I asked.

She wrinkled her button nose. "I've never met anybody English. But I'm sure they're fine."

Frank purred.

I warmed to my theme. "And what about men of letters, lawyers, statesmen and natural philosophers?"

"They all sound terribly serious," said Mo.

Frank raced to the back of the cave, scrabbled about a bit, careered past us to the cave's entrance, did a somersault, and leaped back up on to the ledge where the bell, book and candle had been.

"I love it when he has a mad five minutes," said Mo affectionately. "He's so entertaining. You should take him to the castle with you – they'd love him even more than the pig's bladder."

When Frank had rushed to the cave entrance, I had seen that dawn would break shortly. I really needed to get on my way to stop Duncan going anywhere near the castle.

"What about it, Hemlock, old son?" I said. "Fancy coming with me?"

Frank gave me a disdainful stare before leaping off the ledge to land by Mo.

"Oh dear," she said happily. "It looks as though he prefers staying with me."

"I'll just make my own way, then," I said, heading out on to the moors as the sky began to lighten. I took in the endless vista of rolling hills, distant mountains and sparkling lochs, and

71

wondered yet again what on earth it was that attracted people to wild swimming. I much prefer Edinburgh's Royal Commonwealth Pool.

To my dismay, Birnam Wood wasn't where I had left it, but was significantly closer to the castle. As I approached it, I began going over my plan to send Duncan back home, preventing him from walking into a murderous trap.

I would be so apologetic – I had been sent with a second letter from Macbeth that superseded the first but unfortunately I no longer had it. Duncan would ask me where it was, and I would go into my dramatic explanation of being ambushed by a golden eagle, not any old golden eagle, but one with a two-and-a-half-metre wingspan, which wanted the vellum for nesting material. I would demonstrate how I had fought to keep hold of the letter, while the eagle's wings beat about my face, and its talons grazed my jerkin, its hooked beak tearing the vellum out of my grasp.

So now the message had to be verbal, but since I was the amanuensis who had written it, I knew exactly what it said and could report it accurately: terribly sorry not to be able to receive the king right now, unforeseen circumstances, but of course he would be more than welcome another time, date to be confirmed.

By this time, I had reached the wood. In daylight it wouldn't have fooled a class of toddlers. It was more than obvious that every tree had arms and legs, and was carrying a hewn-down branch in front of itself.

"Hello," said a tree.

I peered at it without recognition.

"We met earlier when we were a couple of miles further back," the tree prompted, beaming through a tracery of leaves. "You told me I wasn't a tree."

"And I'm the one who told him that trees can't talk," said the tree next to him.

"Of course," I said. "I remember you both very well. Sorry, you looked quite different in the dark."

"That would be because of the lack of light," explained the chatty tree.

"Very likely," I said. "I've come to have a word with the king."

"Help yourself," said the tree, shuffling along slightly so that I had room to get in. Once again, I battled my way through the rows, *sorry, gangway, could you shift a wee bit more, message from the Thane of Glamis and the Thane of Cawdor for his Grace, not actually got it with me, bit of a problem with a golden eagle,* until I reached the glade where I had met Duncan and his thanes.

It was empty.

I had a bad feeling.

"Where's the king?" I asked the nearest tree.

The tree shrugged. "Gone."

Gone? While I was off getting transformed by Mo, maybe Macbeth had sneaked into the wood and killed the king. But in that case, why had Gruoch wanted to delay Duncan's visit until Macbeth's brother arrived?

"Gone where?" I asked, trying to keep the anxiety out of my voice.

"Gone to the castle, him and the other toffs. Said he was fed up waiting outside. Meanwhile, we're left freezing our foliage off."

"That's a shame," I said. "I hope you warm up a bit when you go on your defence formation round the castle."

But that might be too late to save Duncan. Once again muttering apologies as I shoved through the tightly packed wood, I set off for Glamis. The sun was well up by the time I hammered on the door – despite having taken careful note of my mouse physiology, I was no longer able to flatten my rib-cage and slide underneath it.

"Knock, knock, knock! Who's there?" asked the querulous porter.

"Me again," I said.

"Are you a thane?"

"No," I said.

"Are you part of the retinue?"

"No," I said.

"Are you a foot soldier?"

"No," I said. "If this is twenty questions, you've only got another sixteen left."

"Do you think I'm a fool?" he demanded.

"No, *I'm* a fool," I said.

There was muttering on the other side of the door, and the creaking of the drawbar being shifted. The small, wild-haired porter peered at me.

"You should have said right away that you were a member of staff," he complained. "Grumpychops is in a terrible mood already, and if she's looking for you and you're not there, we'll both be in trouble."

"What's she in a mood about?" I asked uneasily.

"The king turning up out of the blue. He wasn't expected until tonight, but he just arrived, him and his thanes and his retinue."

I could hear noise coming from the dining hall, shouting, singing, the crashing of drinking horns.

"Says she's never known anything like it, roistering and carousing at this hour of the day. She's going mad, trying to get porridge for them all. There's so many of them, she's having to water it down – it'll be meagre, thin, thin porridge that they get."

I had a brief panic that his words would reverse Mo's spell, turning me back into a mouse, but nothing happened. Maybe they had to be said in reverse order.

"The king," I said urgently. "I'd like to go and check that he's all right."

I went to pass by the porter, but he held up his hand like a traffic policeman.

"You won't find him in there," he said.

I felt a shiver of disquiet.

"Where will I find him?"

"He's gone hunting with the Thane of Glamis and Cawdor. If you ask me, his thaneship was desperate for any excuse to get away from his missus. The pair of them sneaked out together not half an hour ago."

Or that could have been Gruoch's master plan. Separate Duncan from his thanes and retinue, ply them with strong drink and watery porridge, and leave him with the man she had trained to murder him.

I'd only ever been on a horse as a passenger rather than the driver, but if my mission needed me on horseback on my own, then that was what I would do. Lots of film stars ride horses – how hard could it be?

"Do you have a spare horse?" I asked. "One that's not too big and is fairly placid?"

The porter sighed. "I'm not a thane. My poor brain can't cope with your clever jokes. Is the answer a squirrel?"

"This isn't a joke," I snapped. "I need to find the king right away, so I need to catch up with their horses."

"What horses?" asked the porter in surprise. "How would you manage to catch anything if you were crashing around on a great big horse? No, they'll be creeping through the undergrowth, just them and their daggers."

I swallowed hard. "Which way did they go?" I managed to ask.

The porter took me outside. He pointed, I sprinted. I crossed open country until I reached more woods. I looked at the trees suspiciously, but this time, they were real, a genuine part of the Caledonian Forest. Once inside, I got down on all fours and proceeded by doing a bear crawl, close to the ground on my hands and toes, left knee and right arm moving together, right knee and left arm. I could creep up on Macbeth unobserved. It was also possible that I would actually meet a bear – nobody's sure when they became extinct in Scotland, but Macbeth and Gruoch's cloaks suggested they were still around – and this way, there was a chance I could persuade it I was a bear as well.

I was conscious of every small sound: scuttling animals, birds pecking, the creak of mighty tree trunks. And something else. It wasn't loud enough to be roistering and carousing, but it was heading in that direction. I headed in that direction as well, left knee, right arm, right knee, left arm, until I could squint round a tree at whoever was making the noise.

Macbeth and Duncan were sitting opposite one another in a clearing, propped up against tree trunks, belting out all of the old Gaelic favourites. From their enthusiasm, and a slight slurring of the lyrics, I suspected strong mead had been taken.

"That's us gone through the whole repertoire," said Duncan. "Perhaps we should start the hunt. Those thanes take a lot of feeding."

"Don't worry, I've sent my men out to take care of that," said Macbeth. "We can just relax, especially as you've got a big night ahead of you."

The words sounded casual enough, but knowing what I knew, they were chilling.

"I actually composed a song the other day, a tribute to my lovely wife," Macbeth went on, giving his shy smile. "Would you like to hear it?"

"I certainly would," said Duncan. "I envy you that wife of yours. What a mind she has. I don't believe there's any difficulty she couldn't overcome."

Pity you don't realise that you're the difficulty, I thought.

"I'll tell her you said that. She'll appreciate it, coming from you," said Macbeth.

This was horrible, listening to a conversation that was sheer dramatic irony.

"Let's have the song, then," said Duncan.

"It's called 'Red-Headed Gruoch'," said Macbeth, taking a while to find the right pitch. I wondered why he was preventing Duncan from going back to the castle, keeping him in this deserted place.

He began singing. He had a good voice, and it was a catchy little number. Duncan joined in the chorus, clapping to keep time. Under other circumstances, I would have done exactly the same, but I could hardly bear to hear the sinister lyrics, which drew heavily on Ina and Mina's rhyme scheme.

Red-headed Gruoch will dance tonight,
Dance until the morning light.

When Macbeth finished the song, Duncan, who had no concept that Gruoch's dance would be to celebrate his own death, said, "I do hope your good lady will allow me to have a dance with her."

"You're the king," said Macbeth. "Whatever the king wants, the king gets."

Duncan's eyes twinkled, and a stray sunbeam caught his gold circlet, making it twinkle as well. Mediaeval monarchs were supposed to live in constant fear of assassination, but if there was a memo, Duncan apparently hadn't got it.

Macbeth was implying the king would still be around this evening, but that could be a ruse – he could be planning to stab him to death any moment now. There was a reasonable distance between them. I calculated that if Macbeth tried anything, I would have enough time to intervene and disarm him. Since he wouldn't be aiming at me, I would be able to grab his arm with both hands and use his own momentum to send him crashing into a tree.

I was assessing the terrain when a hearty voice, neither Macbeth's nor Duncan's, called out, "Hello? Is there anybody there? I've been walking through this forest for miles."

"In here," Macbeth called back.

A few moments later, a man strode into the clearing. He was larger and hairier than Macbeth, and even more muscular and bearded. He wore a much bigger bearskin cloak, and the dagger in his belt made Macbeth's look like a butter knife.

Macbeth jumped to his feet, and they caught one another in a manly embrace. His arm still round the other's shoulder, Macbeth turned to Duncan.

"This is a surprise for you, my liege," he said. "Allow me to present my brother, MacBhàis."

Macbeth – MacBheatha, son of life. And now his brother, MacBhàis, son of death.

Five

Macbeth's brother, Macdeath, knelt down on one knee and bowed his head.

"My liege," he said.

Duncan now stood. He went over to the newcomer and raised him up, despite the vibes I was frantically sending: *stay well away from him.*

"We don't need formality here, young man," the king said. "I'm glad to meet you. I'm sure I can rely on your loyalty. I have a high regard for your brother."

"And a higher regard for my wife," said Macbeth, and they all laughed.

The laughter made me think of my own new role. I would intervene in my guise as a fool. They wouldn't take me seriously, and I could act as Duncan's bodyguard, ready to take them down the instant they tried anything. They might be big and hairy and have daggers, but I had my martial arts expertise.

I got to my feet and entered the clearing.

Macdeath whirled round. "What do you—" he began.

"I tell the jokes," I said. "This is one specially for his Grace. What do you call a Viking holding a branch in front of himself?"

Macdeath stared at me while Macbeth and Duncan smiled expectantly.

"I don't know," said the king. "What do you call a Viking holding a branch in front of himself?"

"Leif," I said.

"This boy's a fool," said Macdeath.

"I know," wheezed Duncan through gales of laughter. "Macbeth, were I a different sort of king, I'd be pretty peeved that you had such a brilliant fool, and I didn't have any."

"Oh, I don't know," I said. "You've got the thanes."

Macbeth and Duncan were now chortling so much that they had to lean against a tree for support.

Macdeath's hand went to his supersized dagger. "How dare you talk to us like that?" he snarled.

"Are we playing truth or dare now?" I asked. "Right, first question, and if you refuse to answer it, you have to lick your elbow. What's a secret you've never told anyone?"

Duncan and Macbeth stopped laughing and awaited the response.

Macdeath took a menacing step closer to me. "You actually expect me to tell you a secret I've never told anyone?"

"No, but if you don't, I actually expect you to lick your elbow."

"Let's hear the secret," said Duncan.

"My liege," said Macdeath, going red, "I cannot."

"I am your king," said Duncan with sudden force. "Speak."

"Now, now," I said, "that's not the way the game works. He doesn't have to answer the question, but if he doesn't, he has to lick his elbow."

"Lick your elbow," said Duncan.

"My liege," said Macdeath, going pale, "I cannot."

"I am your king," said Duncan.

Macdeath looked pleadingly at me.

"And I'm the adjudicator," I said. "It's truth or dare, and if you won't tell the truth, you have to accept the dare."

Macdeath bent his head towards his elbow and stuck out his tongue. It was miles away. Duncan and Macbeth started sniggering. Macdeath frantically grabbed his elbow with his other hand and tried to pull it closer to his tongue. Still miles away. As he desperately kept trying, he started rotating, faster and faster, like a dog chasing its tail, until he toppled over. Duncan and Macbeth were now completely convulsed.

"I hope I don't die laughing tonight," gasped Duncan, which set Macbeth off even more.

I helped Macdeath up. He was looking distinctly groggy.

"You did very well," I told him. "And you were quite right not to divulge the secret if you didn't want to. Never feel pressurised. I know I said you had to tell the truth or do the dare, but it's just a game, and you could have refused to do either. You would probably have been mocked a bit for sulking, but I'm sure that wouldn't bother you for too long."

"Who are you?" he croaked.

"I'm your brother's fool. That means I'm licensed to be as rude as I want to the gentry. I've been booked for the party tonight."

Macdeath, still staggering slightly, put his finger to his lips.

"Big night tonight," he whispered confidentially. "Have to be on top form to make sure nothing goes wrong. Feeling a bit sick, though."

"You sit down and put your head between your knees for a moment," I said, trying to sound sympathetic. I would normally have been very sympathetic: it's a horrible sensation when the fluid in your ears starts swilling around. But Macdeath had inadvertently confirmed to me that he was in on the murder plot, which was scheduled for night-time. At least that meant I could relax a little, now that I knew they weren't planning to do away with Duncan immediately in the Caledonian Forest, but this evening was going to be tough. I not only had to prevent Duncan being murdered, I also had my first official gig as a fool.

The four of us set off for the castle perfectly amicably, Macdeath having finally grasped that I had a dispensation to poke fun at anyone I liked, including Duncan and himself. Now that I was getting to know him better, I could see that his initial aggressiveness had been a defence mechanism, since he was almost as shy and self-effacing as his brother. He had also been overwhelmed by meeting royalty for the first time, and was anxious to prove to Duncan what a loyal servant he was. That didn't fit well with his grim task of murdering the king. I wondered whether he too would be subjected to Gruoch's special blend of wheedling and bullying.

I could almost have wished myself back to being a mouse to allow me to eavesdrop. But when the porter let us in, the three men went straight to the dining hall to start roistering and carousing. I didn't know whether this was a good thing or a bad thing. It was bad for Duncan, since he wouldn't be on his guard – but he wouldn't be on his guard anyway, since he foolishly believed Macbeth was his loyal friend. The drink might make Macbeth and Macdeath more belligerent and more easily persuaded to go along with Gruoch's evil plot. But alcohol also makes you less coordinated, more careless, drowsy and incoherent, which is why I prefer to stick to tea.

With the men occupied, I decided to check on the mastermind of the ungodly operation. The door to Gruoch's room was slightly open, and as I lurked in the corridor, I caught sight of her pacing up and down, wringing her hands as though she was washing them. I gave a peremptory tap on the door and walked straight in, the licensed fool.

She gave a gasp as she saw me. "You! This is all your fault, you know."

"All what, precisely?" I asked.

A pewter ewer and basin filled with water sat on the small table under the window.

"If it wasn't for you, I wouldn't have got ink all over my hands," she complained. "I've been washing them and washing them, and it still won't come off. I can't go in to dinner looking like a midden. I've got a position to keep up."

Yes, queen-in-waiting, I thought.

Out loud, I said, "I didn't do a thing. You were the one who grabbed the vellum."

"It's all going wrong," she said in a small voice, sinking on to the bed and dislodging more bits of straw from where she had stabbed the mattress. "You said it would wash off, and it hasn't."

All right, she was a murderess, but she was clearly upset, and

I felt the tiniest bit sorry for her. I thought back to the close encounters I had had with ink cartridges.

"It's because you've only been using water to wash your hands," I explained.

"How else would I wash my hands?"

"I'll show you," I said, praying that Miss Blaine was still being proactive about my requirements. I opened my pouch, and there was a small glass bottle.

As I took it out, Gruoch came close to see what I was up to.

"Such a beautiful, delicate thing," she marvelled. "Where did you find such a treasure?"

"Dunedin," I said confidently, since similar bottles were available in Morningside pharmacies.

I pulled out the cork stopper, which also amazed her, and a minty eucalyptus smell permeated the room.

"What a wonderful perfume," she said.

"Nice and antiseptic," I said. "Do you have a bit of clean cloth?"

She went over to the chest I had hidden under when I still had a collapsible rib-cage, and retrieved a torn piece of linen. I deduced that this was part of the material she had ripped up in order to make a tourniquet for Macbeth's leg.

I carefully poured a few drops of tea tree oil on to it.

"Hold out your hands," I instructed.

She put her hands behind her back.

"Are you a witch?" she asked.

"No, I told you, I'm a fool," I said. "Now hold out your hands."

Her response was to retreat across the room to the window, her right hand now hovering near the dagger in her embroidered girdle.

"Have my sisters sent you to me?" she asked.

"I told you your husband hired me as a fool to entertain the king. Why would your sisters send me to you?"

"To kill me," she said simply.

I diagnosed a serious case of psychological projection, a defence mechanism to prevent her having to face up to her own unacceptable thoughts. Because she was planning to have someone killed, she was unconsciously taking this character flaw and ascribing it to other people.

"Why on earth would your sisters want to kill you?" I asked.

"They don't like me," she said.

My immediate impulse was to tell her that was nonsense, but unfortunately I knew it was true.

"There's quite a big difference between not liking someone and sending someone to kill them," I said.

"Maybe, but don't think I haven't noticed you've not answered my question about whether my sisters sent you to kill me. All you've done is ask me why they would do that."

"You're overthinking things," I said kindly. "Just take what I say at face value. Your sisters haven't sent me to kill you. Nobody's sent me to kill you. All I'm trying to do is get the stain off your hands. Now let me see them."

I hadn't taken two steps towards her when there was a sudden flurry of hissing and spitting and I was confronted by a wide-open mouth containing extremely sharp teeth.

"You stay away from her," snarled Frank, who had just emerged from under the bed.

It was an extremely unexpected intervention.

"For goodness' sake, I'm not going to hurt her," I said. "Calm yourself."

"You talk to cats as well?" asked Gruoch curiously. "So do I. My husband says I'm just being stupid because they can't understand a word I say, but sometimes I almost believe that this one does."

"I'm sure he does understand the occasional word," I said. "He looks a clever little fellow."

"How dare you patronise me," spat Frank.

"Got a bit of a temper, hasn't he?" I said.

Gruoch was watching him in surprise. "I've never seen him like this before," she said.

"He probably doesn't like the strange new smell," I said. "Did you know that cats have up to two hundred million scent receptors in their noses? We have only about five million. It wouldn't surprise me if the dear little chap was suffering acute nasal discomfort."

"I'm warning you," spat Frank.

"Perhaps," I said, "you should put him outside the door to stop him being so upset."

"That's a good idea," said Gruoch, at which point Frank shot back under the bed. She laughed. "There – he doesn't seem to want to go. We can pretend that Spot understood our conversation."

"So we can," I said. "Anyway, I honestly am only trying to help. If you show me your hands, I'll rub them with this cloth. It's nothing to do with witchcraft, it's just oil from a faraway land."

She hesitated for a moment. Then she said, "Yes, I hear Dunedin is very far away, and that it takes several days to reach it," and came over to me with her hands outstretched. The ink stains were really quite bad, but as I dabbed at them with the oily cloth, they began to fade and eventually disappeared.

She stared at her palms in wonder, wiggling her fingers. "I thought my hands would never be clean again," she said.

"Tea tree oil's the thing," I said. "I'll leave this bottle with you. And another good tip – if you mix a few drops with whisky and water and dab it on yourself before you go out, it's great for keeping away the midges as well."

She took the bottle and stowed it carefully in the wooden chest.

"I can never repay such generosity," she said. "But I must try. What would you like?"

"Honestly, I'm fine," I said. "I'll easily get another bottle when I'm back in Dunedin." Then I remembered the prop I needed to make the evening a success. "Although if there's any chance of getting a pig's bladder…"

"I'll see to it myself, right away," she said, gathering up her dark green skirts and heading out of the room. I very much hoped she wasn't about to personally slaughter a pig.

Frank emerged from under the bed.

"What was that all about?" I asked. "Those teeth of yours are really quite scary."

"Gruoch's been very good to me," he said. "I didn't know what was in that bottle of yours."

"An antibacterial oil," I said. "You're as paranoid as she is. Mo's been very good to you as well. You can't really imagine that Gruoch's sisters would have hired me as an assassin?"

"Maybe not Mo, but what about Ina and Mina? You can never tell with families," said Frank darkly. "I heard about a man who poured poison into his brother's ear and then married his brother's widow."

"I heard about that too," I said. "It's just a story."

"Just because it's a story doesn't mean it's not true," said Frank. "And a story can give people ideas."

The absurdity of the situation suddenly struck me. I was arguing with a cat.

"One thing puzzles me," I said. "Now that I'm back to my old self, how come I can still understand you speaking when everyone else just hears cat noises?"

"I've been wondering about that myself," said Frank. "I think it must be because we've had a shared experience as humans transformed into other creatures."

"I was able to talk to the owl as well," I said. "Do you think it was a transformed human?"

Frank looked thoughtful. "They say the owl is a baker's daughter."

That was definitely a line from Shakespeare. Given how rude Frank had been about the bard, I thought it was pretty cheeky to quote him without attribution. But perhaps Frank was just saying what any of his contemporaries would say. After all, it came from a popular piece of folklore in which the Messiah went into a baker's shop in disguise and asked for something to eat. The baker put a huge lump of dough into the oven for him, but the baker's daughter objected, whereupon she was turned into an owl for being so mean. I didn't see how that would teach her much of a lesson. Owls are predators who have nothing to worry about apart from the occasional buzzard and fox. From my experience, it would have been a much better story if she had been turned into a mouse.

But the quote reminded me that Frank was a self-confessed man of letters. He could prove useful in my preparations for the evening.

"I'm trying to think up a few jokes for tonight," I said. "I'd be grateful for any help you can give me. But nothing too complicated. As you said, they're not as sophisticated as you."

"Few are," said Frank with a sigh. "If only it were possible just to write for people on one's own level. But you'd never make any money that way. You need smut if you're going to keep the audience's interest."

"I beg your pardon?" I said, my tone icy.

"Smut," he repeated more loudly, as though I hadn't heard. "That's what the groundlings at the Globe want when they come to see a play. Mention drink and sex, that always gets a laugh. Say something about how drink provokes lechery. And then say it provokes it and unprovokes it, because it provokes the desire but takes away the performance, and then—"

"I'll say nothing of the kind," I snapped. I was about to tell him what he'd said wasn't remotely funny, but that wasn't the point. "That's not the sort of material I use. I would never contemplate using suggestive or inappropriate topics just because they might get me a few cheap laughs."

Frank came as close to shrugging as a cat can. "Please yourself," he said. "But don't say I didn't warn you. When that lot are roistering and carousing, they won't want any of your posh intellectual rubbish."

"My jokes are excellent," I said. I decided to try out one of my best ones on him. "Why do elephants paint the soles of their feet yellow?"

"I haven't the faintest idea why they would do such a thing," he said.

"So that they can hide upside down in a bowl of custard without being seen."

He looked impressed. "That's very modern. Very avant-garde."

That wasn't exactly the reaction I'd expected, since I felt it was quite an old joke. "How do you mean?" I asked.

"Custard. It was only invented a few years ago."

I was mortified. He was entirely correct. I had told myself that custard tarts were around in the Middle Ages. But while that was what they were called, they were simply pies whose ingredients were baked in an egg and milk sauce. It wasn't until the beginning of the seventeenth century that "custard" started to mean just the sauce. There was no way my joke would make sense in the eleventh century.

"Thank you for reminding me," I said. "I'll need to change that before this evening."

Frank didn't seem to be listening. "Custard," he mused. "It's got a nice sound to it. It would be a good name for a character in a play. It would definitely get a laugh from the groundlings."

"Never mind the groundlings," I said. "Leaving aside the custard issue, what sort of a laugh do you think my joke would get from the thanes? Be honest."

After a moment's thought, he said, "If this is the kind of thing you're planning to do, take it from a professional – you'll be a disaster."

"I'm not exactly a stranger to public speaking," I said acidly. "I know all about tailoring my material to a particular audience. Why don't you come along this evening, and you'll find out how to be entertaining. Without the need to resort to the language of the gutter."

"If I come along this evening, it'll be so that I can rescue you when they start pelting you with the leftovers," said Frank.

"You wee…" I began, and was wondering how to finish without resorting to the language of the gutter when Gruoch came back in.

"Yes, he's a wee sweetheart, isn't he?" she said. "That's nice to see you getting on better now. But I'm afraid I've got bad news for you. We can't find a pig's bladder. Is that going to be a problem?"

Frank gave a mocking purr.

I definitely wasn't going to look dejected in front of him. "No problem at all," I said briskly. "We performers are always prepared for every eventuality. But could I trouble you for some vellum and a quill and ink?"

"Of course," she said, going back to the door and bellowing, "Vellum, quill and ink for the Thane of Cawdor's fool!"

Moments later, a servant rushed in, laid the three items on the small wooden table by the window, and rushed out again.

I dipped the quill very carefully into the ink, since I didn't want to have to use up any of Gruoch's precious store of tea tree oil. One downstroke, one loop and I was finished. I laid the quill on top of the ink pot, blew on the vellum until I was sure the ink was dry, and rolled it up.

"Thanks," I said. "All done."

She looked doubtful. "That's it?"

"It is," I said, and it was.

It seemed no time before we were off to the feast. It was quite something. There were bannocks, obviously, with butter and cheese and honey, sometimes all three at once. But there was also smoked salmon and salted herring, mutton stew with barley, roast beef with onions and turnip, and venison with kale and nettles. And for dessert, there were apples, pears and cherries. It was all good wholesome fare, but I got the impression that I was the only guest who appreciated the food rather than the drink. The dining hall was packed with thanes, not only Duncan's entourage, but all of the local worthies as well. Everyone apart from Gruoch was roistering and carousing. She sat by Macbeth, biting her Cupid's bow lip, and occasionally prodding him in a way that suggested he should roister and carouse a little less enthusiastically. He was ignoring her, not out of disrespect, but because he was so well away that I doubted he could feel the prodding.

Macdeath, sitting further down the table among some thanes,

was glowering, his hand clenched round a drinking horn. I had been so busy enjoying the food that for a moment I had forgotten Gruoch's evil plan. The plan that Miss Blaine had sent me to thwart.

And suddenly I understood why Gruoch had been so anxious not to let Duncan into the castle until Macdeath had turned up. She had seen how useless Macbeth was at stabbing, despite her best efforts to train him, so she had a Plan B. His larger, hairier brother, who even came equipped with his own hefty dagger, could be sent to carry out the murder if it turned out that Macbeth wasn't up to it. Looking at Macbeth now, his eyes unfocused, his hands unsteady, I would already have jettisoned Plan A. Macdeath could obviously hold his drink, and I doubted he would even need to use Gruoch's dramatic two-handed technique when it came to murdering the king. A glancing blow from him would be enough to finish off most people.

Duncan, oblivious to the machinations, was roistering and carousing with the best of them, occasionally cramming bits of food in his mouth, but mainly getting refills for his drinking horn, his gold circlet slightly askew. He gripped the edge of the long trestle table, and hauled himself to his feet.

"I'd just like to say a few words," he announced.

He could scarcely be heard over the hubbub, but Gruoch started shushing the thanes nearest her, and eventually they were all shushing one another until the noise died down.

"This has been a great evening," said Duncan, "and I'd like to thank Macbeth, the Thane of Glamis and Thane of Cawdor."

"What, all three of them?" shouted a thane who had been in the Birnam Wood glade. In the horrified silence that ensued, he gradually grasped that he'd nicked the king's joke. Pink with embarrassment, he slowly slid off his bench to hide underneath the table, where a fair number of thanes had already landed up.

"I'd like to thank," repeated Duncan, "Macbeth, who was already Thane of Glamis and whom I promoted to Thane of Cawdor."

There was scattered applause. I guessed quite a few of them wished they had been made Thane of Cawdor instead.

Gruoch now got to her feet, looking utterly regal, her Titian hair in two long braids, her green dress complemented by a large bronze brooch. She was also wearing a bronze circlet, which in the torchlight looked rather like gold and not at all like a party hat.

She laid a hand on Macbeth's shoulder, her slim delicate fingers contrasting with his thick bearskin cloak. The effect would have been completely ruined if her hands had been covered in ink. She must be pleased the tea tree oil had cleaned them up so effectively.

In a meek, deferential voice, she addressed Duncan.

"My liege, you honour us too much with your presence. My husband would thank you himself, but he is so overwhelmed by your munificence that he is unable to speak."

As overwhelmed as a newt, I thought.

Duncan waved his arm towards her. "Our honoured hostess."

There was more enthusiastic applause.

"And her husband says I can have a dance with her," he added, which led to a lot of puerile "woohoo"-type noises from the thanes.

I was appalled, first because of the sexist nonsense of "her husband says I can have a dance with her" – the only person whose decision it was was Gruoch. But second, I could see the perfect opportunity for assassination. Gruoch didn't only have a brooch and a circlet as accessories, she also had a dagger tucked into her embroidered girdle.

Duncan would claim his dance, and insist on getting up close and personal with Gruoch. At an appropriate moment, she would access her dagger, turning him from half-cut to full-cut. But she would do it cleverly. You hear about lots of people who've been stabbed saying they didn't realise what had happened; it just felt like a thump. Duncan would be easily convinced that he'd knocked into the table, so wouldn't raise the alarm. But soon, he'd slump to the ground, and Gruoch would say, "Oh dear, I think he might have had a little too much to drink."

Macbeth, or more likely Macdeath, would dash to the rescue, covering Duncan with his bearskin cloak to avoid any blood being seen, before picking the body up and carrying it to the king's bedchamber. The body would then be discovered in the morning, and I was prepared to bet that the blame would be put on Duncan's bodyguards, just as it was in Shakespeare's play.

In short, there was no way I was going to allow the dance to happen.

I jumped up and cried, "But first we must have mirth and merriment."

The thane who had been hiding since stealing Duncan's joke peered out from under the table to see who else was getting on the wrong side of the king. I could see Macdeath staring at me with sudden intensity.

But Duncan was beaming. "It's the fool," he said to a nearby group of roisterers and carousers. "This will be a treat. He's really terribly good."

I crossed to the middle of the hall, where I could be seen and heard at all three of the long trestle tables.

"Hello, good evening and welcome," I began before I was interrupted by a thane shouting, "If you're a fool, where's your pig's bladder?"

I went over to his table. "Right here," I said, unrolling the vellum scroll I had prepared earlier. "This," I said, indicating the line with a circle attached, representing a balloon on a stick, "is a virtual pig's bladder. No pigs were harmed in the making of it. And when I hit someone over the head with it, I want you all to shout, 'Oink oink!'"

I hit the enquiring thane over the head with it.

"Oink oink!" shouted the assembled gathering, roaring with laughter.

It was going tremendously well. Looking at the tables laden with food, I decided to try a joke.

"What do you call a thane with salted herring in his ears?" I asked.

They looked at me with bemusement laced with anticipation.

"Anything you like – he can't hear you!" I announced.

The place erupted. "Anything you like – he can't hear you!" they hooted, and started shoving bits of salted herring in their neighbours' ears.

"Which burns longer, a tallow candle or a beeswax candle?" I asked.

There was a lot of muttering as they tried to work it out.

"Neither – they both burn shorter!" I said, hitting a thane on the head to a chorus of "Oink oink!"

"Which side of a horse is hairier? The outside!"

"Oink oink!" they yelled, without me even having to hit anyone on the head.

"How many Englishmen does it take to batter down a castle door? Ten thousand – a hundred to hold the battering ram, and nine thousand nine hundred to move the castle backwards and forwards."

"Oink oink! Oink oink!" they bellowed.

I was on a roll now. "What gives you the power to walk through walls?" I asked.

"Witchcraft?" ventured someone before being quickly hushed by those around him.

They must all know of the estrangement between Gruoch and her sisters, so anything to do with witches was obviously off-limits. Macbeth leaned over to Gruoch, who was sitting very upright and expressionless, and patted her hand comfortingly.

"It's a very funny answer," I said, trying to sound jovial. "The thing that gives you the power to walk through walls is a door."

There was a ripple of laughter, but it was more relieved than amused. It was time for my best joke, finessed for the mediaeval era.

"Why do elephants paint the soles of their feet beige?" I asked.

There was silence. They all frowned in concentration.

"Come on," I said. "Have a guess."

Nobody answered.

"Do you give up? All right, I'll tell you," I said. "So that they can hide upside down in a bowl of porridge without being seen."

There was another silence.

Then a thane said, "What's an elephant?"

"You must know what an elephant is," I said. "The emperor Charlemagne had one, and that was two hundred years ago. St Augustine was always going on about elephants. Haven't you seen them in books? They're very popular as illustrations."

"I'm afraid this lot aren't really into books," said Duncan. "They're more into roistering and carousing."

"Oink oink!" shouted a thane.

"An elephant doesn't go oink," I said, possibly more sharply than necessary, but it always distresses me when I come across people who aren't into books. "An elephant goes like this." I gave an impressively realistic imitation of an elephant trumpeting. "Elephants are extremely large animals, twice as tall as a person, and about sixty times as heavy."

"I don't understand," said a thane.

"What don't you understand?" I asked.

"If an elephant's so big, how would it manage to hide in a bowl of porridge?"

"Perhaps it's a very big bowl," suggested another thane.

"It would have to be a very, very big bowl if you were going to get an elephant and the porridge in it," said the first thane.

"But if it's upside down in a bowl of porridge, how does it breathe?" asked his neighbour.

I was about to say that this was absurdist comedy – random, incongruous, the whole point being that it made no sense, the humour stemming from its complete lack of logic. But I realised in time that nothing kills an atmosphere like explaining jokes.

Suddenly, Duncan began to laugh. "So that they can hide upside down in a bowl of porridge without being seen! Brilliant – so funny!"

All of the thanes began laughing as well, but in quite an

uncertain way, suggesting they weren't entirely clear why.

"Tell us another," Duncan begged.

Taking account of their terms of reference, I couldn't ask how they knew whether an elephant was in the fridge, or how many elephants they could fit into a Mini. I ran through my list of possible topics: pigs; bears; cats; books – no, not books; thanes; and kings.

And then inspiration struck. I would teach them some knock-knock jokes.

"Right," I called, "we're going to have some audience participation. When I say knock knock—"

My attempt to get them to say, "Who's there?" went unheard as they all began shouting, "Knock! Knock!" and hammering their fists on the wooden tables.

The small, wild-haired porter rushed in. "Knock, knock, knock! Who's there?" he griped. "How can there be knocking from within?"

Duncan and the thanes thought this was totally hysterical. They spluttered mead and ale all over the table, slapped their thighs, slapped their neighbours' thighs, did high-pitched impersonations of the hapless porter. Eventually Duncan managed to control himself enough to say, "Peace, friend. It was the fool who got us all to knock."

"Oh, it was, was it?" said the porter grimly.

He marched over to me and grabbed my jerkin, for all the world as though he was about to give me a Glasgow Kiss.

He was smaller than me, and I could easily have disposed of him through my martial arts expertise. But it would look like a very unfair fight, especially since everyone apart from Gruoch thought I was a man, and in any case, I didn't think I should be brawling at a feast in honour of the king.

I could think of only one other thing to do. I whacked the porter over the head with the roll of vellum.

"Oink oink!" bellowed the assembled gathering, falling about in fresh paroxysms of glee.

The porter shrank back at the new outbreak of noise. "I'm going back to my door now," he growled at me under his breath. "But don't think I'll forget this."

He stalked out of the hall, pursued by shouts of "Oink oink!" and "Knock knock!".

I had made an enemy, but I didn't really care since I was so buoyed up by the roar of the crowd, even without the smell of the greasepaint. And I could see a way to draw the evening to a close, with Duncan hopefully forgetting his plan to dance with Gruoch.

"What we need now," I called, "is a cheeky wee nightcap."

This was met with shouts of approval.

I signalled to some passing servants. "Light a fire in the middle of the hall, bring me the biggest cauldron you've got, and water to fill it."

They looked at me disdainfully, but I drew their attention to Gruoch, and she gave them a brief nod. Now that the mistress had authorised it, it was accomplished in seconds. I manoeuvred the cauldron on top of the fire, and poured in the first bucket of water.

There was a blood-curdling screech and a drenched and furious Frank shot out of the cauldron, where he must have been asleep. Everyone jumped at the sudden caterwauling, and then applauded me as though I had conjured a rabbit out of a hat. Everyone apart from Gruoch, that is – Frank rushed over to her, and she began drying him with the hem of her gown, cooing reassurance.

As I poured in the remaining buckets of water, it struck me that there was probably now cat hair in the cauldron. But I figured the thanes were made of hardy stuff, and I just wouldn't have any tea myself.

My Darjeeling and Earl Grey mixture is fine during the day, but it's important to avoid caffeine before bed as part of good sleep hygiene. I opened my pouch and, sure enough, Miss Blaine had provided me with a camomile alternative. As soon as it had infused, the servants and I filled up all of the drinking horns. Once the thanes started drinking, some of them dunking honey-covered bannocks, the level of boisterousness gradually decreased. Camomile tea is an excellent sedative, containing apigenin, an antioxidant that also acts as a muscle-relaxant.

Before too long, Macbeth was crooning the song he had written for his wife,

Red-headed Gruoch will dance tonight,
Dance until the morning light.

But he was singing it as a lullaby this time, and nobody was showing the slightest inclination to dance. Instead, they sang along gently, swaying in time to the rhythm. Macbeth had his arm around his wife, and she was leaning against his shoulder, Frank nestled in her lap. The cat was still pretty damp, but I hoped he would understand that I had soaked him accidentally.

Duncan waved for me to approach him. I was going to do the kneeling-in-front-of-royalty thing again, but he grabbed me and caught me in an embrace almost as manly as the one between Macbeth and his brother.

"This is a very special night for me," he said huskily. "Thank you for making it even more memorable. I can't imagine there's anybody in the world who could be more of a fool than you are."

I felt he might have worded it better, but it's always nice to have an appreciative audience, and I told him I was very grateful for his flattering remarks.

"I'm really feeling quite tired after all the roistering and carousing and oinking and knocking," he said. "I think I might go to bed."

This was tremendous news. He had completely forgotten about doing a *Strictly* number with Gruoch, so was no longer in danger of being stabbed on the dancefloor. I would see him safely to his bedchamber and all would be well.

I should have known that murderers stay alert even when everyone around them is beginning to nod off. I doubted that Gruoch had even touched her camomile tea. The first indication that she was on the move was an indignant miaow from Frank as she stood up and he fell off. The miaow was just for show – being a cat, he used his righting reflex to land elegantly on his feet. The second indication was the swish of her woollen gown as she moved towards Duncan.

"My gracious lord," she said, "let me conduct you to your bedchamber."

"That's all right," I said. "I'll do it. You stay and look after your other guests."

"But you don't know where the bedchamber is," she said.

"I've got a good Scots tongue in my head – I can ask," I said.

"The king wishes to rest," she said. "We can't have him further fatigued by you dragging him all over the castle."

I felt like saying it wasn't much of a castle, particularly when you compared it to Edinburgh's, but decided that was unnecessarily inflammatory. That didn't mean, though, that I was just going to accept her unreasonable objection.

"Surely you can't be suggesting that your servants are so ignorant they won't know which room is the royal bedchamber? I'm sure they'll direct me to it in less than no time."

Duncan was smiling benignly at the exchange, but the set of Gruoch's jaw suggested she was getting quite cross.

"I am the king's hostess," she said. "What are you? Nothing but a fool."

"The fool doth think he is wise, but the wise man knows himself to be a fool," I declared.

Gruoch's brows knitted together as she tried to work out where that left me.

Frank, who had crept up to huddle by her ankles, gave a low hiss. That cat had a real problem with Shakespeare. I wondered what it was. He insisted that in real life he was a man of letters, so surely he would appreciate the finest writing of his age. But perhaps he was one of these pretentious types who would never admit to liking anything popular.

Duncan, though, was repeating what I had said and murmuring, "Marvellous. Such a way with words."

"As you like it, here are some more – suit the action to the word, the word to the action. Time to go."

I helped Duncan to his feet, and linking my arm in his, rapidly steered him towards the back of the hall where the corridors were.

"Sorry to bother you," I said to a passing servant who was going round with refills of camomile tea, "but can you tell me which is the best way to the royal bedchamber?"

"I'm afraid I'm new here," said the servant. "I know where the kitchens are, if that's any good."

This brief delay had given Gruoch the opportunity to catch up with us. She grabbed Duncan's other arm.

"Allow me," she said.

I could feel Duncan being pulled away from me.

"No, really, allow me," I said, hauling him back.

"The king wants me to escort him to his bedchamber," she said, tugging at him.

"I don't remember him saying any such thing," I said, hanging on to him.

"Then let's ask him," she said, coming to a sudden halt and forcing us all to stop, Duncan almost toppling over in the process. "My honoured lord, wouldn't you prefer me to show you to your room?"

"Your Grace," I said, "I'm sure you'd prefer me."

"Why don't you both take me?" he said genially, and off we went, at least two of us unhappy to be part of a trio.

Of necessity, I had to let Gruoch lead. We didn't go down the corridor leading to her room, but along the other one. She opened a door into a room that was definitely plush by the standards of the day. The large wooden bed with an ultra-thick straw mattress was covered by a purple woollen blanket, the shade suggesting that the yarn had been dyed with crushed brambles. A woven purple wall-hanging placed over the hole that was the window kept the room cosy. Sheepskin rugs on the floor had also been dyed purple. By the bed was a small table with a carved wooden bowl on it.

I wondered how likely it was that thanes always had a room ready for a passing monarch, complete with regal purple accessories. It was much more likely that Gruoch had prepared this room in expectation of Macbeth taking over the throne.

"Lovely," said Duncan. "Very nice." He sat down on the bed and bounced a bit on the straw mattress. "Very comfy. I'll be dead to the world. And what's this?" He indicated the wooden bowl, which I now saw was full of liquid.

"Ale, my liege," said Gruoch. "In case you feel thirsty during the night."

"Very thoughtful," said Duncan.

Except he didn't realise what the thought was; I did. With a shudder, I remembered how Macbeth had reportedly poisoned an army of invaders by lacing their drink with deadly nightshade.

"A fly!" I exclaimed. "You don't want to swallow that by mistake. I'll get it." I snatched the bowl off the table, pretended to slip, and managed to spill all of the liquid on to the floor. "Oops. Butterfingers. Sorry." I shifted a sheepskin with my foot so that it would soak up the alcoholic puddle.

"Don't worry," said Duncan. "I just want to get to bed. If I wake up and I'm thirsty, I'm sure I'll be able to call on a servant."

"Of course, my liege," gushed Gruoch. "Anything you want, just shout."

Yes, just shout, "Stop murdering me", and see how well that works, I thought.

"I'd better get to bed as well," I said. I noticed Gruoch didn't enquire as to where I was sleeping, and whether my accommodation was adequate. Her hostessing skills were clearly restricted to those higher up the social scale. Fortunately, I had worked out my own arrangements.

As we both left the king's bedchamber, she said acidly, "Try not to do any more damage."

"I'll do my best," I promised. Whatever damage I might do, it would scarcely be as bad as murdering someone. I watched her disappear along the corridor towards her own bedroom, and took up my position. I had expected the king would have bodyguards outside his door, as described by Shakespeare, but no one was there. Except now he would have me, Shona McMonagle, making sure he was safe.

I lay across the bottom of the door like a draught excluder, pretending to be asleep. But since I hadn't had any camomile tea, I was awake and alert. If Gruoch, Macbeth or Macdeath turned up with evil intent, they would find themselves in a chokehold before they could say, "Prepare to meet thy doom."

Even if I had been sleepy, I would have had trouble dropping off. The corridor was the main thoroughfare from the dining hall to the kitchens, and there was a constant to-ing and fro-ing of servants carrying platters and flagons and drinking horns and cleaning equipment. Floors had to have the straw on them replaced, and the tables and benches had to be sluiced down. Anyone passing me would have thought my eyes were closed, but in fact I was squinting out from under my eyelashes and taking note of everything that was going on.

I snored in a convincing manner as the activity continued around me, but the servants' clatter must have disturbed the king. With a creak, the heavy wooden door opened and Duncan peered to the left and to the right. Then he looked down and did a double take.

"What are you doing here?" he demanded.

"Just finding a quiet corner for a kip, your Grace," I said.

"Can't you find one somewhere else?" he asked.

"I've looked all over and I'm afraid this is the only space left," I said. "I hope you don't mind."

I was counting on his innate kindness and good manners, and I wasn't disappointed.

"Oh, all right, then," he said. "But do try to get some sleep."

"I will," I said. "Goodnight."

With a muttered "Goodnight," he disappeared back into the room and closed the door.

The next thing that happened was that Macdeath came along

the corridor, his bulk casting sinister shadows in the torchlight. He was heading straight for Duncan's door, and stopped abruptly on seeing me on the threshold. Rather than continue pretending to be asleep, I decided to confront him, and gave him a challenging stare.

"What are you doing here?" he demanded, just as Duncan had done.

"Unlike some, I don't have a bedroom," I said. "So this is where I'm sleeping."

He looked disconcerted, and went back the way he'd come, muttering.

A few minutes later, the door creaked open again, and Duncan popped his head out. It still had the gold circlet on it, but he was wearing a linen nightshirt.

"You're supposed to be asleep," he said accusingly.

"I thought I should stay awake in case you wanted anything, since I spilled your drink," I said.

His face cleared. "That's very kind," he said. "I wonder if you'd be so good as to fetch me some water?"

I stood up and waylaid a passing servant. "Water for the king, quick as you like."

The servant sprinted off to the kitchens.

"Oh," said Duncan. "I thought you would go and get it yourself."

"I wouldn't dream of doing that, your Grace," I said. "After all, I've noticed that your Grace has no bodyguards at the door, so I've taken it upon myself to perform that role."

"I don't have bodyguards because I don't need them," he said, a little testily. "We're all friends here."

"That's very kind of you to say so, your Grace. As your friend, I count it a privilege and an honour to be allowed to sleep across your door. You can't imagine how impressed everyone in Dunedin will be when I tell them."

The servant returned with a flagon and a drinking horn. If Macdeath had gone to the kitchens, he could have overheard the

101

order of water for the king, and poisoned it with deadly night-shade, just as the ale had been.

"I hope these have been properly cleaned," I said. "We don't want our pure Highland water contaminated with rancid mead."

"I cleaned them myself," said the servant earnestly. "They're perfectly safe."

"Prove it," I said. "Pour some out and drink it."

"Oh, I couldn't," gasped the servant. "This is for the king."

He made it sound as though his reluctance stemmed from respect for the crown, but it could just as easily have been because he didn't want to die a hideous death.

"I'm sure the king won't mind," I said. "He's just been telling me how we're all friends here. Isn't that right, your Grace?"

"Yes," said Duncan in an oddly weary tone.

I took a step towards the servant. "So have a taste yourself or I'll pour the whole lot down your throat for you."

His hands shaking, the servant decanted some water from the flagon into the drinking horn and gulped it down.

"It's fine," he spluttered.

"How do you feel?" I asked. "Is your heart racing?"

He nodded. "I've never met royalty before, and you're quite scary."

"Any hallucinations, blurred vision, headache or rash?"

He shook his head. "No, none of those."

His speech wasn't slurred either, so I was pretty certain he hadn't been poisoned.

"All right," I said, taking the flagon and drinking horn from him. "You can get back to whatever you were doing."

"Thank you," he mumbled, and fled.

"There you are, your Grace," I said. "Lovely organic spring water filtered through basalt rock. Would you like me to set these on your table for you?"

"No thanks, I'll manage," he said, and I noticed him wiping the rim of the drinking horn with his nightshirt.

"Goodnight, then," I said.

His reply was quite curt, and he closed the door behind him with a degree of force. If he had been drinking half as much as his thanes, he would have been very dehydrated, which never improves your mood. But he would feel a lot better after the refreshing water.

I settled down in front of the door again, mentally rehearsing my best Taekwondo moves. It was obvious to me now that Gruoch had assigned the role of murderer to Macdeath, and that was why he had been slinking along the corridor. But Gruoch had reckoned without me. Macdeath might be big and burly, but a backfist strike and a roundhouse kick would make short work of him. I would successfully complete my mission to the satisfaction of Miss Blaine, keeping Duncan alive to be killed decently in battle with Macbeth near Elgin. That made me feel a bit sad. I liked Duncan, even if he was being a bit brusque right now. But I had to remind myself that these were different times, different manners, and men spent their time having battles. Duncan and Macbeth seemed to get on perfectly well right now, but if they were going to be in a fight involving armies, the relationship was obviously going to deteriorate. I wondered whose fault it would be, and then told myself that that was unfair – there would probably be faults on both sides.

As I was pondering, a ball of black fur hurtled down the corridor towards me.

"Quick! Quick!" panted Frank. "Come with me!"

"I can't," I said. "I have to stay here to guard the king in case someone tries to assassinate him."

"Don't worry about the king, he'll be fine where he is," said Frank urgently. "It's Macbeth's brother – we've got to go and stop him."

My mind was whirling. I had just mentioned an assassination plot against Duncan, and without any sign of surprise, Frank had immediately started talking about Macdeath. I had no doubt that he kept his ear close to the ground, mainly because he was pretty close to the ground in the first place. He was in and out of

Gruoch's room, Gruoch having no inkling that her beloved cat could understand every word she said. I had deduced her wicked plan; Frank would have heard it directly from her. And now, bless him, he was looking to me to stop things before they started.

I sprang up. "Ready. Where is he?"

Frank was speeding off down the corridor, too intent on his task to reply, and I sprinted after him. He rounded a corner and I found him waiting for me at the entrance to a small, low tunnel that was in complete darkness.

"Down there," he whispered.

I grabbed a nearby torch off the wall and prepared to crawl inside.

"What are you doing?" he demanded in an undertone. "You can't take that in – the light will alert him."

"But I won't be able to see a thing," I pointed out.

"I will. Just follow me."

Cats have excellent night vision, able to see about eight times better than us in the dark, but how I was expected to follow a black cat in an unlit tunnel was beyond me.

Frank disappeared inside. I hesitated. He had another advantage over me: his whiskers, which let him judge the width of what he was getting into. The tunnel was narrow as well as low, and I wasn't at all sure how well I was going to fit into it. And then I realised that if the bulky Macdeath could access it, I certainly could. The only problem was that roundhouse kicks would be out of the question. But a key tenet of Taekwondo is developing an indomitable spirit. I could rely on my punching technique.

I crept into the tunnel on my hands and knees. It had a steep downward incline and it didn't smell very nice. In fact, the smell was downright horrible, an amalgamation of various ghastly things like mouldering kale, old porridge and rotting herring. All I could feel around me was earth, as though it had been dug directly into the hill on which the castle sat. It was disorienting to be in such all-consuming darkness, a darkness so profound that it seemed to have the quality of silence. I found myself holding my breath, feeling that any sound I made would be magnified a thousand-fold. I had no idea how near or how far Macdeath was, and Frank hadn't even briefed me on what exactly Gruoch's brother-in-law was doing. It must have been something alarming, given Frank's state of agitation. Sharpening his dagger, perhaps. I listened for the sound of a whetstone, but could hear nothing. Macdeath was worryingly quiet. I couldn't even hear Frank. I crawled warily forward, my hands stretching out into the darkness. There was a sudden tickle on my nose, a swish from Frank's tail, and I couldn't help it, I sneezed.

I froze. The sneeze must have alerted Macdeath to my presence, and let him know how far away I was. It had been quite a loud sneeze. I have a bit of an allergy to cats. Studies show that the problem isn't actually the cat's fur, but its saliva, and cats will keep licking themselves. I've asked my friends who have cats to sponge the animal down before I visit, but so far, none of them has, which I find a little disappointing.

I strained to hear the faintest sound that would warn me of Macdeath's approach. If I was crawling down the tunnel, presumably he was crawling up. But there was still no sound. Perhaps the tunnel opened out into a wider area where Macdeath was crouched, waiting for me. Or perhaps it even led outdoors. Although I couldn't see, I might be able to feel. I stretched out a hand to check for a faint breeze, but nothing.

And then, in the distance, there was noise. A great deal of noise. People shouting. People running. The noise wasn't coming from in front of me, but behind. Back in the castle. More shouting. More running. I strained to hear what was happening.

Suddenly, there was a piercing scream. It sounded like Gruoch. And then she spoke, her voice trembling in horror, and I was certain it was Gruoch.

"Woe, alas! King Duncan! The king is dead!"

Six

I had been conned by a cat. Lured away from my post so that the assassin could carry out his dreadful deed.

My first thought was that this was typical cat behaviour. Dogs are loyal, desperate to please, reliable. Cats are independent, calculating, sleekit. I was furious.

"Frank!" I shouted. "You get back here and explain yourself."

Nothing. My words echoed back at me along the tunnel, but there was no sound of scampering paws, no touch of a swishing tail or a wet nose.

My second thought, which should probably have been my first, was that I had failed in my mission. Miss Blaine had entrusted Duncan's safety to me and, due to my negligence, he had been murdered. Not only had I destroyed the integrity of Scottish history, with heaven knew what effect on the future, but Miss Blaine would demand an explanation, find it unacceptable, and never send me on another mission ever again. My name would become a byword for failure among current and former pupils alike.

I shuddered, which was quite uncomfortable, given the narrowness of the tunnel. And then I gave myself a firm talking-to. I was catastrophising, yielding to a cognitive distortion that undermined an accurate perception of reality.

Using the skills acquired through the finest education in the world, I reassessed my situation and realised that at this stage, I was completely overreacting. There was circumstantial evidence, true: I had heard Gruoch and Macbeth plotting, had watched

Gruoch trying to train her husband to be an assassin, but did I actually know what had just happened? No.

I was thinking the worst because I thought Frank had acted as a decoy. But Frank and I were, if perhaps not yet good friends, at least good companions. I could be doing him a terrible injustice by thinking so badly of him. The very first time I met Miss Blaine, she warned me that I should never assume, and here I was assuming that Duncan had been murdered. But it was entirely possible that Duncan had died of natural causes, given the average life expectancy in the Middle Ages. If that was the case, I couldn't be held to blame. I couldn't quite work out where this left the unfolding of Scottish history if Macbeth hadn't killed Duncan in battle near Elgin, but that wouldn't be my problem.

What I now needed to do was to check the facts, which involved getting out of the tunnel. I had no idea where it led, so there was no point in going forward. I had to back up. It wasn't easy, given the steepness of the slope. The effort made it seem a much longer journey and since there wasn't enough room for me to turn my head, I couldn't see my goal of the torchlit corridor. The only thing to encourage me was the fact that the shouting and the running were getting louder.

There was a sudden firm grip on both of my ankles and I was hauled out of the tunnel, blinking in the light. I rolled over to find that my rescuer was the porter.

"Thank you so much," I said. "I was afraid I was going to be stuck."

He looked at me with revulsion. I was concerned that he was still cross about the knock-knock jokes when I realised that my hodden grey had acquired a number of unsightly stains. I suspected that I might also have acquired some of the tunnel's pungent odours.

"What were you doing in there?" the porter demanded.

Sometimes a partial truth can work even better than a lie. "I saw Gruoch's cat, Spot, go in. If anything happened to him, Gruoch would be terribly upset, so I thought I'd better follow him to make sure he was all right. Except it was so dark in there that I couldn't see him, what with him being black."

The porter grunted. "The cat can look after itself. It'll be outside by now, hunting all the wee animals, and it'll come back in when it's good and ready."

Meanwhile, thanes and servants were still running past us, shouting and exclaiming in horror. The porter had obviously come to check out all the commotion, but seemed utterly unconcerned by it, presumably because as yet it was having no impact on his door.

"Excuse me," I said to the porter. "I'm going to go and see what's happening."

The corridor was jammed full of spectators. The shouting had decreased to excited chattering, and I was able to push my way to the front, using much the same technique as I had with Birnam Wood: *sorry, don't mind me, I'm just the fool, could I squeeze through.* I got a few surreptitious "oink oinks" in recognition as I went past.

Gruoch was outside Duncan's door, the very picture of shock and horror, one hand over her open mouth, the other clutched to her bosom. At this point, Shakespeare's play refers to people having to go off to hide their naked frailties, so I was relieved to see that any frailties she had were decently covered by her green dress.

"What's happened?" I asked.

Gruoch pointed at the door with a trembling finger, as though words were too much effort.

"Apparently the king's dead," said a thane.

"I'm sorry to hear that," I said. "But perhaps not surprised. Being a king must be very stressful. He probably had all sorts of underlying conditions. Had he been complaining of any health problems recently? What did the doctor have to say?"

I was trying to sound matter-of-fact, though my mind was whirling. It was crucial to find out what had happened. I needed confirmation that Duncan had died of natural causes, and not been murdered. In that case I wouldn't have failed in my mission to stop him being murdered. There was nothing about stopping him dying naturally. And I also felt quite sad that he had died. I'm an egalitarian, believing that we're all Jock Tamson's bairns, and I have very little time for the upper classes. But Duncan was the sort of king who gives the monarchy a good name.

"I don't think a doctor's seen him," said another thane. "Just the undertaker. He's in with him now."

A doctor would have been preferable, but surely an undertaker would have an idea of how the king had died.

I walked up to the door of the bedchamber. Just as I reached it, Gruoch, doing a good impersonation of someone overcome by emotion, collapsed against it. I was pretty sure she was doing it just to stop me going into the room.

"Could somebody get this lady a chair?" I said. "I'm just going to have a quick word with the undertaker."

Gruoch made an amazing recovery, rapping on the door and calling, "Undertaker!" in a remarkably strong voice.

The door opened a crack, and to my astonishment, I was face to face with Macdeath.

"The fool wants a word," said Gruoch. "You'd better come out."

He eased himself round the door and closed it behind him.

"You're the undertaker?" I asked.

His brow furrowed in confusion.

"Of course I'm the undertaker. That's how I got my name, the son of death."

Trying to look as though I'd known that all along, I said, "Well then, undertaker, can you tell us what the late king died of?"

"I certainly can. He died of stab wounds."

Even as I asked my supplementary question – "Self-inflicted?" – I could hear a mixture of reactions from the thanes and servants. Some were groaning in dismay while others cheered in undertones. I was appalled by the reaction. Duncan was such a nice man that I had thought he was universally beloved. And then I saw money changing hands. The rabble had actually been placing bets on the cause of death. But I couldn't waste any more time being appalled. Everything hinged on Macdeath's answer. If Duncan had, for whatever reason, sadly decided to take his own life, I was in the clear.

"Self-inflicted?" echoed Macdeath, disappearing back into the king's bedchamber. "Not unless you think he was limber enough to stab himself in the back a dozen times. No, he died in a frenzied attack."

At last I had my answer, but it was the answer I never wanted. I had destroyed Scottish history and turned it into nothing more than a piece of seventeenth-century drama.

"I'm so sorry, Miss Blaine," I whispered, but there was no response, no sharp pain in my big toe as though someone had trodden on it, no words carried faintly on the wind.

What I did hear was a thane further back in the crowd calling, "I have a question. Who did this most bloody piece of work?"

Macbeth, whom I hadn't even noticed, stepped forward.

"Me," he said. "I did it. I'm the murderer. I killed Duncan so that I could claim the throne. The king is dead. Long live the king. Which is me."

Gruoch curtsied low. "Long live the king," she said reverently.

The crowd repeated the words, but didn't sound terribly enthusiastic.

I was upset enough by my terrible failure not to care what I said. "You?" I scoffed. "You killed the king?"

"Yes I did," said Macbeth defensively.

"I don't believe it for a moment," I said.

Behind me, I could hear whispers of agreement.

"Of course he did," said Gruoch, rushing over to him and clinging to his arm. "Look how strong and manly and murderous he is." She ran her hand over his bicep. "Deliciously terrifying. How could anyone look at him and think he wasn't a murderer?"

"He's big and hairy and muscular, I grant you that," I said. "But a murderer? No way."

"He is," Gruoch insisted. "He's a big, hairy, muscular murderer. At last we have a worthy King of Scots. Not the sort of man you'd want to argue with."

"I want to argue with him," I said. "He says he's a murderer. I want to know how he did it."

If they had had headlights in those days, Macbeth would have looked like a rabbit caught in them. Gruoch gave him a nudge, but nothing happened.

"You heard the undertaker," she said. "My terrible husband, who's now the king, stabbed Duncan to death in a frenzied attack. So everybody had better watch out and do as he says."

"How did he stab him to death?" I asked.

Gruoch was at her sardonic best. "With a dagger."

That raised almost as big a laugh as my jokes.

"I'm not asking about the means; I'm asking about the method. Maybe the so-called king could give us a demonstration of how he went about it?"

Macbeth glanced nervously at his wife, and she gave him a faint nod. He pulled his dagger out of his belt, and I noticed something very interesting.

"That dagger hasn't got any blood on it," I said.

Macbeth looked panicky, but Gruoch riposted, "He cleaned it. He likes things to be neat and tidy. That's the sort of methodical man we need as a king, alongside the murderous rages. By the way, fool, speaking of cleaning things, you could do with a wash. You look as though you've been dragged through a tunnel backwards."

If she was trying to browbeat me, she had picked the wrong fool. I ignored her personal comment.

"I'm just asking the Thane of Glamis—"

"Great Glamis!" she snarled. "Worthy Cawdor! Greater than both, by the all-hail hereafter!"

"I think we'll leave the all-hail hereafter for the moment, until we're quite sure that the king was murdered by great Glamis and worthy Cawdor," I said.

"What, both of them?" came a voice from the back, which got another laugh. I wondered why Macbeth needed a fool, since they were all perfectly able to entertain themselves.

"What we'd like is for your husband to show us how he carried out the frenzied attack," I said.

"Of course," she said smoothly. "We'll need a volunteer to be the late king. Since you're so keen to find out what happened, I think it should be you."

I'd walked straight into that one. I couldn't refuse without a serious loss of face, but being the volunteer could lead to a serious loss of blood.

Gruoch got the crowd to move back a little, so that I could lie down and pretend to be asleep. I made sure my eyelids weren't completely closed, giving me the chance of a rolling side escape if I was about to be skewered.

"Prepare to tremble," Gruoch told the assembled gathering. "The king's strength is surpassed only by his ruthlessness."

"Not yet the king," I was about to point out when I realised that Gruoch was still talking, but under her breath. Rather than interrupt, I listened.

"Just remember what we practised, darling – arm up high to start with, and when you bring it down, don't stab yourself in the leg."

"Up high, don't stab leg," Macbeth repeated in an undertone.

"You've been doing brilliantly, my darling. Just this one last hurdle and the crown is yours."

As Macbeth turned towards me with the dagger, I distinctly heard him mutter, "Oh, great. Just what I want."

Squinting from below my eyelashes, I saw him raise the dagger aloft. Just as he plunged it downwards, he inexplicably stumbled, and the dagger ended up in the wall and stayed there, vibrating. I opened my eyes completely at this point to see a ball of black fur disappear down the corridor behind Macbeth. I wondered if Frank had deliberately intervened to ensure no harm was done, and then remembered that he was a cat – independent, calculating, sleekit – so would simply be off at speed to the kitchens to check out the leftovers from the feast.

"The king has shown mercy," Gruoch called to the crowd. "He is prepared to commit regicide in order to give you a better ruler, but he has spared the fool. Is this not a king who cares about his people, even the lowest of them?"

I decided to take the word "lowest" as referring to my lying on the floor, so I got up.

"I'm sorry," I said, "but that was completely unconvincing. While I appreciate not being murdered in a frenzied attack, nothing I've seen so far persuades me that the Thane of Glamis and Cawdor would be capable of such a thing."

I addressed the crowd directly. "Am I right?"

There was a bit of shuffling and looking at the floor from those at the front who could be identified. But there was loud agreement from those further back.

Macbeth's shoulders were hunched, as though he wanted to disappear inside his bearskin cloak, and lumber off into the Caledonian Forest. But Gruoch drew herself up to her full, impressive height, her button nose in the air, her jawline firm, her braided red hair gleaming against the green of her dress. She was back in sardonic mode.

"And if not my husband, pray, who else do you suggest killed the king?"

"That's easy," I said. "Your brother-in-law, the undertaker."

The reaction I got was even more gratifying than the laughter at my jokes. Gasps, intakes of breath, low whistles and more than a few mumbles of approval.

"In fact," I continued, "why don't we ask him?"

I rapped on the late king's bedroom door. "Hello? Have you finished undertaking yet?"

The door opened a fraction and Macdeath peered out.

"Almost," he said. "What do you want?"

"I want you to admit before all these people that you murdered the king," I said.

"Me?" said Macdeath in a surprisingly shrill voice. "Why would I kill anyone? I'm not an assassin. I'm an undertaker."

"Why would you kill anyone? Isn't that all too obvious? You're drumming up business. A royal funeral – that's got to be a nice little earner."

This time, there were mutterings of disquiet and dissent from the crowd behind me.

"How could you have the nerve to charge for a royal funeral?" demanded a thane.

"You couldn't. It wouldn't be right," said his neighbour.

Macdeath waited for the muttering to diminish before saying with great composure, "I would not accept a single bawbee for my work tonight. The sole reward I seek is knowing that I have done everything I can to prepare King Duncan for his passage from this world to the next."

"Everything you can, including stabbing him to death in a frenzied attack?" I asked. "That's certainly an effective way of preparing him for his journey."

"How could I have done it?" he asked. "I was nowhere near here. I've been roistering and carousing in the dining hall. Seven hundred drunken thanes will testify to that."

"You've been doing way too much roistering and carousing if you think there were seven hundred thanes in the dining hall," I said. "That's practically seeing quadruple."

"But it's where he was, and we can corroborate that," said a thane near the front. "He was with us the whole time, never shifted from his seat."

"That's right," said another thane. "We weren't moving while that venison with kale and nettles was still on the go. We came to see what was happening only when we heard the lassie – sorry, the lady of the house – saying the king was dead."

A lot of nodding and voluble agreement, which I didn't find at all convincing. The lot of them had been roistering and carousing, and I didn't believe any of them had the faintest idea who had been there and who hadn't. But they were insistent on their story.

Gruoch gave Macbeth a furtive shove. He cleared his throat nervously.

"My brother has been wrongly accused," he said. "There is only one person here who is responsible for the death of the king, and that's me. I did it, all by myself, which means I'm now king."

He looked anxiously at Gruoch and she gave him a confirmatory smile.

Someone was pushing through the crowd. Someone small and wild-haired.

"I'd like to say something, if I may," he announced as he elbowed his way towards the front.

A cheer went up as the gathering recognised the porter, and there were cries of "Knock knock!".

Glaring, the porter reached the space outside Duncan's door where Macdeath, Macbeth, Gruoch and I were standing.

"I can tell you who killed the king," he said.

"Yes," said Macbeth, "it was me."

"Excuse me for contradicting you, your thaneship, but no, it wasn't. The person who's responsible is that man there."

I looked behind me to see who he was pointing at. Gradually everyone shuffled to one side, and I realised he was pointing at me.

Seven

The thanes and the servants all fixed me with baleful looks.

"The fool killed our king?" said someone. "That's not funny."

"I didn't kill the king," I protested.

"I killed the king," said Macbeth, beginning to sound ever so slightly querulous.

"Yes, he did," said Gruoch. "My big muscular, murderous husband did it."

"With respect, your ladyship and your thaneship," said the porter, "I don't think there's a single person here who believes that's true." He turned to the crowd. "Anybody?"

Nobody looked directly at Macbeth and Gruoch. They raised their eyes to the ceiling, admiring the craftsmanship of the wood, they stared at the floor, fascinated by the tight-packed earth, they carefully adjusted their shirt sleeves and smoothed their breeks. Nobody was prepared to go along with Macbeth's insistence that he was a murderer.

But I couldn't see why they weren't prepared to go along with mine that I wasn't. It was obvious that the porter was making this completely unsubstantiated allegation because he was still cross about the knock-knock jokes, and being hit over the head with a picture of a pig's bladder. I could have understood if he had attached a bit of vellum to the back of my jerkin with "Kick Me" on it. But accusing me of murder was going too far.

"I've no idea what the porter's talking about," I said. "I was nowhere near Duncan's room."

"Yes you were," came a chorus of voices.

A middle-aged serving wench raised her hand as though to get a teacher's attention. "I was going along the corridor and that fool there was lying on the ground in front of the royal bedchamber. King Duncan found him and asked him what he was doing there, and he said that was where he was sleeping, and King Duncan told him to find somewhere else and he said no."

An old crone added, "I saw the undertaker come to bid the king goodnight, but he went away when he found the fool lying on the ground blocking the way into the bedchamber. The fool was stopping him seeing the king, who I warrant he had already murdered in a frenzied attack."

And then a young manservant piped up, "The king asked the fool to fetch him some water, but the fool ignored the royal command and told me to get it instead."

Encouraged by the reaction he got, the young servant continued, "And when I came back, the fool threatened me, and said he would pour the whole flagon of water down my throat. He's a violent man."

The crowd was beginning to back away from me.

"I think you're all missing the point here," I said. "Which is that the king was perfectly well and extremely alive."

"Maybe he was then," said the porter darkly. "But what about when I caught you trying to escape?"

"Escape? When was I trying to escape? This is a complete fabrication."

The porter addressed the mob. "He was escaping down the waste disposal tunnel."

Expressions of disgust flitted across various faces, including mine. I wondered if I could borrow a change of clothes. But first I had to challenge the porter's assertion.

"I was not escaping," I said. "I was coming back."

"You were wriggling into the tunnel. I grabbed your legs and pulled you out."

"I was wriggling *out* of the tunnel."

"All right," said a thane. "Let's suppose we accept that for a moment. What were you doing in the tunnel?"

"Do you know what he told me?" asked the porter. "Wait till you hear this. He told me her ladyship's cat was in the tunnel, and he was following it to make sure it was all right."

Everyone burst out laughing, including Gruoch.

"What's so funny?" I demanded.

"Spot's a cat, not a rat," said Gruoch. "You really think a fastidious creature like that would go down a waste disposal tunnel?"

"But he did," I insisted. "He told me…" The words died away as I realised that telling them about my conversation with Frank wasn't going to do me any good at all.

"I think we can all see the fool's evidence for what it is: worthless," said the porter. "He obviously killed King Duncan."

"No I didn't," I said.

"No he didn't," said Macbeth. "I did."

A thane who appeared to have drunk slightly less than everyone else took the floor. I had great hopes of him.

"We all know and love our fellow thane, Macbeth," he began.

The others stamped their feet in approval at this.

"You couldn't meet a nicer man or a better host. He's just not the sort to kill a king, especially not a king who, under the laws of hospitality, he has sworn to protect. This fool, on the other hand – a fool talks nonsense, and this is what he is doing when he tells us that he did not kill King Duncan."

"I think you'll find," I said, "that a fool speaks truth to power, which is exactly what I'm doing. I don't know how I can put it more strongly. I didn't kill the king."

"And I did," Macbeth added. "Which means I now get to take over the throne."

I latched on to using this argument in my favour. "If you persist in saying that I murdered Duncan, then that must mean I'm the king. And I can't believe you want a fool as your monarch."

"It's happened before," muttered someone.

The slightly-less-drunk thane, whom I decided to dub the Thane of Sobriety, said, "You can't be king precisely because you're a fool. You're common."

Another thane, glancing at my stained hodden grey, and wrinkling his nose, added, "Common as muck."

I got the message. Only thanes and such as thanes were allowed to become king. I bit back my views on Jock Tamson's bairns and said, "Just let Macbeth be king, then."

"But we've got a conundrum here," said the Thane of Sobriety. "The Thane of Glamis and Cawdor says he killed King Duncan, but we don't believe him. You say you didn't kill King Duncan, but we don't believe you."

I caught Macbeth's eye and he gave me a sympathetic smile. I thought that was quite sweet of him, given that his claim to the throne was being comprehensively rubbished. And then I remembered that despite all his protestations, he didn't actually want to be king, so presumably was quite happy with the way things were turning out. I, on the other hand, was accused of murder, and since I was common as muck and my alleged victim held the highest status in the land, I would probably be executed. That unnerved me. I concentrated hard on sending a message to the Founder. I hoped she might somehow overlook the failure of my mission, so I didn't mention it directly: *Miss Blaine, I apologise again that things didn't work out as well as I expected. Please would you get me out of here?* Nothing. Not a tremor.

The Thane of Sobriety stretched his arms wide and addressed the throng. "So, lads, how are we going to settle this? The usual way?"

I'm normally quite phlegmatic, but my heart rate increased quite dramatically. I didn't want to think what the usual way might involve. But even though I didn't want to, I did. The stocks? Beheading? Gralloching? *Miss Blaine? Hello? Can you hear me? I really need to leave now*, I thought with fresh intensity. Still nothing.

The thanes were all roaring agreement. "The usual way? Aye!"

I assessed my surroundings – an apt word, since I was surrounded. The servants might be on my side, since they were probably also in the common-as-muck category, but the thanes weren't. There were too many of them, and they all had fearsome daggers stuck in their belts. I had no chance of escaping down the corridor in either direction. Macdeath was standing in front of the door to Duncan's bedchamber. I imagined he was still cross with me for identifying him as the murderer, but even if he let me into the room, I was still trapped, since the castle's windows were deliberately too small for a person to fit through. Out of the corner of my eye I could see the porter going round checking that all of the doors were locked. My best strategy was to wait until I was arrested, and use my martial arts skills to incapacitate my gaolers when it was just me and them.

But there was no sign of anyone coming to arrest me. I glanced towards Macbeth again. His smile had gone and he seemed suddenly paler.

"That's settled, then," said the Thane of Sobriety. "The usual way. Our dear friend Macbeth, and this fool, in single combat."

The thanes all began chanting, "Fight! Fight! Fight! Fight!"

I found myself grabbed and propelled back to the dining hall, where Macbeth and I were left facing one another with the Thane of Sobriety standing by as referee, while the other thanes and Gruoch took the places at the trestle tables, and the servants started running round with more mead and ale.

"What's your weapon of choice?" the Thane of Sobriety asked Macbeth.

I found myself staring at the dagger in my opponent's belt. My expertise is in unarmed combat. The only weapon I've ever used has been a lacrosse stick. Gentle soul though Macbeth undoubtedly was, he was also a warrior, as well as being significantly bigger and hairier than me, and whatever weapon he decided on, he would win.

Macbeth drew himself up to his full height. The bearskin cloak emphasised his broad shoulders, the tilt of his bearded chin gave him a heroic look. Gruoch gazed at him in mute adoration and I could understand why she had fallen for him. But my current concern was what weapon he would go for.

In a strong, clear voice, he said, "I leave the choice to the fool."

There were raised eyebrows, then murmurs of approbation and loud applause.

The Thane of Sobriety bowed to him. "A true Highland gentleman," he said.

The attention now focused on me, waiting for my decision. I guessed that hitting each other over the head with pigs' bladders wasn't going to cut it. I couldn't think what to suggest. My martial arts skills enable me to defend myself or to save someone. But to get involved in a fight just for the sake of it – that was unimaginable.

And then inspiration came to me.

In a voice as strong and as clear as Macbeth's, I said, "I choose words as weapons – I choose flyting."

There was confusion all around me. Thanes and servants alike hesitantly repeated the word in a questioning tone.

"I don't know what flytings are," said Macbeth.

I was a few hundred years too early, but if I had already destroyed the timeline of Scottish history, I didn't see that it would do much more harm if I explained it now.

"We disparage one another," I said. "Poetically."

"Poetically?" asked Gruoch sharply, and I remembered the estrangement between herself and her sisters.

"It's all right," I said. "It's not in trochaic tetrameter."

The Thane of Sobriety was frowning. "You said words as weapons. But words aren't weapons. With weapons you can see who's winning, who draws blood, who ends up dead."

"Words can be the most powerful weapons we have," I said sternly. "It will be perfectly obvious who's wounded, and who's landed a killer blow."

"I still don't understand what I'm supposed to do," said Macbeth.

"Don't worry, it's easy," I said. "The idea is to be as rude and offensive as possible. So I'll start off by saying something like this:

> *You lousy loathsome lump, you useless thane,*
> *I've never known a character more flawed,*
> *You've clearly got an acorn for a brain,*
> *Your face needs slapping with a moistened cod."*

The audience, refuelled with alcohol, cackled as though this was the funniest thing they had ever heard.

"There," I said. "Have you got the idea? Give it a try. There are lots of rhymes for fool, if that helps."

"Hang on," said the Thane of Sobriety. "We don't have an adjudicator. I could easily do it if you were fighting with proper weapons..." He caught sight of my expression and quickly corrected himself, "... with actual weapons, but I'm not qualified to judge poetry."

Macbeth seemed to have a sudden thought. "Poetry," he said. "My sis—"

I just knew he was going to say, "My sisters-in-law would be good adjudicators." And that was going to cause all sorts of ructions with Gruoch.

I spoke over him. "Exactly. Your suspicion is correct – there's nobody here competent to be the arbiter. So I suggest we leave it to the popular vote and judge it by the clap-o-meter."

"The what?" asked Macbeth and the Thane of Sobriety in tandem.

"We hear how loudly this lot cheer and applaud," I said. "The contestant who gets the loudest support wins."

I turned to the trestle tables. "Let's have a practice. Give me a cheer for Macbeth, the Thane of Glamis and Thane of Cawdor."

"What, all three of them?" shouted someone.

There was loud laughter until someone else shouted, "That's the late king's joke. It should have been allowed to die with him", after which it tailed off into embarrassed silence.

I tried again. "Let's hear it for your gracious host."

This resulted in sporadic applause and a few muted cheers. I felt bad for him. We were fighting on my terms, not his, and it wasn't fair if he already felt he was a loser. At least when I asked for the audience's support, I would get even less, since they thought I was a murderer, and that might give Macbeth a bit of encouragement.

"And now let's hear it for me, a fool."

The applause was thunderous, interspersed with whoops and shouts of "Oink oink!". That wasn't at all what I intended, though it boded well for my winning. I wondered what would happen if I won. Would I simply not be executed, or would I win a prize?

Politely keeping my face expressionless at the acclaim of the crowd, I said to Macbeth, "Give it a go. I'm sure you'll do very well."

"I don't think so," he said in an undertone. "I usually try not to be rude to people."

"You're only being rude to me in the context of a literary competition, and I'll take it in good part," I assured him.

He adjusted the bearskin cloak over his shoulders, and strode round the dining hall like a prize fighter in the ring. I could see his lips moving as he tried out some lines. It was impressive that he was going to try to string a few words together. Even if the thanes didn't like it, I resolved to applaud him in a sportsperson-like manner.

He squared his shoulders and declaimed:

> *"You fool, you dolt, you simpleton, you clown,*
> *You should be flung into a squalid cell.*
> *How dare you fight a man of my renown?*
> *Your rhyming stinks, your jerkin stinks as well."*

The thanes were on their feet now, stamping, whistling and cheering. This was the sort of poetry they appreciated.

Striding round the room again, like a prize fighter who had just won the top prize, he whispered anxiously to me as he passed. "Was that all right? It was really difficult trying to work out the rhymes and the rhythm at the same time, and I'm not sure I did it properly."

The next time he passed me on his circuit, I whispered back,

123

"You were great. Really good – are you sure you haven't done this before?"

He gave his shy smile and mouthed, "No, never."

That was impressive. He hadn't even used "fool" as a rhyming word. "Clown" was much more difficult for a beginner, but he had managed it with style. I was going to have to up my game. As the thanes' cheering died down, I shouted:

> *"I don't know why they call you son of life,*
> *You'd get more life out of some soggy peat.*
> *You're absolutely henpecked by your wife—"*

The sudden dreadful silence warned me that my second verse wasn't as popular as the first. It continued for some time before Macbeth curtly addressed the Thane of Sobriety. "My chosen weapon is the axe."

There were loud cheers and cries of "This is more like it!". In an instant, the thanes had transformed themselves from a literary audience to a bloodthirsty mob who would have been at home in the Colosseum, giving all of the gladiators the thumbs-down.

The Thane of Sobriety held up an admonitory hand. "I'm afraid that it is too late to change. My lord has already allowed the fool the choice of weapons, for both combatants. The word-weapons it must be."

Macbeth gave him a look, and the thane dropped his hand as though he had been scalded. There was a pile of discarded weapons in the corner of the dining hall, and Macbeth strode over to it and selected an axe. He returned to where the Thane of Sobriety and I were standing, making all sorts of precise and fluid movements with the axe as he went, twisting, sweeping, slicing.

The Thane of Sobriety signalled to a servant to bring me an axe as well.

"It takes a lot to upset him," he said to me in an undertone, indicating Macbeth, who was now practising lunges and turns. "But once he's upset, he's like one of those Viking berserkers. I'm sorry, because I thought your jokes were very funny, and I wouldn't have minded hearing a few more. If I can give you some advice, don't bother fighting back, because you'll only get injured. Much better just to stand still and let him take your head off with a nice clean swipe."

He handed me the axe. It was about the length of a golf umbrella, but there the resemblance ended. I do regular weight-training, so the axe's weight didn't bother me. But the axe-head did. It was like a crescent-shaped meat cleaver, and the edge was razor-sharp.

I had faced the prospect of being killed on previous missions, and the same question came to me every time, and was never answered: What would happen to me? Would I simply never reappear in the library, cursed by my colleagues as they tried to cover my shifts? Or would my remains suddenly turn up, my headless body slumped in a chair, my head rolling off the desk into a wastepaper basket like a victim of the guillotine? It would be the talk of the Morningside steamie for weeks. I didn't care for either option, so there was only one solution: not to let Macbeth kill me.

I cradled the axe the way I had cradled my lacrosse stick on the playing field, and immediately I felt more confident. I no longer saw Macbeth as a large, hairy warrior whose prowess was far beyond mine. Instead, I saw him as a girl from an opposing team, in her Aertex shirt and pleated games skirt, whom I had absolutely no doubt I could beat.

Macbeth bore down on me, axe raised, and I couldn't help smiling. How often had I parried this move, an opponent thinking she could slice downwards on my stick and knock the ball out of my net.

"Stop!" The voice wasn't the Thane of Sobriety, but Gruoch.

On hearing his wife, Macbeth stopped instantly, and looked round in surprise.

Gruoch was on her feet at the top table, her red hair glowing in the light of the torches. "This duel," she said, "is being fought to determine who killed King Duncan. It is no longer necessary. I shall tell you who killed the king. It was me."

I practically dropped my axe in astonishment. I had honestly thought Macdeath was responsible. I waited for the cries of shock and disbelief, but instead everyone, servants and thanes alike, were nodding in a "that makes sense" sort of way.

"In case you're interested in how I did it," she said, pulling the dagger out of her embroidered girdle, "it was like this."

She held the dagger above her head in both hands, then drove it downwards towards the table, snatching it back up just before it slashed into the wood, repeating the move again and again until she finally left the dagger juddering in the table.

"It was a frenzied attack," she explained.

The Thane of Sobriety bowed to her. "The demonstration was completely unnecessary, my lady, since all we needed was your ladyship's word."

Everyone nodded vigorously.

"But it was very informative, thank you," he added. "I take it your ladyship now claims the throne? And may I say, how very appropriate, given your ladyship's lineage as granddaughter of Kenneth III. I think I speak for all of us when I say we'll be very happy to have you as queen."

"Your happiness or otherwise is of no interest to me," snapped Gruoch. "I murdered Duncan, so that makes me queen."

The thanes were all beaming and nodding, saying things like, "She's good, isn't she?" and "That's the sort of strong ruler we need."

"And," she said, her voice cutting across the chatter, "I shall be queen alongside Macbeth the king. There will be no nonsense about consorts. We will be equal partners."

There were a couple of resigned shrugs, but nobody seemed inclined to argue. Gruoch held out her hand to Macbeth. Smiling shyly, he walked over to her, took her hand and kissed it. The next thing, she grabbed him and kissed him. This gave rise to a few ribald comments, but in the main, the reaction was that they made a good team.

Eventually the kiss ended and Macbeth, looking a bit pink, turned to the gathering and said, "I think what we all need now is another drink."

This met with universal approval.

Even the Thane of Sobriety said, "I suppose since we're celebrating, I could have a wee sensation."

A servant rushed over with a drinking horn full of mead, and he drained half of it in one go before holding it out for a refill.

"Don't worry," he said to Gruoch, "I'll limit myself to six or seven. I need to keep a clear head if there's a coronation to organise."

This led to more shouting and applause. I took advantage of the new outbreak of roistering and carousing to make my escape into the corridor before they could start demanding that I caper, or tell more knock-knock jokes.

This was getting worse than I had feared. Not only had Scottish history turned into a Shakespeare play, it had turned into an inaccurate Shakespeare play. The bard had left Lady Macbeth with a scrap of humanity that meant she was incapable of carrying out the murder herself, but Gruoch was positively flaunting her homicidal tendencies.

I slumped to the ground, distraught to think that I was responsible for this whole mess. And then I saw a ball of black fur unconcernedly heading in the direction of the kitchens.

"Oi, you!" I called. "You're a very, very bad cat!"

Frank ambled over to me. "Gruoch thinks I'm a very, very good cat," he said.

"I bet she does," I said bitterly. "You deliberately got me out of the way. If you hadn't been a decoy, getting me away from my post outside Duncan's door, her plan would never have worked."

"Exactly," said Frank. "But I did and it did. If you'd stayed where you were, it would have spoiled everything."

I was going to berate him and ask him if he knew what he had done, but of course he didn't. Even if he had been a man of letters, a lawyer, a statesman and a natural philosopher in the seventeenth century, right now he was a cat, and was unlikely to comprehend the fact that he had changed the entire course of history. In any case, I had no right to blame him. I was the one who had left my post. It was all my fault.

But I couldn't stop myself saying, "Why did you do it?"

"I wanted to help her," said Frank nonchalantly. "She's a nice lady."

"And I'm not?" I demanded.

"You don't feed me," he said. "And you threw water over me."

That was one thing I wasn't going to take the blame for. "I didn't do it deliberately," I said. "And it was your fault for going to sleep in the cauldron."

"It wasn't my fault," he said indignantly. "Sleeping is what cats do. We can sleep for twenty hours out of twenty-four, you know."

"Of course I know," I said. "But you need to be more careful. Sleeping in cauldrons is dangerous. If you tried it at Ina, Mina and Mo's, you could end up boiled into a spell."

"That wouldn't happen," retorted Frank. "Mo would make sure I was all right. I like Mo. She's a nice lady."

He stalked off in the direction of the kitchens.

There was nothing more I could do here. I couldn't put things right. I sent a message to the Founder: *Miss Blaine, it's me again, Shona McMonagle. Please may I come home now?*

Nothing. Zilch. Nada.

And then I thought of Mo. Frank was right, she was a nice lady. And talented. She had transformed me back from being a mouse. Why shouldn't she be able to get me back to twenty-first-century Edinburgh? There was no point in sitting around moping. I would go and see the witches.

I've trained myself to be unobtrusive and I switched to that mode to go through the dining hall. But I needn't have bothered. Nobody would have paid me the slightest attention. Macbeth and Gruoch were dancing in the open space between the tables, gazing adoringly into one another's eyes, while the thanes sang the song Macbeth had written for his wife,

Red-headed Gruoch will dance tonight,
Dance until the morning light.

The Thane of Sobriety was singing louder than anyone else, except out of tune and to a completely different rhythm. I wondered when he would remember that he had a coronation to organise.

The small, wild-haired porter was snoozing by the main door, but his subconscious was working well since his eyes snapped open as I reached him.

"I'm sorry you got disturbed when I was doing my turn at the feast," I said. "I wasn't calling for you – I was telling a special kind of joke called a knock-knock joke. It's very popular where I come from, and it's a tribute to porters. I can't think of any other profession that has a series of jokes in its honour."

He looked at me warily.

"It goes like this," I said. "You say, 'Knock knock', and then the other person says, 'Who's there?', and then you say something like, 'Luke', and the other person says, 'Luke who?', and you say, 'Luke through the spyhole and find out.'"

I laughed to show what a funny joke it was, and he laughed a little as well, but I felt he was just doing it out of politeness rather than being amused.

"And," I said, "I'm sorry for hitting you over the head with the vellum scroll with the picture of the pig's bladder on it. It's a sort of instinctive thing that we fools do. I didn't mean to upset you."

"That's all right," he said. "I'm sorry I accused you of murdering King Duncan, although I really did think it was you. So old Grumpychops did it herself. Imagine! It makes you proud to be part of her household, doesn't it?"

I made a non-committal noise. I was shocked by how impressed they all were with Gruoch for having stabbed a perfectly nice king to death in what she herself admitted was a frenzied attack. He could have had years of happy ruling ahead of him. And I was hugely disappointed in Macbeth for just going along with it. He came over as such a nice, quiet man and now here he was dancing in the dining hall with his murderer of a wife. But I remembered that, despite their apparent closeness, he had concealed from her that he had just been visiting her sisters. I had seen more evidence of how two-faced he was when he met Duncan in the Caledonian Forest and pretended to be his friend. But I had tried to make allowances, telling myself that he had been pressurised into it by Gruoch. Now I had to accept that they really were in it together, and that despite his shy smile, Macbeth was just as devious and evil as his wife.

And I was disappointed in myself as much as in him, for not having realised all of this earlier, since I'm usually very astute when it comes to assessing character. But most of all, I was dejected that I had let Miss Blaine down by failing in my mission to stop King Duncan being murdered.

"I need to get out for a breath of fresh air," I told the porter.

He pulled open the drawbar and began chuckling.

"When you come back, you could do one of those jokes of yours," he said. "You could say, 'Knock knock', and I could say, 'Who's there?', and you could say, 'The fool', and I could say, 'Come in.'"

I felt he hadn't fully grasped the formula, but he was still chuckling away, so I let it go.

"That advice about looking through the spyhole was good too," he said. "Now that we're going to be a royal castle, I think I'm going to ask if I can have a spyhole. It would stop me having to shout so much."

"That's a good idea," I said. "And it should be quite easy to create. Just get Gruoch to shove her dagger in the door, twist it round a bit, and there's your spyhole."

I meant it sarcastically, but the porter slapped me on the back, saying, "That's a brilliant idea. As soon as I've closed the door after you, I'll go and ask her."

In his excitement, he practically threw me out, the drawbar clanking into the brackets behind me.

It was still dark, but I knew my way back to the witches' cave well enough. Orienteering has always been a hobby of mine, and I eat a lot of carrots, so I have good night vision. But before I set out, now that I was in the open air, I had one last try. *Miss Blaine, there's nothing more that I can do here. I'd like to come home, please.*

I think I knew before I started that there would be no reply. Miss Blaine was so angry about my failure that she was ghosting me. She had been cross with me before, but I had redeemed myself by succeeding in my mission. This time, redemption was beyond me. Waiting until she calmed down could take long enough: given that she was well over two hundred years old, she must work on a different time frame from the rest of us.

I was pinning all my hope on Mo now. I clambered down the steep hill from the castle, and set off in the direction of the cave. I couldn't have gone more than twenty paces when I walked straight into a tree.

"Hello again," it said.

"Hello," said the tree next to it. "He's the one you said wasn't a tree, and I'm the one—"

"Yes," I said, "I recognise you both. It's nice to see you again."

I had completely forgotten about the trees forming a protective honour guard round the castle during Duncan's visit. Much good had it done him. I wondered whether I should let them know what had happened.

"Have you heard anything?" I asked cautiously.

"Loads," said the tree. "Owls hooting, animals snuffling, Hamish here snoring."

"I do not snore," said the other tree indignantly.

"How would you know?" said the first tree. "You're asleep when you do it."

Snoring can be really disruptive to those around you, quite apart from affecting your own quality of sleep, so I taught him some throat-strengthening exercises and told the first tree to make sure he did them regularly.

But my heart wasn't in it, and I returned to my original question. "You haven't heard anything from inside the castle?"

"How could we, with all the racket out here?"

"I've got something to tell you," I said. "But I think you should sit down first."

"Orders to sit down, lads," called Hamish.

That hadn't been my intention: I was planning to tell just Hamish and the first tree, and let them pass the message on. But the next thing, all of the trees sank to the ground, still holding their boughs before them, and I was confronted by a bonsai Birnam Wood.

"I'm afraid I've got bad news for you," I called. "Good King Duncan has been foully murdered."

"Oh no," groaned the first tree. "That's terrible news."

"The absolute worst," said Hamish, a catch in his voice.

I was a wee bit surprised that such rough fighting men were so upset by Duncan's death. It was another reminder of what an exceptionally nice person he must have been.

"You know what this means, lads," said Hamish. "Iona."

Amid the outburst of whingeing and complaining, I said, "What?"

"The Isle of Iona," said the first tree, "where all the kings are buried. We'll have to take him there, and it's miles."

"Miles and miles," said Hamish. "Why couldn't he have got himself murdered in Oban? Then all we would have had to worry about would be the ferry."

"I forgot about the ferry," said the first tree. "I get seasick. This is a nightmare. Who murdered him, anyway?"

"Gruoch," I said. "Macbeth's wife."

"A woman?" said Hamish derisively. "What did she do, poison his porridge?"

That made me cross. "You don't think women can be proper murderers?" I demanded. "I'll have you know that she stabbed the king to death in a frenzied attack. You'd better be careful she doesn't come down and carve her initials on your trunk. You're her soldiers now, you know."

He brightened. "Maybe she'll just want us to chuck him down a well, and we won't have to go to Iona after all."

"She's a lady of great refinement and class," I said. "I'm sure she'll want King Duncan buried with full military honours in the royal cemetery." There was possibly something a little contradictory in my springing to Gruoch's defence, but I felt I had to contest such outdated eleventh-century views. "And now, if you'll excuse me, I've got a visit to make."

I pushed my way through the bonsai wood and began trudging in the direction of the witches' cave. It was going to take ages. It might not be as far as Iona, but it was very hilly, and I'd had quite a trying day and night.

I had reached the summit of one of the many hills, and was preparing to descend, when there was a swooshing sound, followed by another swooshing sound. A moment later, Ina and Mina were standing beside me, holding their broomsticks.

"Greetings, fool, how do you do?" said Ina.

"Could you make another brew?" asked Mina hopefully.

"All right," I said, not wanting to admit that I was actually on my way to theirs, though only in order to see Mo. "But it'll take me a while to get to the cave with all these hills. I'll see you there."

"But by then we'll be in bed," said Mina.

"Don't walk – come with us instead," said Ina.

The next thing I knew, they had each grabbed one of my hands, and I was being dragged into the sky as they set off again on their broomsticks. I had mixed feelings about this. It was certainly exhilarating to be flying about two thousand feet up, although my appreciation of the topography was limited since it was still dark. But dangling by my hands felt as though my arms were about to be wrenched out of their sockets. I engaged my bicep and latissimus dorsi muscles, the way I would when doing pull-ups in the gym, bent my elbows and lifted myself up to reduce the pressure on my arms.

I was inhaling and exhaling to make the exercise easier when I became aware of Ina breathing loudly as well.

"Mina, I feel really hot," she panted. "He's much heavier than I thought."

"As I told you before, it's muscle," I said with dignity. "If you did as much weight-training as I do, you wouldn't find it difficult to carry me at all. But wouldn't it be easier to let me ride pillion?"

"Pillion? That's a funny word. Not one that I've ever heard," said Mina.

"That's because it's normally used in connection with horses rather than broomsticks," I said, avoiding "motorbikes" just in time. "It means I sit behind one of you on your broomstick. If you land somewhere, we can sort that out."

The descent was rapid, and since I was much lower than the broomsticks, I was in danger of being splattered on a desolate moor, or at least breaking both my ankles.

"Let go of me!" I shouted, and thankfully they did in enough time for me to make a perfect parachute landing fall, touching my feet on the ground for only a nanosecond before rolling sideways to absorb the shock.

Then I scrambled on to the broomstick behind Ina. It creaked quite a lot, and needed a few words of encouragement in rhyme, but eventually it lurched upwards. By now there were faint traces of light in the east, and I could begin to make out the landscape. There was a river below us, which had to be the River Isla, and I calculated that Macbeth's Glamis Castle was quite far away from the Glamis Castle that was Queen Elizabeth the Queen Mother's childhood home. I wondered whether I could persuade the witches to take me on a daylight reconnaissance. The monograph could be illustrated. Perhaps being able to add so conclusively to Scottish historical research would redeem me slightly in Miss Blaine's eyes, if I ever got back to Morningside.

We landed with a thud, which Ina rhymingly blamed on me, and went into the cave, where Mo sat up, rubbing her eyes, obviously having been asleep. She perked up when she saw me, and then I noticed she wasn't looking at me but beyond me.

"Where's Hemlock?" she asked.

Given the family split, I thought it would be unwise to say he was in the castle. Instead, I said, "Sorry, I've no idea where he is" – which wasn't really a lie, since I didn't know exactly where in the castle he was. Her face fell.

Meanwhile, Ina and Mina had lugged the tea cauldron into the centre of the cave, and said the appropriate words to fill it with water and light a fire under it.

"Now the water's boiling well, this time can I do the spell?" asked Mina.

"I'm the eldest, I go first, making tea to quench our thirst," said Ina.

It was Mo's help I had come for, and she wouldn't be inclined to oblige if I sided with her sisters against her.

"Sorry, ladies," I said. "It would take too long to train you up, and I don't want anything going wrong. Mo showed real aptitude last time." Mo shot me a grateful smile. "But I'll let you turn down the heat, and fetch the goblets," I told the other two.

"Surely you need milk as well?" began Ina, but before Mina could reply, I retorted in metre she could understand, "Do you mind? Who's doing this spell?"

They had said they were going to bed shortly, so it would have to be camomile, and camomile tea with milk is just wrong.

I proffered the bag of leaves to Mo; she took a handful, and we both chucked the leaves into the cauldron on my count. Once the tea had infused, the four of us settled down round the fire with our gold goblets. Ina and Mina were complimentary about it in rhyme and even had a second goblet. But before too long I could see Ina yawning and Mina's eyelids beginning to close. I had to speak before they nodded off. Seeing Mo was the purpose of my journey, but there was something I should tell them all.

"I'm afraid I've got some bad news," I began. "Your sister's done it again."

"What, exactly? She's been mean?" asked Ina.

"That's her only side we've seen," snorted Mina.

Mo was looking at me with justified trepidation.

"She's murdered King Duncan so that she can be queen, and Macbeth can be king," I said.

"That's terrible," Mo burst out.

"It's just like we prophesied," said Ina with interest.

"We never said that Duncan died," commented Mina.

Ina tutted. "If Macbeth's to be our guy, surely Duncan had to die?"

Mina subsided and, after a moment, they both wrapped themselves in their cloaks and fell asleep.

"You're not going to bed as well?" I asked Mo.

She shook her head. "No, I'm a lark. They're owls."

I had a ghastly memory of my close encounter with an owl. Had it been Ina or Mina who fancied eating me? "Real owls?" I enquired.

"No, I mean I like to be awake during the day, but they do their work at night. We meet up at dawn and dusk. They say it's just more proof that I'm not a proper witch."

Her sisters had a lot to answer for, sapping her confidence.

"Ina and Mina brought me here by broomstick," I said. "But when you left me near the castle, you didn't have a broomstick."

"I don't need one," she said. "I can fly by myself."

"Quite. And they can't. Doesn't that tell you something?"

"That I can't work a broomstick?" she said.

I sighed. "Mo, don't you see? You're a much better witch than they are. You were able to turn me back into me, and you turned Fr— Hemlock into a cat to save him from Hecate."

She refused to accept the obvious. "I may have turned him into a cat, but I'm too stupid to turn him back."

"You're not," I said earnestly. "I've already explained to you, he doesn't want to be turned back. He's made that perfectly clear in our conversations."

She stared at me. "Are you serious? When you said you talked to him, I thought you were joking."

I was about to tell her about my jokes, possibly introducing her to the knock-knock ones, but reckoned that right now, she

136

wouldn't be particularly receptive.

"I'm completely serious," I said. "We were able to communicate when I was a mouse, and we still can."

She clasped her hands. "Tell me about him," she demanded.

"For a start, his real name is Frank."

"Frank," she said, sounding slightly disappointed. "I think Hemlock sounds better. And is he a warlock?"

"Not quite," I said. "He's a man of letters, a lawyer, a statesman and a natural philosopher."

In an instant, she turned despondent. "He sounds very clever. Far too clever for someone as stupid as me. I suppose he talks about Ina and Mina all the time?"

"He's never mentioned them," I told her. "But he talks about you. He's says you're lovely looking, and he'd like to consort with you, but he knows you could do much better than him."

"You've just made that up," she said dolefully.

"Surely you know if I'm telling the truth?"

She gave a dexterous sweep of her hand and said, "Say it again."

I said it again.

Her eyes widened in wonderment. "You *were* telling the truth. But why is he here? Did his sorceress send him, like yours did with you?"

"About my sorceress…" I began, and then I stopped. The reason I was here could wait. Mo was desperate to know more about Frank and it wouldn't be fair to change the subject.

"Frank doesn't have a sorceress," I said. "He came here by accident. He's having a few money worries, so he was trying to turn base metal into gold, and something went wrong."

She frowned. "What's base metal?"

"Something that isn't gold or silver. Iron, for example, or copper or bronze."

"I've never turned base metal into gold, but it doesn't sound very complicated," she said. "I can turn thin air into gold." Another sweep of her hand and she was holding a gold goblet to match the ones we had been drinking tea out of. I wasn't sure what to do with this information. Mo's skill with thin air would definitely make her more attractive to Frank, but given my most recent experience of him, I wondered whether that was a good idea. After all, he had now proved to be a devious, deceitful creature who deliberately drew me away from my post so that Gruoch could launch her frenzied attack on Duncan. And on balance, not the sort of person Mo should be consorting with. But if I tried to warn her against him, I could see a Romeo and Juliet situation arising where she just wanted to consort with him even more.

"Conjuring up gold from nothing – Frank will be really impressed by that," I said. "But don't show him yet. It has to be a surprise at the right time. I'll tell you when." I wasn't ever going to tell her.

"I haven't seen him for ages," she said anxiously. "I don't think he's ever disappeared for this long before. I hope he hasn't fallen in a peat bog."

"He's fine," I said. "He's with Gruoch." I could have bitten my tongue out when I saw the change in her expression. I might not want her consorting with Frank, but I didn't want to upset her.

"I thought he might prefer Ina and Mina to me, but I never thought he would prefer Gruoch," she said in a small voice.

"I misspoke," I said. "I don't mean he's with Gruoch, I mean he's up at the castle, and he's only up at the castle because it's got a bigger kitchen."

"I don't understand why he would do that," she said miserably. "I can conjure up anything he wants to eat."

"It's a cat thing," I said. "Just as dogs are utterly loyal and would never leave you, cats like going to different places and pretending that's their home, because no matter how good the food in their own home, they're always on the lookout for more."

I wasn't going to criticise Frank directly, but a few general remarks about cats might begin to sow the seeds of doubt in her mind.

She swallowed. "That's awful news you brought us about Gruoch," she mumbled. "I wish she would stop murdering people. And I hate it that Ina and Mina just accept it now and don't expect her to behave any better. I kept hoping that she had improved, but obviously she hasn't. Macbeth is such a lovely man. I thought he would be a good influence."

"I'm afraid it's the other way round," I said. "She was trying to train him to murder Duncan, but he was no good at it, so she had to do it herself."

Mo clamped her hand over her nose and mouth. I thought she was trying to stop herself crying, but instead she said, "I'm terribly sorry, do you mind? I really can't stand it any longer."

She gave another sweep of her hand, and I found myself clothed in a completely new and unstained outfit of hodden grey. Fortunately, I had retained my DMs, and they were still muddy, but it was a good clean mud. And Miss Blaine's pouch was still on my belt, in the unlikely event that she would send me any more assistance. Still, at least I had tea.

"I was in total awe of Gruoch when I was wee," Mo confided. "We all were, with her not being a witch. Imagine how organised and competent and busy you have to be if you can't call on magic to do things for you."

I briefly imagined a Morningside Library where I would give a wave of my hand and the books would stack and dust themselves, with name slips and rubber bands attaching themselves to reserved items of their own volition.

"We all felt really stupid beside her, not able to do anything ourselves," Mo went on. "She was so clever and glamorous. Her wedding was lovely – her first wedding, I mean. They made such a lovely couple. Her poor husband – we liked him. We had no idea she would go to the bad the way she did."

"One thing I don't understand," I said. "If you're not talking to her, how come you're so friendly with Macbeth? And from what I gathered at the castle, she doesn't know he's in touch with you."

"Oh, no, she can't know. She'd go completely mad. I don't mean mad like walking in her sleep and talking to herself, I mean she'd be really cross. He's so lovely, just like her first husband, and really family minded. He knew she had three sisters, but he didn't know we'd all fallen out because of her being a murderer."

"Did he know she was a murderer?" I asked.

"Of course he did. Everyone knows. Nobody believes her first husband was gralloched accidentally."

Something didn't make sense. He couldn't be that lovely a guy if he was prepared to marry a murderer, could he? Or perhaps he hadn't wanted to get married, and Gruoch wasn't guilty only of murder, she was also guilty of coercive control.

"He came to find us after the wedding, with some honey and bannocks from the reception. We hadn't even been invited, but she didn't tell him that. She told him we hadn't been able to come because we weren't well. How stupid was that? We're witches, we cure things. We've never had a day's illness in our life. And he'd found out where we stayed, and came to see if we were all right – that's how nice he is. He wants to have the family all together."

"That doesn't seem to have completely worked," I said.

"Of course it hasn't," said Mo. "Ina and Mina put a spell on him. It means he comes round every few weeks for a chat, but by the time he gets home, he's forgotten, so he doesn't tell Gruoch."

That explained why he had been so composed when Gruoch said they had no contact with her sisters. He didn't know he'd just been visiting them.

"It sounds a very complicated spell," I said.

Mo shrugged. "Not really. We're witches. We've got spells and potions for everything."

I wondered whether I should suggest that she say, "wise women" instead of "witches", and "mantras and herbal remedies" instead of "spells and potions," although what they'd been putting in the cauldron wasn't entirely herbal.

And then I thought now wasn't the time to say anything that might further sap her confidence, especially as it was a spell I wanted, and definitely not a mantra or a herbal remedy.

"When I met your sisters tonight, I was actually on my way here to see you," I said.

I had scarcely finished the sentence when I noticed she was looking utterly despondent. "It's to bring me bad news about Hem— Frank, isn't it?" she said. "You're either going to tell me that he's staying with Gruoch and never coming back, or that he really has fallen in a peat bog."

"Frank is absolutely fine, and I'm sure he'll be back any minute," I said. "I came to see you because you're the most gifted witch I know, and I need your help. I seem to have got stuck here, and I wondered if you could send me back to where I came from? In case it helps, that's Morningside in Edinburgh in the twenty-first century."

She clasped her hands and cracked her knuckles a bit, which I deduced was preparation.

"That shouldn't be too difficult," she said. "In fact, it should only take two shakes of a lizard's tail."

She quickly drew a pentangle on the ground and got me to stand in the middle. Instead of bringing the bell, book and candle into play, she fetched a mirror. That made sense. A useful prop for time-travelling spells, time reflecting back on itself. It struck me that there weren't any mirrors in the castle, despite the fact that Gruoch liked to cut a dash as well as visiting royalty. Cost couldn't be a problem, with Macbeth being a thane. And then I remembered this was a period when mirrors lost their popularity because of fake news that the devil was lurking on the other side. Mo had said how she wanted to be a good witch, but maybe witches didn't mind the thought of the devil hanging around.

As Mo went to hand me the mirror, I saw a hideous visage reflected in it. It was the devil, wearing a black hooded cloak. And the devil was definitely a she.

Eight

For a terrible moment, I wondered whether I'd seen a reflection of myself, and that the stresses of the last few hours had taken their toll. But no – I was wearing hodden grey, not a black hooded cloak.

I had seen that face before, though. The face of a hideous old woman with a sharp nose and jagged teeth.

Simultaneously, Mo and I said, "Hecate!"

"You're in real trouble now, my girl," she said.

She sounded so like a Marcia Blaine teacher that I thought she was talking to me. But of course she wasn't, since she thought I was a man, a man whom she'd turned into a mouse. She was talking to one of her girls.

Mo had gone very pale and was beginning to shake. Hecate, sneering and wrathful, was such a menacing figure that I couldn't imagine even a self-confident witch standing up to her.

"Why," asked Hecate, "are you not asleep?"

"I…" stammered Mo. "I…"

"Yes, you," said Hecate. "And you needn't think I don't know the answer. You're awake when all decent witches are abed because you're seeking to conceal your misdeeds under the cloak of day."

"I…" stammered Mo again. "I…"

"No, I," said Hecate. "I, to whom you owe your unquestioning allegiance, transformed this, this *man* to prevent you continuing your disgraceful behaviour. My instincts were right, to seek you out at this ungodly hour and catch you red-handed just as by some accident, you reverse my spell."

"It wasn't an accident," mumbled Mo.

"What did you say, girl?" demanded Hecate in a dangerous tone.

"I said it wasn't an accident." This time, Mo spoke loudly and clearly. "I did it on purpose, I did it ages ago, and it was actually quite easy."

"You dare to interfere in what I have ordained?"

Hecate pointed her finger at Mo and at that very moment, Mo pointed at Hecate. Nothing happened. And then I realised that Mo must be blocking whatever it was Hecate was trying to do. They were both beginning to breathe hard, as though they were doing a particularly tough gym workout, and I could see Mo's arm beginning to tremble.

"Quick," she whispered to me. "Call on your sorceress, the one who's much more powerful than Hecate."

"That's the problem," I whispered back. "I can't get through to her. That's why I came to you."

I saw a spasm go through her arm and suddenly she dropped her hand, simultaneously diving sideways. A fireball shot into the space where she had just been. Her agility was impressive. I could see she would be very good at judo.

Hecate aimed at her again.

Mo had assumed I would be able to help. Miss Blaine had warned me at the start of my time-travelling missions that I should never assume, and Mo's current predicament was proof of the danger it could lead to. But I felt I should do something.

"Oi!" I shouted. "Over here!"

Hecate shifted her aim and the fireball came straight at me. I forward-rolled away from its trajectory and it smashed harmlessly into the stone wall of the cave. I wasn't entirely sure what to do next. If she had a limited store of fireballs, Mo and I between us could goad her into using them up. And then I remembered the book on the shelf. It might get hit by stray flames and, as a librarian, I could never do anything that might harm a book.

Hecate pointed both her left and right index fingers, aiming at Mo and me simultaneously. This was getting tricky. She might put an unexpected spin on the fireballs, or go for a drop shot.

Mo scrambled to her feet, both of her hands up in the air. I didn't know whether she was preparing to return fire or surrender.

And then I saw Ina and Mina unwrapping themselves from their hooded cloaks, awakened by the stramash. They blinked a couple of times and their acumen was second to none since, before Hecate had even registered that they were there, they had swooped round to stand between her and Mo.

"Leave our little sis alone!" shouted Ina.

"Sod right off, you putrid crone!" shouted Mina.

They both raised their hands as well, which was obviously a witch thing, and began chanting, "Avaunt! Avaunt! Avaunt!"

The seriousness of the situation was underlined by this total abandonment of trochaic tetrameters.

Mo ran to join them, adding her voice to theirs, "Avaunt! Avaunt! Avaunt!"

Hecate seemed to stoop and diminish. She took an unwilling step backwards, then another.

"Avaunt! Avaunt! Avaunt!" the three sisters continued, now extending their arms and pointing towards her in time with the words, like football fans jeering at the opposition. They could have gone back to trochaic tetrameter and sung "you're not spelling any more" at her.

Hecate, hissing imprecations, was gradually retreating. Eventually she reached the entrance to the cave, and with a final curse, flew off into the daylight.

Ina and Mina hugged Mo.

"Are you okay, little sis?" asked Ina.

Mina glared in the direction Hecate had taken. "How dare she treat you like this?" she fumed.

"Thank you for rescuing me," said Mo shakily. "But this is awful. She'll wreak a terrible revenge on us. What are we going to do now?"

Ina looked at Mina and shrugged. "Now that we've seen off the creep, might as well go back to sleep."

After giving Mo a final hug, they lay down, wrapping their cloaks round them, and within moments there was the sound of gentle snoring.

Mo sat down on the ground, looking bewildered. "I don't know how we did it. She's the most powerful witch in the land, but somehow we defeated her. Our combined force must have been a scintilla stronger than hers."

"A scintilla is all it needs," I said.

Mo looked at her sisters and shook her head. "I don't believe this. She'll never forgive us. I wish we could get away from her. She'll make an example of us so that no witch ever tries to stand up to her again. How can those two be so calm?"

She needed reassurance. "It's because they know Hecate won't do anything immediately," I said. "She'll need time to think up something truly diabolical. And she'll attack you when you least expect it. So right now you might as well relax too."

Despite my soothing words, she didn't look relaxed.

"What truly diabolical thing is she going to think up?" she asked. "What if she kicks us out, says we can't be witches any more? I couldn't bear that. All I want is to be a witch. Ina would be devastated – she loves her poetry. And I know Mina wants to be a scriever, but she wants to be a witch who scrieves."

I tried again. "There's a story about a man who was condemned to death by the emperor, but won a reprieve for a year by saying that by the end of that time, he would have taught a horse to talk. Everyone said he was mad, but he said, 'A lot can happen in a year. I may die. The emperor may die. Or the horse may talk.'"

"Was it you?" asked Mo.

I didn't follow. "Was what me?"

"The man who taught the horse to talk."

"No, it's a story, and the point it's making is that you shouldn't worry about anything beforehand because it may all work out."

"Oh," she said, sounding unconvinced, "I just thought it might

145

be you because you're able to talk to Hem— Frank. I thought you might be able to talk to horses as well. Are you sure Frank's all right?"

"Of course Frank's all right," I said. "And even if he's not, it doesn't matter because cats have nine lives." I realised this might have unintended consequences. "Cats don't literally have nine lives – it just means that cats are really good at getting out of difficulty. So don't throw him in a cauldron when you're making a potion. In fact, if you're doing anything with a cauldron, it might be wise to check he's not sleeping in it first. But I wonder, could I trouble you for that mirror spell now?"

She rallied immediately, her professionalism confirming my view that being a witch was the right career for her. And then she gave a cry of dismay. The mirror had fallen victim to the battle with Hecate, and now lay on the ground in a hundred pieces.

"Never mind," I said. "I'm sure you must have a spell to put it back together."

"Of course," she said, "but mirrors are tricky. If you don't put them back together exactly as they were, it can cause no end of trouble." She concentrated hard for a moment, then snapped her fingers. The mirror reconstituted itself and she picked it up and studied it carefully.

"It looks all right," she said. "But you can never tell."

I had a simple question. "What's the worst that could happen?"

"You could end up about half a mile from your destination," she said.

"That's fine," I said. "I don't mind walking."

But she hadn't finished speaking. "Or you could find yourself in the middle of the ocean. Or cast into outer darkness."

I weighed up the odds. I really wanted to get home. There was some sort of problem in communicating with Miss Blaine. If I ended up in the middle of the ocean, or in outer darkness, the signal might be better. And of course, Mo was a very good witch who had probably put the mirror back together perfectly. I was prepared to take the risk.

Mo redrew the pentangle, which had got irreparably scuffed as we avoided the fireballs, and I stood in the middle.

Her eyes shut tight in concentration, she intoned, "*Brochan lom, tana lom.*" We were back to the meagre, thin porridge. Perhaps the words never changed: it was just the way you said them, or the props you used.

I braced myself. Nothing happened. Mo tried again. Still nothing.

"I'm really sorry," she said. "I can't do it."

"That's all right," I said, although I had a sudden uncharacteristic feeling of despondency. "You warned me that mirrors were tricky things."

"It's not that," she said. "This is beyond my power. You were sent here by your sorceress, and she's the only one who can summon you back."

I thought quickly. "You said the three of you together had the power to defeat Hecate. Perhaps the three of you have the power to send me back."

"Perhaps," she said.

She sounded doubtful, but it was definitely worth a try. I went over to the sleeping figures and prodded them awake. They were somewhat crabby, but I eventually persuaded them to team up with Mo to do the spell again.

They chanted in unison about thin and meagre porridge. Nothing happened. This was troubling. Given that Miss Blaine had an affinity with wise women, surely a triumvirate of them would get through? Something was wrong, and I didn't know what.

"Don't worry," I said, putting on a brave face. "I'll just go back to the castle now, and keep trying to get hold of my sorceress. It's a shame about the mirror."

"I told you it's not the mirror," said Mo earnestly. "The mirror's working perfectly well. See."

I had scarcely registered the words "meagre, thin porridge" when I felt the abdominal twinges that signified a bout of time-travelling was about to take place. My heart leaped. This was nothing to do with the mirror, but with the Founder. My pleas had at last got through to her, and I was going to be reunited with my beloved library, which I hoped hadn't been burned to the ground.

I closed my eyes in preparation for the unpleasant experience of passing through the vortex of the centuries.

"Hello," said a voice, "where did you spring from?"

I opened my eyes to find myself in the middle of a cluster of trees, one of whom was talking to me. Through his branches, I could see the steep hill topped by the big barn of Glamis Castle. The twinges had been nothing to do with Miss Blaine; it was all down to Mo and her mirror. The mirror was working, but Mo had used it to transport me from the cave into Birnam Wood.

"Long story," I said.

"Not as long as our route march," said the tree gloomily. "We're going to be heading off with the king's remains any moment. We're not even allowed to go to the coronation at Scone. That would have been okay, twenty-five miles and then a bit of a rest. But oh no, King-Designate Macbeth's orders, that's us off to Iona, and the minute we get ex-King Duncan into St Oran's Chapel, we've got to come right back."

"Two ferries in one day. I feel seasick already," said the neighbouring tree.

I would normally have sympathised, but right now I was feeling too miserable. In my mind, I had been halfway to twenty-first-century Edinburgh and finding myself still in eleventh-century Angus was an unwelcome shock. I also hadn't eaten for a very long time, which never enhances my mood. I would go to the kitchens and see if I could snaffle a bannock and honey.

I trudged up the steep hill to the castle and knocked on the huge wooden door.

"You have to say, 'knock knock'," came the porter's voice from the other side.

"Knock knock," I said wearily.

"Who's there?" asked the porter.

"The fool," I said.

"Come in," said the porter, pulling back the drawbar. When he saw me, he punched the air in triumph, excitedly bouncing on his heels. "We did it – we did the joke!" he proclaimed.

He looked so happy about it that I felt obliged to muster a smile. "So we did. It was very funny," I said. "Excuse me, I'm off to find something to eat."

The dining hall was packed with thanes and servants but there was no roistering and carousing going on. Out of respect for the late king, his body still in the castle, they were speaking in hushed tones, and serving, eating and drinking with the minimum of noise. I can tiptoe very quietly in my DMs, and the press of people meant I could go into unobtrusive mode and pass unnoticed. I was just going along the corridor that led to the kitchens when I spotted two thanes further down. With only two of them, and a narrow corridor, they couldn't fail to see me. Despite the sombre mood, I knew what they would be like. They would start mouthing "oink oink" and want me to murmur my routine, and I really wasn't in the mood. I shrank into the shadows and waited for them to go away. But they stayed where they were, whispering to one another, and with my excellent hearing, I was astonished to find they were discussing the flyting.

"What King Macbeth and the fool did was great," whispered the first thane. "Do you want to try it?"

"Yes, that would be brilliant," whispered the second thane. "You say your insulting verse and then I'll punch you, and then it's my turn."

The first thane thought for a while, trying out rhymes under his breath, then whispered as loudly as he could:

"We all know that you're useless as a thane.
You're always drunk, and probably insane."

"Oh, very good," whispered the second thane. "Great rhyming. Right, how dare you say that about me?" He punched the first thane on the nose.

The first thane held his sleeve to his nose to try to staunch the bleeding.

"Beginner's luck," he whispered modestly. "But it's actually not as difficult as you'd think. Go on, you have a go."

The second thane pondered. "I could start with – no, that doesn't work. Wait a minute, I think I've got one:

> *They talk behind your back, it's really sad,*
> *They say you're stupid, then they say you're mad."*

"Brilliant," whispered the first thane, laying into his friend for all he was worth.

I was aghast. They had totally misunderstood the whole point of flyting, which was the complete avoidance of non-verbal violence. Instead, they had invented an utterly distorted version combining flyte and fight. They would never have thought of it, if it hadn't been for me. Yet again, it was my fault.

They were both bleeding copiously now and a serving woman coming in the opposite direction handed them a manky dishcloth. She scarcely broke her stride, which suggested that she was used to seeing them beating each other up.

"Thank you," they both whispered after her.

She had nearly reached me, and since the servants had been oinking as enthusiastically as the thanes at the feast, I didn't want her to notice me. I needed time on my own to weigh up my situation. There was a door behind me. I pushed it, it opened, and I slipped round it to find myself in a darkened room. It was daylight outside, but the window had been shuttered, and the only illumination came from two candles at either side of a long rectangular oak chest with intricate carving on it. There was a soothing smell of beeswax mixing with another scent, like wood shavings.

I sat down on the floor and curled into a ball, with my head on my knees, and my arms round my head. Why was I getting no reply from Miss Blaine? When she had first recruited me, she had said I was allowed one calendar week to complete a mission, but she had never explained what the sanctions were if I missed the deadline or if, as now, I failed completely. Perhaps the punishment was to be left where I was. But for how long? A month? A year? For ever? My mind veered away from such a terrifying thought, and in doing so, conceived an even more terrifying one.

If I had destroyed the course of Scottish history, what did the future hold? Perhaps Edinburgh never became the nation's esteemed capital, never progressed beyond a small settlement on top of the Castle Rock – which wouldn't be the Castle Rock since there wouldn't be a Castle. And if there was no city to expand to the east, the west, the north and, most importantly, the south, then – I could feel my heartbeat race in panic – there would be no Morningside. And without Morningside, there would be no Morningside Library.

I'm normally very resilient. Like anyone else, I have the occasional moment of self-doubt, but it doesn't last for more than a second or two before I'm able to draw on the resources of the finest education in the world to overcome whatever problem I'm confronting. But right now, I was faced with the hideous possibility that the Marcia Blaine School for Girls would never exist. Because of my failure. I had destroyed generations of Blainers, all of whom, like myself, had the goal of making the world a better place. I had made the world a worse place.

That was why Miss Blaine was no longer answering my desperate pleas: thanks (oh, was ever a word less appropriate) to me, there was no longer a Miss Blaine.

A Scotland without Edinburgh, without the school, without Morningside, without the library. I couldn't help it, I burst into tears.

And then I stifled a yelp as a large hairy hand patted my shoulder.

"Whatever's the matter, fool?" came a gruff voice.

I recognised the hand and voice as belonging to Macdeath. I had inadvertently crept into King Duncan's bedchamber and the undertaker in his dark clothes had been hidden in the shadows where he was keeping vigil over the deceased. The rectangular chest, illuminated by two beeswax candles, was the king's coffin.

Not even the shock of finding that I wasn't alone, that I was closeted in a room with Macdeath and a corpse, was enough to deflect my mood of utter misery. On the contrary, it deepened my anguish.

I found myself starting to sob all over again as I blurted out, "It's all my fault. I should never have left my post outside the king's door. He was murdered because I wasn't there, and nothing will ever be the same again. I'll never forgive myself for abandoning him. Never."

There was a creaking noise followed by a crash. The carved lid of the coffin was on the ground. A figure was sitting up. The late king, still wearing his gold circlet, his nightshirt stained with his own blood.

I told myself that I didn't believe in ghosts. But then, until Miss Blaine turned up in Morningside Library one rainy day, I didn't believe in time travel.

The bloody corpse began to emerge slowly from the coffin. Under other circumstances, I might have been intrigued or curious, anxious to ascertain whether this was a genuine manifestation of the paranormal, or whether there was some clever trick behind it, as with Victorian ectoplasm. But I was at such a low ebb that all I felt was terror.

I could feel a scream bubbling up in my throat as the corpse began to move towards me, and in an instant, Macdeath grabbed me and clamped a hand over my mouth.

"Ssh," he said. "It's all right."

I tried to struggle free, but I was held fast.

The corpse was still approaching, its hand outstretched. It patted me benignly on the head, its hand warm, not bony and icy as I had feared, and said, "I can't tell you how moved I am by your heartfelt words." Its voice sounded perfectly normal, just like the late king's.

"I'm going to let go now," said Macdeath. "You mustn't scream. Understood? We don't want anyone bursting in here and finding the king isn't dead."

He loosened his grip on me and took his hand away from my mouth.

"The king isn't dead?" I whispered.

"Well, obviously not," said Macdeath drily. "Or do you think this is a ghost?"

Duncan laughed merrily at that, and Macdeath allowed himself a small chuckle. I joined in, to show that I understood what was going on. Except I didn't.

"What's going on?" I asked.

"I think we can tell the fool, don't you?" said Duncan. "It's only fair, given the esteem in which he holds me. And he does tell very funny jokes."

Macdeath bowed his head. "As you please, my liege."

There was a sudden rap at the door, making me jump. I really wasn't myself. Duncan put his finger to his lips and indicated that he and I should slip into the shadows.

Macdeath opened the door a crack, and as he did so, a delicious smell of cooking wafted into the room. My mouth started watering: I realised I was very hungry.

Whoever was on the other side of the door said something, but I couldn't catch it because their voice was particularly low, out of respect for the death chamber.

"No, just leave it outside," said Macdeath, his own voice solemn and subdued. And then he began to bring in trencher after trencher of freshly cooked food, rivalling the feast we'd had the previous night. He lifted the heavy coffin lid off the floor with no more difficulty than if it had been a piece of vellum, and set it down as a table, and the next thing, we were sitting round it, having an indoor picnic.

"I told them I wanted a snack, and they know I'm a big lad," he explained. "But we mustn't eat it all. Some of it's to sustain the king on his final journey."

"Final journey?" I repeated through a mouthful of bannock and cheese.

"It's a good job you're an undertaker and not a storyteller, because you're telling it all wrong, starting at the end instead of the beginning," said Duncan, who was tucking in to venison stew. "What you have to understand, fool, is that I've been king for long enough."

"Six years," I said.

"Is that all?" he sighed. "It seems longer. I just want a quiet life. I'm sick and tired of having to go into battle. Leading the troops, sleeping on the ground, field rations, trying to avoid getting killed. It takes its toll."

"Basically you thought sod this for a game of soldiers?" I said.

He burst out laughing. Or rather, he began to burst out laughing and in an instant, Macdeath was at his side, clamping his hand over his mouth.

"Forgive me, my liege," he said. "But laughter heard coming from this room wouldn't be seemly."

Once Duncan was released, he said, "You're right, of course. But it wasn't my fault. It's the fool's wonderful jokes. Fool, can you stop being so witty?"

"Forgive me, your Grace, but no, I don't think I can," I said, and we all had a quiet chuckle.

"Anyway," said Duncan, "I decided it was time to give up, and what better way than to fake my own death?"

"Couldn't you just abdicate?" I asked.

Duncan and Macdeath looked shocked.

"The king is the Lord's anointed," said Macdeath.

"Faking your own death it is, then," I said.

Even as I spoke the words, I suddenly realised their full import. If my mission was to stop Duncan being murdered, then I hadn't failed, and I hadn't changed the course of Scottish history. Although something strange was still happening. Macbeth was definitely supposed to kill Duncan in battle near Elgin, but the two of them seemed to be such good friends that I couldn't understand how that would happen.

"Are you planning to visit Elgin at any point?" I asked.

"Oh no," said Duncan. "I'm fed up with the mainland. That's why this is so handy, being taken to the royal burial ground on the Isle of Iona. Once I get to the Western Isles, that's where I'm staying."

I could see a potential problem. "Do your troops know the way? I mean, might they end up in Elgin rather than Iona?"

"Bless them, some of them aren't the brightest," said Duncan. "But they're pretty good at navigating by the sun, and they know they've got to go west, stop when they reach the sea, and then get a boat. Why do you mention Elgin? Have you got relatives there?"

"Certainly not," I said. "All of my relatives are in Dunedin." And then I thought that sounded a bit dismissive about Elgin, so I said, "I've been there, of course. It's a very pretty place. The cathedral's still impressive, even though it was burned down."

"Burned down?" said Duncan, looking puzzled. "I didn't even know it had been built. You must be thinking of somewhere else."

"You're right," I said quickly, mentally smacking my wrist. Elgin Cathedral, built in 1224, burned down in 1390 – no wonder Duncan didn't know anything about it. I obviously still hadn't quite recovered from the mental trauma I had gone through, but I would have to concentrate more.

And that was difficult, because I was very confused about what I was supposed to be doing. Was I still trying to stop Duncan being murdered? And who might the possible assassins be?

"Do the troops know that you've faked your own death?" I asked.

Macdeath gave me a look that suggested he thought this was a silly question. "Of course not," he said. "They're the last people we would want to know the king's plan. We need all the soldiers and the thanes to believe that King Duncan is dead so that they transfer their loyalty to King Macbeth. That's the only way to ensure the stability of the kingdom."

"All right," I said cautiously. "Who does know about the plan?"

"You," said Macdeath. "Me. My brother. And my sister-in-law."

"It was actually the lady Gruoch who came up with the whole idea," said Duncan. "She was talking about her husband – her first husband, that is."

Macdeath sniggered quietly.

"It's not funny," said Duncan severely.

"Sorry," said Macdeath. "But it is quite funny. I mean, the way he died."

"I suppose it is," said Duncan, with a quiet snigger of his own.

I was shocked by this display of callousness. Being gralloched by your own wife didn't seem to me to be a matter for levity. But I reminded myself that these were earlier times, when people had a different attitude towards violence, evidenced by the two thanes in the corridor quietly knocking lumps out of each other.

"Your nightshirt," I said, indicating the blood stains.

"Crushed blaeberries," said Duncan cheerfully. "Just in case anyone takes a look in the coffin en route."

"And we'll tell them the food's for the journey to the after-world," said Macdeath, beginning to gather up what we had left. "We still hang on to a few pagan beliefs."

"You're putting food in the coffin?" I asked. "That's never going to work."

"It's a very fine coffin," said Macdeath stiffly. "Made to my own design. There are air holes in the lid, but you can't see them with the way I've carved the designs."

"That's very clever, and it looks a wonderful coffin," I said. "But if it's getting transported, all of the different bits of food will get mixed up together." I picked up a honey-covered bannock. "Look at this, for example. It'll just disintegrate into crumbs, and you'll end up with honey in the mutton."

Then it struck me that if my mission hadn't already ended in failure, as I had feared, I should still be getting a degree of support, even if Miss Blaine wasn't answering my calls. I opened my pouch. This was the confirmation I needed, that I still had work to do. There sat a roll of compostable bags, suitable for home recycling.

The bags definitely hadn't been there earlier.

"Here," I said, tearing bags off for Duncan and Macdeath, "These will keep things safe and separate."

They held the bags wonderingly, running their fingers over them as though they were exotic silk.

"Where did such a thing come from?" asked Duncan.

"Dunedin," I said. "And the best way to open it is to rub it between your hands, like this."

In no time, we were stuffing bannocks, herring, eggs, nettles and all the rest of the picnic into the bags, Macdeath and Duncan constantly exclaiming about how marvellous this was. We had just finished when there was a quiet tapping at the door.

Macdeath opened it slightly, and then just enough to admit the caller. It was Macbeth, bowing low to Duncan, murmuring, "My liege."

"Don't be silly," said Duncan. "I'm not your liege, I'm dead. Macbeth, my noble thane twice over, I can't thank you and your good lady and your brother enough for organising everything." He gave a long exhalation. "I don't think I could have stood another day as king. It's a young man's game."

I bristled slightly, given that he was quite a bit younger than me.

"I can't wait to get to Iona," he sighed. "Sea, sand and sleep."

"We'll miss you," said Macbeth. "But hopefully we can get over to visit you from time to time."

"That would be nice. Just don't expect a fancy castle like this," said Duncan. "I'm going to be a crofter."

"That was Gruoch's first husband's dream," said Macbeth. "It was a shame he died."

Macdeath let out a snigger. "Sorry," he said, not sounding sorry at all. "But the way he died, it's funny."

"Stop it," said Macbeth, and then he started sniggering as well, closely followed by Duncan.

"Excuse me," I said. "If it's not seemly for laughter to be heard coming from this room, I don't think sniggering's much better."

They shut up, but in the manner of naughty schoolboys who

would start sniggering again the moment my back was turned. I resolved not to turn my back.

"I just came to tell you that we're ready when you are, my lie— we're ready when you are," said Macbeth. "The trees have formed an honour guard for you, and eight of the tallest ones have volunteered to be pall bearers. They're all quite upset."

"Aww," said Duncan. "That's nice."

I knew their upset was much more to do with having to walk to the other side of the country than because the king was dead, but it would be churlish to point that out.

Right now, I continued trying to puzzle out my mission. It had seemed obvious that it was to prevent Duncan getting murdered, but now he was still alive. That didn't mean, however, that the threat of his being murdered had disappeared. I decided to approach the matter forensically. Who might be trying to murder him? Given that the trees genuinely believed Duncan was dead, I reckoned I could rule them out as potential killers.

Macbeth I judged congenitally incapable of murdering anyone. Macdeath I wasn't sure about. He and Duncan were very matey, but that might all be an act on Macdeath's part. I thought back to Shakespeare's line where Lady Macbeth exhorted her husband to "look like the innocent flower, but be the serpent under it". Macdeath was far too hairy to look like an innocent flower, and far too large to be a serpent, but the metaphor still held good. As the undertaker, at any point he could say he needed to make adjustments to the coffin, and nobody would be able to contradict him. I imagined the tree pall bearers would be only too happy to go and have a rest, and Macdeath could turn those blaeberry stains into bloodstains at his leisure.

And then there was Gruoch. She had already gralloched her first husband, something the three men seemed to find inordinately funny. She had then pretended to murder Duncan. Given that everyone apart from Macbeth and his brother believed she had, why try again? The obvious answer was in order to conceal the murder from Macbeth and his brother. Why she wanted to do that was another question, and one I couldn't answer right now.

As I was pondering, there was another quiet tap at the door.

"That'll be the missus," said Macbeth. "Come to pay her respects."

"Well, don't keep the lady waiting," said Duncan to Macdeath, who opened the door and let Gruoch in, Frank at her heels.

"My liege," she said, making a deep curtsey.

"None of that," said Duncan genially. "Your good man and your good self are about to be king and queen. Thank you for such a lovely evening yesterday. It was the perfect send-off. Come and give me a goodbye hug."

Gruoch was crossing the darkened bedchamber towards him when Frank greeted me by hissing and she registered my presence.

"What's the fool doing here?" she demanded.

"He was a key part of the evening's entertainment," said Duncan. "He's really very funny."

"That's as may be," said Gruoch. "It's one thing telling jokes to all and sundry. It's quite another knowing when to keep your mouth shut."

She looked at her husband. "Did you know about this?"

"Not a thing," he assured her hurriedly.

She turned to Macdeath. "Why did you let the fool in? You were meant to be guarding this room. You know it's only the four of us who are supposed to know what's going on."

Macdeath shuffled his feet. "I didn't let him in. He came in."

"And you couldn't have dealt with him?" She made it sound quite sinister.

"He was very upset about the king being dead, and the king wanted to reassure him," mumbled Macdeath, clearly intent on shifting the blame on to Duncan.

"Very upset," agreed Duncan. "You should have heard how movingly he spoke about me. It would have been cruel to let him go on believing I had shuffled off this mortal coil."

"Really?" said Gruoch with a grim smile and Frank bared his

teeth. I know cats don't like water, but he was taking his indignation about being soaked to ridiculous lengths. After all, there was no doubt it had been an accident.

"Anyway, what about that goodbye hug?" said Duncan, holding his arms wide. "Your man tells me the trees are ready."

"They are," said Gruoch, "and they're looking very smart." She went over and gave him what appeared to be an affectionate hug. It looked genuine enough, but that just proved how devious she was. I determined to stay close to Duncan from now on in order to protect him, even if that was going to mean a very long walk.

"But I don't see why this should be goodbye," Gruoch added.

"I'm afraid it has to be," said Duncan. "I'm going to Iona for my burial and you're going to Scone for your coronation."

I'd forgotten all about the coronation. I wondered if they would insist on my being there, although jokes at a coronation didn't sound very appropriate. In any case, even though I'd agreed to being Macbeth's fool, I hadn't signed a contract, so I didn't see how they could make me stay. My path would be with Duncan and the trees.

"I'll join the pall bearers if that's all right," I said to Duncan. "I can always lend them a hand if necessary."

I gambled that he was so impressed by what he thought was my grief at his demise that he would immediately agree, and I was right.

"Of course, of course," he said heartily. "Delighted to have you as part of the team."

Gruoch put her hand on Macbeth's arm and pouted prettily. I was immediately suspicious, but the poor sap beamed down at his wife.

"Darling," she purred, "wouldn't it be lovely if we could spend just a little more time with your predecessor? Why don't we all go to Scone together?"

Her sudden suggested change was definitely part of some devious plan. But Macbeth wasn't the pushover she expected. He frowned and said, "That would mean going south and taking the trees out of their way. They should head directly for Dunkeld."

I was impressed that he'd managed to thwart whatever she was up to.

And then Duncan said, "Going to Scone's a great idea. From there to Dunkeld will only add another day to my journey, and I'll be able to stock up with more provisions at the abbey."

"I don't think that's a terribly good idea—" I began, and Gruoch rounded on me.

"Nobody's interested in what you think," she snarled. "You shouldn't even be here."

Duncan laughed, but quietly, for fear of being heard outside. "You mustn't take him seriously, my dear. He's joking. He's always joking."

Gruoch's and my eyes met. We both knew I wasn't joking. And of course we both knew I wasn't a he.

"So that's settled then," said Duncan. "We're all off to Scone. I'll leave it to one of you to alert the funeral cortege, since I'm no longer in a position to give orders. Undertaker – your assistance, please."

Macdeath helped Duncan into the coffin and carefully arranged the compostable bags round him before fitting on the lid with its carefully camouflaged air holes.

"Right," came Duncan's muffled voice. "Off we go."

He sounded so cheerful. But he wasn't out of the woods yet. And neither was I.

Nine

The departure for the coronation was quite something. The eight pall bearers marched slowly down the steep hill from the castle, the rest of Birnam Wood standing to attention on either side, and then regrouping to surround them for the journey.

Macbeth and the thanes were on horseback, with most other people walking, but there was also a procession of ox-drawn carts carrying kitchen equipment and provisions, and no doubt paraphernalia for the coronation. The oxen were massive creatures, with horns to make any self-respecting Highland cattle feel completely inadequate, and I could see they would be useful since there was a definite dearth of roads.

The last person to leave the castle was my friend the porter, who pulled the door to.

"Aren't you going to close it properly?" I asked.

I got the sort of look a professional gives a member of the public who asks a particularly asinine question.

"The drawbar is on the inside, to stop people getting in," he said.

"But we're going out," I said. "People could get in while we're away."

"What people?" he said. "Everyone's going to the coronation. Afterwards, I'll be back in time to not let them in if their credentials are in doubt."

There was no point in arguing. It was his door. I saw it now had the addition of a spyhole, no doubt thanks to Gruoch and her dagger. I had a moment's nostalgia for my previous incarnation. It would have been fun to scamper up the door, collapse my rib-cage to squeeze through the spyhole, and scamper down the other side.

I was hurrying to catch up with the pall bearers when Gruoch herself called me. As befitted her superior status, she was in a cart, albeit one stacked high with cooking pots, bowls, bags of bannocks, sacks of barley and piles of nettles.

"Come and join me," she said.

I was going to demur, but then I thought back to the spyhole she had so expertly carved out, a reminder of how handy she was with a dagger. Being her travel companion was the perfect way to keep an eye on her. I clambered on to the cart, carefully avoiding the nettles, and squeezed in beside a cooking pot.

As we trundled off, I cast around for a topic of conversation. I'm an excellent actor, as those who saw my performance as Lady Bracknell in the school's production of *The Importance of Being Earnest* will attest, but I still found it difficult to know how to chat to a murderer. She might not have murdered Duncan yet, and she wasn't going to if I had anything to do with it, but she had still murdered her first husband.

"Not a bad day for the time of year," I said.

"No," she said.

We lapsed into silence, which continued until the procession stopped for a break. I busied myself making tea for everyone, to go with the bannocks. The pall bearers were particularly grateful, and I made sure I was between Gruoch and the coffin at all times.

When we set off again, I felt it was her turn to take up the conversation, but she didn't utter a word.

Eventually I asked, "How are you finding the tea tree oil?"

"Good," she said.

"Good," I said.

There was another stop for a round of refreshments, after which neither of us said anything until we reached the abbey at Scone. The trees had arrived first and arranged themselves to make it look particularly scenic. Duncan had already been offloaded into the abbey's small chapel, a building on its own, and Macbeth was waiting to escort Gruoch to the guest house where the top tier was staying. Everyone else started setting up rudimentary tents and pavilions.

I made for the chapel, where Macdeath was helping Duncan out of the coffin. It was just as well we would be restocking, since Duncan had managed to get through most of the food. He noticed me looking critically at the small amount remaining.

"It was basically boredom eating," he said apologetically. "There wasn't anything else to do."

"You'd better pace yourself from now on, or your supplies will run out long before you reach Iona," I said. "But isn't it dangerous, you wandering around in here? Won't the monks be in at any minute to sing requiems and so on?"

"I told them not to bother," said Macdeath. "They'll have to do a lot at the coronation tomorrow, what with the praying and crowd control, so they're really pleased. They're a lazy bunch."

This was perfect. There were no other buildings nearby, and the chapel was made of thick stone, preventing any noise from getting out. Duncan was safe for the night.

"Anything I can get anyone?" I asked.

"I wouldn't mind a pie," said Duncan. "This abbey's famous for them."

"That sounds good," I said. "I think I'll join you."

"I'd like one with onion," said Macdeath.

I went off to find the kitchener, who was busy with the contents of the ovens.

"Hello," I said. "I'm with the royal party. Could I please have two pies and a third with onion?"

He stared at me blankly. I repeated myself, more loudly, still to no effect. And then I realised: he couldn't understand my Edinburgh accent.

"Twa pehs an an ingin ane an aw," I said, and was shortly back on my way to the chapel with my order.

When I came back into the chapel, I could scarcely believe the horror of the scene in front of me. I should never have left Duncan's side for an instant.

Macdeath had been joined by Macbeth and Gruoch. Macbeth was busy filling compostable bags with a fresh supply of food. Duncan was sitting on a stool in the apse and Gruoch was standing behind him, stretching her hands towards his neck.

"Duncan!" I yelled, dropping the pies. "Save yourself! She's going to strangle you!"

He didn't move from his seat but peered at me in a puzzled way.

"I'm sorry, I don't get it," he said. "Is that the end of the joke, or are we still waiting for the punchline?"

There was no time to answer him. I was already halfway up the aisle, and an instant later, I brought Gruoch crashing to the ground in a perfect rugby tackle.

"I may not know how to gralloch someone, and even if I did, I wouldn't," I panted. "But I warn you, I'm prepared to do almost everything else to stop you murdering Duncan."

I had her pinned down to ensure she couldn't grab her dagger when there was a flurry of fur, which was hissing and spitting, and Frank was on me, literally trying to scratch my eyes out.

I tried desperately to defend myself against him, an assailant far more deadly than any human, but he was like quicksilver, impossible to evade or to capture.

And then I was the one getting captured, hoisted up with such force that my feet didn't reach the ground, Frank attached to my hodden grey by his back paws and still trying to claw at my face with his front ones.

I had been seized by Macdeath, and as I fought to free myself while simultaneously keeping out of range of the ferocious cat, out of the corner of my as yet unscathed eye I could see Macbeth approaching.

"How dare you attack my wife, you pest-ridden villain?" he roared.

I thought it was a bit much to call me pest-ridden when Mo had provided me with a fresh set of clothes, but that wasn't my major concern. I had always considered Macbeth a gentle, non-violent soul, apart from that uncharacteristic outburst during our flyting when he went for me with an axe. But right now, his arm was pulled back preparatory to punching me in the face. Frank had seen the same thing, and had rapidly detached himself from me to avoid becoming collateral damage.

If Macbeth connected with me, I was going to be in a great deal of trouble, and I doubted that even Miss Blaine would be able to put me back together again.

"Stop right there!" Gruoch's voice rang out across the chapel.

"Yes, dear," said Macbeth meekly, stopping right there, inches away from me.

"And you," she commanded Macdeath, who let me drop to the ground.

I leaned forward, resting my hands on my thighs, letting my breathing return to normal. When I looked up, I found Duncan glaring at me in a distinctly hostile manner.

"I know we allow you some latitude because of your profession, fool, but to attack a defenceless lady – that's completely outrageous," he said.

"I'm fine, don't worry about it," said Gruoch, dusting herself down. "And you should probably know that the fool's a lady as well, although obviously not that defenceless."

The three men stared at me.

"I thought you were a beardless youth," said Macbeth eventually.

"Well, I'm not," I said.

"But you've got a man's name," he said.

"In Dunedin, it's a woman's name," I said.

"Peculiar sort of place," grunted Macdeath.

"Yes, I think I can see it now," said Duncan consideringly. "Not a beardless youth but a woman. One who's had a hard life by the look of it."

Now Gruoch was approaching, but thankfully she showed no sign of either punching me or gralloching me. In fact, she seemed positively friendly. I watched her warily in case she was looking like the innocent flower, but being the serpent under it.

"I owe you an apology," she said. "I was completely wrong

about you."

"In what way?" I asked.

"I've been trying to protect our beloved Duncan from you," she said.

"But I've been trying to protect him from you," I said.

"Sorry, what's all this?" said Duncan. "Why do I need protecting?"

"I thought she wanted to kill you," Gruoch and I said at the same time.

"Why on earth would you think I wanted to kill him?" I asked.

"It's a perfectly reasonable assumption," said Gruoch. "You turn up out of nowhere, having persuaded my husband to hire you as a fool—"

"She didn't persuade me," said Macbeth a trifle querulously. "It was my own idea."

"Of course it was, my darling, and a very good idea, too," cooed Gruoch. "I just meant she obviously presented herself to you as a fool."

Macbeth nodded. "Yes, that's exactly what she did."

She looked at me. "And the next thing you were weaselling your way into everything, trying to stop me showing the king to his bedchamber, lying on the floor outside his room, then turning up unexpectedly when he was being stowed in the coffin."

Looking at it from Gruoch's point of view, I could see my behaviour might have been construed as slightly suspicious. But her behaviour looked even more so.

"I'm sorry I flattened you just now," I said. "But when I came in, you definitely looked as though you were about to strangle the king."

"She was very kindly about to give me a neck massage," said Duncan tartly. "I'm feeling quite sore after being stuck in that coffin for hours."

"You poor thing," said Gruoch, darting over to him. "Let me get on with it."

I tensed, preparing for a second rugby tackle if necessary, but she proceeded to provide what looked like a very therapeutic massage.

"It was a logical presumption," I said. "What was I supposed to think? The minute I suggested travelling with the pall bearers, you suggested that we all go together to Scone. Why would you do that unless you were contemplating murder?"

Gruoch continued unknotting the muscles at the top of Duncan's shoulders. "And what was I supposed to think? It was totally suspicious when you suggested travelling with the pall bearers. I decided we should all travel together so that I could keep an eye on you. And the moment I became queen, I was going to have you arrested and locked up."

"Too kind," I said.

"Common sense," she said, her fingers working on Duncan's shoulder blades now.

He moved his head experimentally from side to side and gave a sigh of relief. "That's wonderful, my dear, thank you. This conversation is very interesting, but I'm a simple old soldier who does his killing on the battlefield, so I don't quite understand. If everyone thinks I'm dead apart from the five of us in this room, what would be the point of either of you two ladies murdering me?"

"I didn't understand that either," said Macbeth.

"Neither did I," said his brother.

I hadn't been able to work it out myself and waited for Gruoch to provide the answer.

She shrugged. "I have no idea. It makes absolutely no sense. She's the one who was talking about it."

They all looked at me.

"Well, it was because – it was a perfectly natural supposition – I mean, she's a murderer, after all," I said lamely.

"Are you calling my wife a murderer?" shouted Macbeth.

"Yes," I said. "It's well known that she murdered her first husband."

I waited for the sniggering, but there was none.

"Is it indeed?" said Macbeth in quite a dangerous tone.

Gruoch crossed over to him and linked her arm in his. "Come on now, darling. She doesn't know what happened. I think we should explain to her."

She sat down gracefully on the stone flags, her long green dress spreading round her like a lily pad. I sat down as well, and Macbeth and Macdeath leaned against the wall.

"My first husband was a warrior because that's what men are," she said. "Unless they have a profession like being an undertaker."

Macbeth and Macdeath nodded sagely.

"But my husband never took to it," she said. "All he wanted was to have a wee croft in the Western Isles."

Duncan gave a sympathetic sigh.

"I have to say I wasn't wild about the idea, since I'm a town girl at heart," she said.

"Is that why you murdered him?" I asked.

"I did no such thing," said Gruoch. "I was very fond of him. I was perfectly prepared to move if he wanted to. And because of that, he and I thought up a plan where he could fake his own death."

I could see there was a theme here.

"I told everyone I'd accidentally gralloched him. They all thought I'd murdered him, and that was what they were supposed to think. You get less trouble when you're seen to be a strong woman."

"I hear you," I said. "But surely it's difficult to prove you've accidentally gralloched somebody when you haven't?"

Gruoch smiled at Macdeath. "It helps when you've got a friendly undertaker nearby. This gentleman and my late husband were good friends. The three of us concocted the plan, which included a specially designed coffin with breathing holes in it."

There was definitely a theme here.

"So what went wrong?" I asked.

"Absolutely nothing," she said. "It went like a dream. We said we were transporting him back to his birthplace for burial, and the minute he was out of the local area where he would be recognised, he got out of the coffin and headed for the Western Isles, where I was to join him after a suitable period of mourning."

"One thing strikes me," I said. "That's two men faking their own deaths to get away from the pressures of warfare. Why not just stop fighting?"

There was a sharp intake of breath from the men.

"We couldn't do that," said Macbeth. "Warriors fight. That's what they do."

Gruoch had the sort of expression the Marcia Blaine teachers bestowed on you when you'd correctly answered a particularly difficult question. Except I'd asked a question, not answered it.

"We're going to make a few changes," she said. "I remember how this all started – the king and my husband and I were chatting over dinner, and the king—"

"Honestly, you don't need to keep calling me that," said Duncan. "There's another king now."

"Not until after the coronation," said Gruoch. "Which means the title's still yours." She appealed to Macbeth, "Isn't that right, my darling?"

"Whatever you say, my dear," said Macbeth affectionately.

Gruoch returned to her story. "The king told us how fed up he was, and I told him how my late husband had arranged things to get out of a dead-end job, and we decided to repeat the plan. But then there was the question of what to do next. Macbeth didn't want to be king."

"Yes I did," said Macbeth automatically.

"You really didn't," said Gruoch. "But you do now, because we decided it would be a partnership with me as your queen, didn't we?"

"Yes we did," said Macbeth.

"Macbeth will host parties and I'll cover policy," said Gruoch. "The thanes are all a bit scared of me, because they think I'm a murderer, so I'm not expecting any opposition. We'll organise a couple of skirmishes, just so it's not a complete change of pace, and then let things settle down and stop all the fighting so that we can concentrate on peace and prosperity. They can all beat their swords into ploughshares and their spears into pruning hooks – that'll keep the vassals happy when they're working in the fields. Then they can turn their axe-heads into cauldrons and the handles into spurtles – that'll please the kitchen staff."

"It all sounds great," I said. "I'm sure things will work out so well that you'll be able to take a wee holiday. You could have a leisurely trip through France, and then go on to Italy, call in on the Pope while you're there."

Macbeth gave Gruoch his shy smile. "A continental holiday with you – I'd really like that."

She smiled back. "I'd really like that too."

But there was something I still didn't understand. "You say you're not a murderer, but you keep talking about your late husband."

There was a terrible snort behind me. I turned to see Macdeath, who now had both hands over his face.

"Sorry," he choked. "Sorry."

Meanwhile, both Macbeth and Duncan were overtaken by fits of coughing.

"It's not funny," said Gruoch severely, and I realised they had all been trying to stifle sniggers.

"Forgive me, my lady, but it is," gasped Macdeath, which set them all off again.

"It isn't," she said. She turned to me. "Tell me if you think this is funny. My husband duly reached the Western Isles. One day he was out walking on the beach under a cliff when a pig toppled over the cliff and fell on top of him. He was killed outright."

The three men clutched one another, now laughing uproariously, interspersed with cries of "oink oink".

I gazed at Gruoch with horror and sympathy. "That's not funny, that's dreadful. I'm so sorry. What a terrible thing to happen."

"Thank you," said Gruoch simply.

I confronted the men. "I am a professional fool and as such, I know what's funny and what isn't. This isn't funny. You're going to stop laughing about it right now, and you're never going to laugh about it again. Do we understand one another?"

"Yes," they muttered and I distinctly heard Macbeth whisper to his brother, "She wasn't as scary as this when she was a man."

In the silence that followed, we could hear a slurping noise from near the chapel door.

"That damned cat!" said Macdeath. "Look, it's eaten all the pies."

"Don't use that sort of language about Spot," snapped Gruoch. "It's offensive, and it makes you sound like the porter."

"Sorry," said Macdeath. "I'll go and get some more pies."

"Good idea," said Macbeth quickly. "I'll come with you and see what they've got."

It was obvious that the pair of them just wanted to escape in case we gave them more of a hard time.

"Can I come as well?" pleaded Duncan.

"Of course not," said Gruoch. "How would it look, a dead king wandering around the abbey?"

"I could pretend to be a ghost," Duncan suggested.

"Ghosts don't buy pies," said Gruoch. "Those two will have to manage without you."

He looked so woebegone that I wondered whether I might have a solution. I surreptitiously opened my pouch. Perfect.

"Here," I said, handing Duncan the Jimmy wig with its straggly red hair and tartan tam o' shanter, "try this."

He was unrecognisable.

"Nobody would know it's you," said Macbeth. "Apart from anything else, they'll be so busy looking at that amazing hat that they won't pay the slightest attention to your face."

"Right, let's go and get those pies," said Macdeath and the three of them headed towards the door.

"But you can't go out in your nightshirt, especially as it's covered in blaeberry juice," I objected, and Duncan's face fell.

I looked around for inspiration and there, in a corner, I spotted a pile of monks' habits. We found one to fit, and Duncan was set to go wherever he liked.

"Don't engage with people," I warned him. "If anyone asks you anything, just say 'yes', 'no' or 'that would be an ecumenical matter'."

But there probably weren't too many denominations around to be ecumenical about and there was always the danger that someone would recognise his voice.

"No, scrap that. Let the others do the talking," I said. "You can be from a silent order."

They set off, leaving Gruoch and me together. Frank curled up and went to sleep.

"Thank you for being sympathetic about my first husband," she said. "You're the only person who hasn't laughed."

"Because it's not funny," I said.

"I suppose it is a bit," she said. "Having a pig fall on your head."

"Maybe a bit," I conceded, and before I knew it, we were both having a guilty giggle.

"It was awful at the time," she added. "And then my lovely undertaker introduced me to his even lovelier brother. I couldn't be happier with Macbeth, and I know he's going to be a wonderful king."

"I'm sure he will be," I said, reluctant to tell someone who was neither a witch nor a time traveller that I knew it for a fact. "And particularly because you'll be in charge of policy."

I wondered if that sounded bad. "You do realise that during the flyting, when I said he was henpecked, that was purely because the object of the exercise is to be as rude as possible? I didn't mean it seriously."

She looked astonished. "Of course I realise that. How could anyone possibly think he was henpecked?"

"Unimaginable," I said. Something else had bothered me about that whole incident. "When you stood up and took the blame for murdering Duncan when we were in the middle of our axe fight – I hope you didn't intervene because you knew I was a woman. I'm perfectly capable of looking after myself."

"Don't be silly," said Gruoch. "I intervened precisely because I could see how capable you were. I was afraid you might hurt my poor darling."

I was about to protest that my only intention had been to parry the attack from her poor darling rather than attack him myself when I remembered some of the terrible injuries sustained by

Blainers on the lacrosse pitch. It confirmed me in my view that weapons are a bad idea, and I was glad that under Gruoch and Macbeth's governance, the country was moving towards a policy of non-violence.

"That was good, what you did when you came in and thought I was strangling Duncan," she said. "You completely knocked me off my feet. Will you show me how to do it?"

She was quite serious, and I found myself instructing her in how to hurl herself at me, shoulder first, while wrapping her arms round my legs and still continuing to move forward. She was a quick learner and it was disappointing that there wasn't yet a rugby team she could try out for.

One particularly energetic tackle sent me careering down the aisle to land inches from Frank, still enjoying his post-prandial snooze. He jumped up with an indignant yowl and stalked off into the shadows.

"Poor Spot, being disturbed like that," Gruoch whispered to me. "We shouldn't have been so noisy. Did you know cats can sleep for twenty hours out of twenty-four?"

"Yes," I said. "I did."

I was just letting my breathing get back to normal when the chapel door opened and Duncan, Macdeath and Macbeth appeared, the latter proudly carrying the pies.

"Welcome back, my darling," said Gruoch. "The fool has just taught me the most wonderful new skill."

"That's splendid, my darling," said Macbeth. "Is it a joke?"

"Absolutely not," she said, and, before I could stop her, she was dashing towards him, connecting exactly as I had trained her, and Macbeth was toppling like a skittle.

"The pies!" yelled Macdeath, and even as the king-designate collapsed towards the ground, he threw the pies to his brother, who caught them neatly. It was a perfect pass, which made the lack of a rugby team even more disappointing.

Gruoch jumped back up, and hauled a groaning Macbeth to his feet.

"There," she said. "Are you impressed, my darling?"

Macbeth groaned a bit more before wheezing, "Tremendously, my darling. You never cease to amaze me. Actually, if you don't mind, I think I'll sit down for a moment."

After a while, he felt well enough to try a piece of pie, and we sat in a companionable group enjoying our late meal, and chatting about the coronation.

"I wish I could be there," said Duncan sadly. "But I'll be back in that stuffy coffin. No offence – the air holes are really good. It's just that there isn't much space in there, especially with the food."

In his monk's habit and the straggly red hair of the wig, it was impossible to imagine him as a king.

"You don't need to go back in the coffin," I said. "You can stay as a monk. Come to the coronation. And then when the trees set off for Iona, we'll tell them you've been sent to travel with them as a mark of respect from the abbey. Just remember you've taken a vow of silence until you get to Iona."

Gruoch gave a gasp of excitement. "That's a brilliant idea. It would be so lovely if you could join us on our special day. Wouldn't it, my darling?"

Macbeth was nodding enthusiastically as Duncan took the idea on board.

"Nobody recognised me in the abbey," he admitted. "A lot of people said they liked my hat. I remembered not to say anything in reply – I just blessed them."

And then his face fell. "It wouldn't work," he said. "If I'm not in the coffin, it'll be too light and the trees will get suspicious."

Macdeath held up the pie he was eating. "That's not a problem. We just fill the coffin with more food. You won't need to eat it en route because the trees will feed you. When you get to Iona, it'll take a while to grow your own produce on your croft, and this way, you'll have something to tide you over."

Duncan laid down his own pie, and didn't even notice Frank creeping out of the shadows to start nibbling at it.

"Genius," he said. "There's nothing I would like better than to be at your coronation. I can scarcely remember mine, I was so nervous. Not that either of you will be nervous, obviously. There's absolutely no need, since it's going to be a very happy occasion, surrounded by friends and family."

I swallowed my last mouthful of pie. Now that I had a whole new perspective on Gruoch, there was something I had to tell her, and I was going to have to confess that I had made a bad situation a whole lot worse.

"Speaking of family," I said, "I need to talk to you about your sisters."

It was as though a dark cloud passed over her.

"I can't imagine why," she said, her tone clipped.

"Because I've met them," I said. "And they've got completely the wrong idea about you. I'm afraid they think you murdered your first husband. And I'm afraid I told them that you'd murdered the king, because I thought you had. So now they're convinced you're a double murderer."

She tossed her head. "I really couldn't care less. If that's what they're prepared to believe, then they're not worth bothering with."

Macbeth caught her hand. "Please don't talk like that, darling," he said. "Family's important. If it hadn't been for my brother here, you and I wouldn't be together now. Misunderstandings should always be put right. And I'd really like to meet your sisters." Ina and Mina's forgetfulness spell was working well – he had no idea he'd met them just the other day.

Gruoch pulled her hand away from his. "Well, they have absolutely no interest in meeting you. They couldn't even be bothered to come to our wedding."

Macbeth looked at her in surprise. "You told me they couldn't come because they weren't well."

Gruoch got to her feet and began pacing up and down the aisle. "I told you that because you're so into family and everyone getting on, and you and your brother have such a great relationship, and I didn't want to admit how dysfunctional everything was on my side."

Macbeth was beginning to stand up, but she held out her hand to stop him.

"Can you imagine what it's like, being the eldest of four, and you're the only one who's too stupid to be a witch? Even little Mo could do spells in her cradle. Particularly the hairdressing ones – my hair's never been the same since I left home. The three of them have always despised me."

I was about to tell her that she had it all wrong, that they were in awe of her non-witch abilities, but she saw me draw breath and said with dignified firmness, "I'm speaking." She was going to be an impressive queen.

"I sent them letters explaining everything about my first husband's apparent demise. If they choose not to believe me, and to listen to popular gossip instead, that's their problem. But I decided to take the generous view, that the letters might not have reached them, and I sent them the wedding invitation by courier, with instructions to hand it to them directly." She paused, biting her lower lip, and took a moment to compose herself. "They returned it defaced with a message telling me never to try to contact them again or they'd turn me into a midge, and everyone would hate me, and I'd get swatted."

Macbeth jumped to his feet, his hand on his dagger. "Did they indeed? Where will I find these sisters of yours?"

That forgetfulness spell was really impressive.

"Wait a minute," I said. "That can't be right. They told me you never invited them to the wedding."

Gruoch gave a gasp of outrage. "The little liars! How dare they?"

I was a bit shocked by her hasty reaction. If there's one thing I've learned, it's never to jump to conclusions, but always to sift the evidence carefully. That way, you won't go wrong.

"Let's just go over a couple of things," I said. "You sent them a wedding invitation, and they sent it back with a nasty message. You're sure it was their handwriting?"

"I've no idea," she said. "I don't know what their handwriting's like. They've never been good correspondents."

"So we can't be certain they're the ones who sent it," I said, feeling rather like a Golden Age detective. "And we can't actually be certain they ever received the invitation. If they were upfront enough to send your message back, why would they claim they never got it? If you ask me, everything points to the courier."

Gruoch and Macbeth looked at one another.

Macbeth said, "To think we've put our entire safety in the hands of that two-timing, conniving little—"

"Sorry, who's this we're talking about?" I asked.

"The porter," Gruoch shot back. "I thought I could rely on him since he always seemed to do such a good job with the door."

"He's probably getting ready to let in every assassin in the country," said Macbeth.

"Now then," I said. "We don't know any of this for a fact, do we? We're just speculating, and we really shouldn't do that."

"Keep out of this, fool," warned Macbeth. "I'm going to find the villain who upset my wife, and when I do..." He let a thrust with the dagger in his hand finish the sentence.

"Do you know where he is?" I asked.

"Not yet, but I shall search through every tent, under every bush until I find him."

"That could take a while, especially as it's the middle of the night. And you've got a coronation in the morning, remember." I got to my feet. "I think I might know where he is."

Macbeth stepped forward eagerly, the dagger still in his hand. "Then take me to him."

I shook my head. "If I find him, I'll bring him back here. That's on the firm understanding that you're not allowed to kill people in a church."

I motioned for Macbeth to put the dagger back in his belt and he reluctantly complied. Then I left the chapel, crossed the courtyard and went into the main abbey building, the only one in the monastic enclosure to lead to the outside world. And at the end of a long corridor, I found what I was looking for: the front door. The porter was sitting on a stool beside it, kicking his heels against its legs.

"Oh hello," he said when he spotted me. "This place is so boring. Nobody comes in, nobody goes out. Do me a favour and nip outside for a moment – we could do our joke again."

"Sorry," I said. "No time for that. Macbeth and Gruoch want to see you."

He folded his arms. "This door won't watch itself, you know."

It was a very delicate situation. A large part of me hoped that the porter wasn't to blame in any way for the unfortunate message, but a small part of me knew that he had a very flawed sense of humour, so might have thought it was funny. Because of that, another part of me wanted to urge the porter to flee to the farthest end of the country. But around fifteen per cent of me knew that Macbeth was so enraged, he was quite capable of scouring every last inch of his realm. I had to present the porter in the best possible light, and the longer the delay in getting him to the chapel, the longer Macbeth would have had to seethe.

"It's not your door," I said. "I'm sure the monks have their own system. Come on, we can't keep the king-and-queen-designate waiting."

He followed me unwillingly, muttering, "It's not right leaving a door unattended. Very poor show, not having anyone on duty."

I thought back to the door of Glamis Castle, which wasn't even locked, but this was his area of expertise, and I felt unable to question it. Maybe there was an important distinction between the inside of a door and the outside. But in the matter now at issue, he had been a courier, not a porter, which allowed for something having gone very badly wrong.

As we walked back along the corridor, he said, "So what do old Grumpychops and her man want, anyway?"

I saw no harm in forewarning him. "It's to do with the wedding invitation Gruoch gave you to take to her sisters."

He gave a cheery gurgle. "I remember that. It was quite a laugh."

My heart sank. I liked the wild-haired wee soul. He might have done something dreadful in concocting the fake reply, but he didn't realise it – to him, it was just a joke, and there was no evil intent. I resolved not to let anything bad happen to him.

When we went into the chapel, we found both Gruoch and Macbeth now pacing up and down the aisle. Macdeath and Duncan obviously wanted no part in the drama. They had taken themselves off to sit by the coffin, and were making inroads on the food they'd just acquired from the abbey.

Macbeth began heading in our direction and I wasn't entirely sure he remembered that killing people in church wasn't allowed. I made sure the porter was safely behind me.

"We are going to discuss this in a civilised manner," I said in my best prefect's voice and was gratified to see Macbeth stop in his tracks.

"The porter has kindly agreed to help us with our inquiries," I went on. "This is not in itself an admission of guilt, and we will do him the courtesy of listening to what he has to say."

The porter had by this time picked up that there was something of an atmosphere, and was nervously running his fingers through his hair, making it even wilder.

"We also have to remember that being a courier is outwith his normal terms of employment." I turned to the porter. "Did you receive any additional training to prepare you for your new role?"

He blinked. "I was just told by her lady thaneship to take a wedding invitation to her sisters. I didn't realise I needed any additional training."

"Delivering wedding invitations is a responsible task, which requires care and precision," I said. "Did you feel the information you were given was adequate?"

"She told me where they stayed, if that's what you mean."

"And did you deliver the invitation as instructed?" I asked and I saw Gruoch hold her breath as she waited for the reply.

The porter seemed more bewildered than offended by my question. "Of course. That's what her lady thaneship told me to do, so I did it."

Now I was the one to be bewildered. Mo had quite explicitly

told me that the three sisters had never received an invitation. I didn't like to think she had lied to me.

"You're sure you delivered it to the right address? Did you just throw it into the cave?" It might well have been eaten by a passing newt or toad before anyone saw it.

This time, the porter was definitely offended by my question. "I know how to deliver a wedding invitation. I'm not stupid. I handed it directly to one of the lady thaneship's sisters."

Gruoch made a small sad sound and Macbeth put his arm round her.

The porter, completely missing the poignant moment, said, "It was so funny. She looked at the invitation and she said, 'We witches don't attend civilian events', and then she waved her hand around and all these funny black marks appeared on the other side of the vellum, just like magic. And then she said, 'Take this back where it came from.'"

Gruoch gazed at me more in sorrow than in anger. "Now we know for certain that it was my sisters. Do you need more proof that they despise my non-witchness? What a fool I was to imagine for a second that our loyal porter could have written such a spiteful, malicious message to me."

The porter beamed and then his smile faded as he fully grasped what she had said.

"Your lady thaneship," he said reproachfully, "I would never write you a spiteful, malicious message. I would never write anyone a spiteful, malicious message, because I can't write."

Gruoch accepted the rebuke meekly, and Macbeth gave her a comforting squeeze.

But my little grey cells were firing on all cylinders. I had one more question. "Was it daylight when you gave the witch the invitation?"

"Yes, of course it was," said the porter. "The cave's very out of the way. I would never have found it at night."

And there it was, proof positive that the poison pen writer was Mo. The one who was a lark, awake during the day, while her two sisters were owls. She had lied to me.

"I've got some good news and some bad news," I said to Gruoch.

"Is this a new joke?" called Duncan expectantly through a mouthful of barley. Thankfully, the barley disguised his voice enough for the porter not to realise this was the ex-king.

"I'm afraid not," I said. "The good news is that two of the lady Gruoch's sisters may know nothing about any of this, so a reconciliation may be possible. The bad news is that we now know which sister's responsible. My lady Gruoch, I'm sorry to have to tell you that it's Mo."

Gruoch let out a heart-rending wail. "Little Mo!"

"She wasn't little at all," said the porter.

I was about to explain that it was simply a reference to Mo being the youngest, but the porter hadn't finished.

"She was a great big old – sorry, your lady thaneship, I mean she was quite an elderly lady. With a big pointy nose and big pointy teeth. And a horrible pointy finger that she pointed at the vellum."

That wasn't Mo. Like all of the sisters, she had a button nose, and her teeth were perfectly standard. And I well remembered that finger, the one that had turned me into a mouse and fired fireballs.

"It's Hecate!" I said excitedly. "Lady Gruoch, it's not any of your sisters – it's their boss, the queen of the witches. She's horrible to them. They can't stand her."

The chapel suddenly seemed very quiet. In an ominous way. And then, speaking quite conversationally, Gruoch said, "Where will I find this Hecate?"

"I'm not sure," I said. "She seems to fly around a lot. I suppose you could give her a shout."

"I'll give her a shout all right," said Gruoch. "Let's go."

Duncan and Macdeath nervously stood up, but she waved them and Macbeth away.

"We'll see you later," she said. "This is women's work."

Ten

"Hecate!"

Gruoch's voice rang out into the cold night.

We had left the abbey far behind, the porter delightedly opening the door for us and slamming it shut behind us. We had walked silently through a somnolent Birnam Wood, which surrounded the abbey perimeter, then past all of the sleeping figures who were camped near the Moot Hill in anticipation of the coronation. And then we trekked far into the hinterland until we found ourselves on a blasted heath.

I had told Gruoch everything I knew about her sisters, including how much danger they were in after saving me from Hecate. That made her quite a bit more cross.

And now she was positively incandescent with rage when there was no response to her summons.

"Hecate! I'm warning you – get yourself over here right now!"

Suddenly a tall, black-cloaked figure materialised in front of us in the moonlight, jagged teeth exposed in a snarl.

"Who dares summon Hecate, queen of the witches?" she rasped.

"Gruoch, who in a few hours will be Queen of Scots."

I could see this shaping up to be quite a fight.

But Hecate was already pulling rank. "A mere mortal? Kneel down at my feet."

"Don't bother," I advised. "I didn't."

Hecate turned her fearsome gaze on me. "And I see you've brought the troublesome man whom I transformed for his temerity in consorting with one of my witches."

"She's talking about Mo," I explained to Gruoch. "But she's got it all wrong. There was no consorting – Mo was just directing me to your castle."

"What, she doesn't even realise you're not a man?" said Gruoch. "It strikes me you don't have to be too bright to be queen of the witches."

"What did you say?" screeched Hecate.

"And her transformation spell wasn't that great, because it took Mo only a few seconds to turn me back from being a mouse," I told Gruoch.

"Stop talking about me as though I'm not here!" Hecate shrieked.

"Sorry," I said. "I didn't realise you wanted to be included in the conversation. I was just saying you're a pretty rubbish witch compared to Mo. This is Mo's sister, by the way."

Hecate's thin lip curled. "Ah, the civilian of the family. To think I've been wasting my time trying to stop you contaminating those girls when they're beyond recovery."

"I hear you prevented them getting the invitation to my wedding," said Gruoch.

Hecate cackled. "That, and all of the other messages you sent them. The minute they officially became witches, I made sure they would have nothing more to do with you. I wasn't going to let you explain you hadn't murdered your husband. And I was quite proud of sending you that threatening message, since then you wouldn't have anything more to do with them. It was a duty and a pleasure – as their queen I protected them from all profane outside influences."

"I'm afraid that's another instance of you failing miserably," I said. "This lady's husband has been visiting them regularly for a chat and to make sure they're all right."

"Has he really?" whispered Gruoch. "I had no idea."

"Neither does he," I whispered. "They put a forgetfulness spell on him."

"I might have known it," raged Hecate. "They're foul, treacherous creatures, completely unfit to be witches. You disturbed me while I was dealing with them – now you can see what happens to traitors and renegades."

She snapped her fingers and there in a heap on the heath were Ina, Mina and Mo. They were in the clutches of some terrible enchanted plant that looked a bit like sugar snap peas. It had twined round their hands and over their mouths so that they had no means of casting spells. They looked at us with wide, frightened eyes.

"I'm about to strip these reprobates of all their witchly powers, and turn them into snails to be eaten by toads," said Hecate.

"You can't do that," I said.

"Watch me," she said.

"No, I mean you can't do that. Being a witch is like being a librarian. It's something that runs in your veins, it's in your DNA." I wondered whether I should give a brief explanation of what DNA was, with reference to Franklin, Watson and Crick, but decided that would lessen the impact of what I was saying. "Even if the City of Edinburgh Council fired me tomorrow, I wouldn't stop being a librarian. You can throw Ina, Mina and Mo out of whatever pathetic wee members-only club you think you're running, and you can turn them into snails, but they'll still be witches. Witch-snails."

"They can be witch-snails if they like, but it won't stop them being eaten by toads, especially when I throw them into my toad cauldron," sneered Hecate.

"Don't you dare," said Gruoch.

"Or what, mortal?" Hecate demanded, lifting up her hand preparatory to letting the spell loose.

"Or this," said Gruoch.

And a second later, Hecate had been felled in the most beautiful rugby tackle I've ever seen. But Gruoch, as I had taught her, had grabbed Hecate's legs, which left the witch's hands free. She was already beginning to point with a deadly digit. We were all in terrible danger.

Gruoch had hurtled an impressive distance, and the few seconds it would take me to follow her could mean I would be too late.

I shouted a warning. "Her finger! Get her finger!"

And then Hecate gave an unearthly shriek. Something black had sprung out of the darkness and latched on to her finger with its sharp white teeth.

"Frank!" I said.

"Spot!" said Gruoch.

"Hemlock!" said Mo, who I noted was now free of her sugar snap pea ligatures.

Frank didn't make a sound since that might have loosened his grip on Hecate, but he swished his tail in greeting.

Ina and Mina, also sugar snap pea free, were right behind Mo and the three of them stationed themselves round Hecate with their hands upraised, which left their queen unable to move.

"You're not fit to call yourself queen, and I speak as one who knows," Gruoch grated. "How dare you threaten these witches? They no longer belong to you, they're their own women. They're about to have royal blood flowing in their veins. You're going to promise to stay away from them from now on, do you understand me?"

Hecate's eyes bulged as she tried to answer while incapacitated. Ina tilted her hand slightly so that Hecate could speak.

"Curses on you, vile and loathsome creature!" Hecate croaked. "Yes, I understand, yes, I promise. But what are you? How can a mortal Queen of Scots have such power over the queen of the witches?"

"It's nothing to do with being a queen," said Gruoch. "I've got more power than you can imagine because I..." she paused for effect "...am a sister."

She turned on her heel, her dress swirling spectacularly as she went.

"Spot, darling," she called, "you can let go of the bad lady now and come along."

I saw a flash of white in the darkness as Frank trotted after her, with Ina, Mina and Mo following.

As she went, Mo said carelessly, "Avaunt", and with a swoosh, Hecate avaunted.

The four sisters waited for a moment to see whether she might come back, and when there was silence, they fell into one another's arms.

"We heard everything," sobbed Mo. "Hecate brought us with her, but we were invisible to start with. You really invited us to your wedding?"

"Of course I did," said Gruoch with a catch in her voice. "How could you think I wouldn't invite my little sisters? And how could you think I was a murderer?"

Mo extricated herself from the group hug and stared at me accusingly. "The fool said you murdered King Duncan."

"That was a misapprehension on my part," I said. "Largely because your sister told everyone she'd murdered him. King Duncan's alive and well, but only four of us know that. And now the three of you. You mustn't tell anybody."

Gruoch drew Mo back into the circle. "And tomorrow I'm going to be crowned queen, and now you can all come to the coronation."

That led to a further outbreak of tearful excitement from the witches, two-thirds of it in trochaic tetrameter.

"It's well after midnight," I pointed out. "So the coronation's actually today. We'd better get back to the abbey before everyone wakes up. It's a long walk."

"Walk? That's daft when you can fly," said Ina.

"Come and give our brooms a try," said Mina.

"I'll give it a go this time as well," said Mo with a determined air.

The three of them snapped their fingers, and a moment later were all clutching brooms. It was decided that Gruoch should go with Ina, I would go with Mina, and Mo would take Frank.

"Come along, Hemlock, jump on to my lap," said Mo.

"That's my cat Spot, not your cat Hemlock," said Gruoch. "You can recognise him by the white spot on his chest."

"Yes, that's how I recognise my cat Hemlock," said Mo.

Gruoch turned to me. "And you called him something else."

"Yes, Frank," I said. "That's his real name. Don't worry, I'm not laying claim to him – he's actually a person, and Mo turned him into a cat to save him from Hecate. He says he's quite happy as a cat. I'm able to talk to him because Hecate turned me into a mouse."

Even as I spoke, I was aware of how completely insane my words would sound. But Gruoch just said, "Oh." I supposed if you had three wee sisters who were witches, you would develop a certain tolerance of this sort of thing.

Then she said to Mo, slightly diffidently, "Can I ask you a favour?"

"Not if you want me to give you Hemlock," said Mo. The four of them had enjoyed an emotional reunion, but there were obviously still some tensions. I wondered which of them would end up keeping Frank.

"Nothing to do with Spot," said Gruoch. "If you transformed him, that gives you first dibs. I wanted to ask if you could do my hair for the coronation?"

"I would love to," said Mo. "Thank you for asking me."

Harmony was restored and the three broomsticks with their drivers and passengers took off into the night sky, Mo exclaiming about how easy it was. All she had lacked was confidence.

"One thing I don't understand," I said to Mina. "The three of you were tied up in all that green stuff and then suddenly you weren't, but surely Hecate hadn't freed you?"

"What you said about our veins, helped us shed our verdant chains," said Mina. "Thanks to you we had an inkling we could get free just by thinking."

Mo, who was just behind us on her broomstick, Frank clinging on to her by his claws, called, "When Hecate tied us up to begin with, we thought that was all our power gone. Then you gave us the confidence to realise that we didn't have to chant or use our hands, we could just access the power within ourselves."

It all sounded a bit New Age-y, but it had worked, so I wasn't going to argue with them.

We landed neatly outside the abbey's front door and Gruoch knocked.

"Who's there?" came the response from the porter.

"Lady Gruoch and party," she said.

The drawbar was pulled back, and the porter peered round the door.

"I'll need to process you all separately," he said in delight, slamming the door shut.

I had to explain about his joke, expecting Gruoch to have none of it. But she was obviously still feeling guilty about thinking the porter had written Hecate's threatening letter and said, "We'd better just go along with it."

So one by one we said, "Knock knock", were asked our names, told him who we were, and were invited to come in. I was last, Frank having slipped in right at the start, no doubt off to check on the kitchener's pies. By this time the porter was helpless with laughter, and I had to close the drawbar myself.

"It's the best joke I've ever heard," he guffawed. "I can't wait to get back to the castle and try it out on the thanes." Processing all of them individually was going to put a dampener on their roistering and carousing.

As we crossed the courtyard from the main abbey building to the chapel, dawn was beginning to break.

"You're not going to get much sleep before the coronation," I told Gruoch.

"I'm far too excited to sleep, reunited with my little sisters," she said.

"We're the same the other way," said Ina.

"We won't sleep throughout the day," said Mina.

Inside the chapel, the men apparently weren't remotely excited by the prospect of the coronation since they were all lying on the floor, snoring loudly, surrounded by pie crumbs. With a disapproving snort, Ina snapped her fingers, and the debris disappeared.

Mo got Gruoch to sit on the chair Duncan had been sitting on, said the magic words about thin and meagre porridge, and Gruoch's hair turned into a cascade of ringlets. A snap of Mo's fingers, and she was holding a mirror.

"Careful," I shouted. "You don't want to send her to the middle of the ocean, or outer darkness."

"This is an ordinary mirror," she said. "I know what I'm doing."

"Of course you do, you're really great," said Ina.

"Your witch skills are so innate," said Mina.

They had changed their tune. Mo was no longer the useless wee sister. She showed Gruoch her reflection.

"That's amazing," said Gruoch. "It's gorgeous."

"There are a couple of other styles I can show you," said Mo. She created two long braids. She added a fringe. She swept the hair back in a ponytail. She pulled it into a bun.

Gruoch enthused over the different looks and then said, "Can I have it like hers?" indicating Ina, her hair plaited in a circlet on top of her head.

Another snap of the fingers and it was done.

"That's the one. You look a dream," breathed Ina.

"Perfect for a Scottish queen," sighed Mina.

Then it was decided that Ina's hairstyle had to change to avoid detracting from the royal one. Then Mina's had to change to complement Ina's, and Mo did a quick renovation of her own hair to blend in.

"Have you thought about doing this professionally?" I asked. "You're no longer in thrall to Hecate. You can do whatever you want. You could be a witch slash hair stylist."

Mo wrinkled her button nose. "I'd prefer something more challenging. Styling hair's too easy. I'll keep it as a hobby."

Ina looked critically at her sisters. "Now Mo's fixed our locks and tresses, we need beautiful new dresses."

She snapped her fingers and Gruoch was suddenly clad in an emerald silk dress with long flared sleeves that looked as though it had come straight from Byzantium. Another snap of the fingers and the three sisters were no longer in black hooded cloaks but in pale pink versions of Gruoch's frock. They looked a bit like bridesmaids, which I supposed was appropriate since they'd missed out on being at the wedding.

Mo suddenly snapped her fingers at me and my hodden grey turned hodden silver.

Macbeth was prodded awake to admire the results.

"You look even more lovely than usual, my darling," he said. "That colour suits you so well. And what a smart fool. But who are these lovely ladies?"

Despite having visited the witches so recently, he had no recollection of it. The forgetfulness spell they had put on him was obviously effective.

Now Ina snapped her fingers like a stage hypnotist. Macbeth blinked like a volunteer from the audience being brought out from under.

"Ina? Mina? Mo? What are you doing here?"

"They've come for the coronation," said Gruoch. "Which will start fairly soon, by the way."

"I should go and get changed," said Macbeth.

"There's no need, we'll kit you out," said Ina.

"Family's what it's all about," rhymed Mina sententiously, snapping her fingers. Macbeth was no longer in his dark woollen tunic and trousers, but in robes of cloth of gold redolent of Venice. He looked simultaneously majestic and stylish.

Mo eyed him critically, snapped her fingers, and his hair and beard were neatly trimmed.

"Well now," murmured Gruoch, "don't you look handsome?" She glided towards him with a glint in her eye.

"With the coronation imminent, I think we should wake your brother-in-law and King Duncan," I said quickly in order to prevent an embarrassing public display of affection.

Gruoch changed trajectory and gave Macdeath's shoulder a bit of a shake. He lurched to his feet.

"This is my brother," said Macbeth.

"And these are my sisters," said Gruoch.

There was a polite exchange of "Nice to meet you".

Frank meanwhile was standing on Duncan's chest, batting at his face. Duncan sneezed loudly, dislodging his visitor, and sat up.

"This is King Duncan, who isn't dead," said Gruoch. "My liege, may I present my sisters?"

Ina, Mina and Mo boggled a bit at the sight of the Jimmy wig with its tartan toorie, but quickly hid their reaction with low curtsies. Duncan gave a self-effacing wave of the hand, insisting he was no longer king, while Gruoch insisted he was king until the coronation.

"So this proves I'm not a murderer," she said.

There was a furtive conversation among the sisters and then Ina, who seemed to have been designated as spokes-sister, said, "Gruoch, if you didn't kill your first man, are you wed still?"

Macbeth, Macdeath and Duncan had another coughing fit. Gruoch glared at them and I thought it wise to intervene.

"He's sadly deceased because of a pig."

The three sisters nodded as though this made perfect sense, but I distinctly heard someone mumble "oink oink" and decided there needed to be a rapid change of subject. The witches' future employment seemed as good a topic as any. I had unsuccessfully suggested hairdressing to Mo, but her sisters already had aspirations.

"Lady Gruoch and your thaneship," I said, "you'll soon have a peace dividend, which means you can focus on being a sophisticated European court, fostering the creative arts. May I suggest that you sponsor a makar and a scriever?"

"A what and a what?" asked Macdeath.

"A poet laureate and its prose equivalent," I said. "They could write things to celebrate special events, like birthdays, and do wee personalised pieces for visiting ambassadors. It would give you international cachet."

Gruoch considered this. "What do you think, my darling?" she asked.

"Whatever you think, my darling," said Macbeth.

"I think we should do it," said Gruoch. "Although it's going to be difficult to find people with the necessary skills. We may have to import them from the continent."

"Look no further," I said. "Allow me to present witch slash makar Ina and witch slash scriever Mina."

"Oh, girls," said Gruoch emotionally. "That would be wonderful. Ina, from the moment you could talk, you were always making up poems. But Mina, what about you? You always made up poems as well."

Ina gave Mina a dismissive look. "She just copies. I'm the poet."

Mina gave a gasp of outrage.

But Ina, undeterred, said, "That's the truth, and well you know it."

For a moment, I thought there was going to be trouble. Then Mina said slowly, "Too much rhyming, I suppose. Time to try my hand at prose."

This led to another group hug, punctuated by squawks of "Mind my hair!"

The chapel door opened and in walked a monk, his appearance so distinguished and imperious that he could only be the abbot. His jaw dropped as he took in the scene.

I rushed up to him. "Father Abbot," I said, my tone sombre. "We've been holding a vigil for the late king in preparation for the coronation. The future queen is in terrible distress over his passing, and is being comforted by her ladies-in-waiting."

The abbot put his hand up to his mouth and said in a low voice, "But I thought she murdered him."

"Yes, of course she did, but it's important to keep up appearances," I whispered back. More loudly, I said, "If you could give us a little more time to allow the future queen to compose herself. And some breakfast would be nice."

He didn't respond and I saw he was peering beyond me, at Duncan. For a moment, I thought we had been rumbled. And then I realised he was particularly focused on the Jimmy wig with its vibrant tartan hat.

"I see you have your own priest, and a high-ranking one at that," he murmured. "This is really embarrassing, but I don't recognise what order he's from."

I remembered the Gaelic phrase for freelance, which I'd already found useful. "He works on his own head," I said.

"I see that," said the abbot. "That's a remarkable mitre he's got on it." He bowed low to Duncan with a reverential "Your Venerability". No bow for impending royalty, I noticed, since their power was purely temporal, but he recognised a superior churchman when he saw one.

He showed no sign of leaving and I realised he was waiting for a greeting from Duncan.

"Vow of silence," I explained. "And he's never at his best until he's had his breakfast."

"I'll get that organised at once," said the abbot, dashing off, and shortly afterwards we had porridge that was neither thin nor meagre but creamy and solid. I was just about to start on my bowlful when Macdeath tapped me on the shoulder and indicated that he wanted to talk to me on my own. Gruoch and her sisters were chatting away, making up for lost time, and Duncan was giving Macbeth lessons in kingship, so there was no problem slipping away to a transept, taking my porridge with me.

"Can I help?" I asked. It's every Blainer's *raison d'être*, helping wherever we can.

"Do you remember when we first met, you wanted to know a secret I'd never told anyone?" he asked.

"That's not entirely correct," I said. "It was a game of truth or dare, and there was no expectation on my part that you would tell me."

"But I want to tell you," he said.

This was a change from when he had been rotating wildly in a bid to lick his elbow. I was immediately on my guard, wondering what on earth he was going to say.

"Being an undertaker," he said. "It's a good job. Steady work."

I hoped he was going to tell me that was because of the warriors all killing one another, and the generally reduced life expectancy in the eleventh century, not that he had been murdering people in the interest of boosting his wages. People seemed to take a very phlegmatic view of murder in this era.

And then it struck me that he could be incredibly useful in providing information for my monograph. There are no accurate figures for life expectancy in the early Middle Ages because of the paucity of records. But who could provide more accurate information than an undertaker?

"I wonder if you could—" I was beginning as he burst out, "I don't want to be an undertaker. I want to be a fool."

I was so taken aback that I nearly dropped my porridge.

"There," he said defiantly, "I've said it."

He must have seen my change of expression as the porridge bowl tilted, and misinterpreted it, since he added, "You were so helpful with my sister-in-law's sisters, getting them court appointments. But please don't think I'm after your job as court fool. That could never happen – you're an expert, and I've never told a joke in my life. But would you consider giving me a couple of lessons? I'm not getting any younger, and I'd like to start practising as soon as possible."

I looked round. The rest of them were still chatting so much that they had barely started their porridge.

"No time like the present," I said. I taught him the basics, and he was really good, with a perfect grasp of the knock-knock jokes.

"Knock knock," he said.

"Who's there?" I asked.

"Dozen," he said.

"Dozen who?" I responded.

Neither too quickly nor too slowly, he delivered the punchline, "Dozen anybody want to let me in?"

"What you really need," I said, "is your own schtick."

"Like a spurtle?" he asked. "Or for the pig's bladder?"

"Not a stick," I said. "You need a gimmick. A catchphrase."

"Like oink oink?" he said. "Or knock knock?"

"Exactly," I said.

I was going to suggest a few things when he suddenly dashed over to the coffin with a look of dismay.

"The coffin is too light!" he exclaimed. "There's not nearly enough food in here to convince the pall bearers that they're carrying a body."

I forbore to mention that this was because he and Duncan had been scoffing the latest provisions.

"We can't ask the monks for more food now just as we're going to the coronation – it would be too suspicious," he said. "My liege, I'm sorry, you're going to have to get back in."

"Oh," said Duncan sadly. "I was looking forward to being at the coronation. Still, I suppose I'll hear the trees talking about it en route to Iona, and that will be almost as good."

Gruoch clutched his arm. "But you must be there, my liege. We wouldn't be having a coronation if it weren't for you. It wouldn't be the same without you."

"Well, someone's going to have to get in the coffin to make up the weight," said Macdeath stubbornly.

Under other circumstances, I might have volunteered, but first I wanted to go to the coronation as well, and secondly, I had had a close encounter with a coffin on a previous mission and the recollection was making me feel a bit queasy.

"Can I help?" asked Ina hesitantly. "What is it you need sorting?"

I counted the beats and it definitely wasn't trochaic tetrameter.

"Ina, I think you might be speaking in prose," I said.

She beamed delightedly. "You recognised it? I thought I would have a go. Now that I'm a makar, I want to keep my poetry for special occasions. I'm going to create epics about how brave Macbeth is and how lovely Gruoch's hair is."

"And how Gruoch overpowered the queen of the witches," I reminded her. "But in the meantime, could you conjure up food in the coffin that amounts to the same weight as King Duncan?"

Ina measured up Duncan with a professional eye. I could see her making some quick calculations.

"Could I have some more nettles?" asked Duncan. "I'd like to make soup when I get to Iona, and they might not have nettles there."

We had only just finished stacking the compostable bags when the tree pall bearers turned up. They were now part of the coronation ceremony. The trees had been desperate to stay for the festivities, but the clincher was the accompanying thanes, who weren't going to miss a party before setting off on the trek to Iona.

The procession began to take shape: first, the pall bearers, followed by Macdeath the undertaker, then Macbeth and Gruoch, followed by the ladies-in-waiting slash bridesmaids. The abbot appeared with a phalanx of monks and the future king and queen halted to let the Church take precedence.

"But where is his venerability?" called the abbot anxiously. "He must lead us, since he will crown the new monarchs."

"Give Duncan the crowns," hissed Gruoch to Macbeth.

"What?" said Macbeth uneasily.

"Our crowns. The gold things that get put on our heads. You did remember them?"

He hesitated, then whispered, "I think they must be back at the castle. Sorry."

Gruoch gave a snort of exasperation. "It's the wedding all over again," she muttered to her sisters. "Could he find the rings? Eventually it turned out he'd left them with the porter, who wouldn't leave the door in case of gatecrashers."

"Have you still got your circlet?" I whispered to Duncan. "Then at least we'd have one crown."

"Yes, but it's under my wig," he whispered back. "I daren't take the wig off or everyone will recognise me."

There was one last hope. I glanced in my pouch.

"Don't worry," I began, "I can give—" but the abbot, having caught wind of all the whispering, looked in our direction and spotted the tartan toorie.

"Your Venerability! Your Venerability!" he called, scuttling down the line towards us. "Please, come with me. We must set out immediately."

The procession began to move.

"Wait," said Macbeth in a commanding, kingly way and the procession stopped.

"This is a day of celebration," he said. "We need joy, laughter. Fool, join us."

I slipped in behind the witches and off we went again. The porter opened the door to the outside world for us, and I could see his lips moving. He was counting us all out, and I was pretty sure he would insist on counting us all back in individually.

The route to the Moot Hill, the ceremonial mount, was lined with Birnam Wood and well-wishers, all cheering, the citizenry waving their hands while the trees waved their branches. When we reached the bottom of the hill, the pall bearers set down the coffin with its filling of compostable bags, leaving Macbeth and Gruoch to walk on past it. It was a particularly significant piece of symbolism, I thought, reminding everyone that Gruoch had murdered Duncan, and they had better watch it.

The flat top of the Moot Hill wasn't that big, so the abbot and his phalanx of monks also peeled off. Duncan set off up the slope, followed by Macbeth, Gruoch and the witches. I joined on the end, so that I could sort out the problem of the crowns. I didn't intend to steal the royal party's thunder, but as we climbed up the hill, amid the wild cheering of the throng below, I heard a distinct ripple of "oink oink".

When we reached the summit, I nearly fell over in excitement. There sat a block of red sandstone, the sacred Stone of Destiny itself, used for centuries at the coronation of Scotland's monarchs.

Back in the twenty-first century I had seen it in Edinburgh Castle – or at least I thought I had. There's long been controversy about whether it's the real one or a fake. But now here I was, right next to what was definitely the original. If only I could take a photo, I could compare and contrast. I glanced in my pouch in case Miss Blaine had let me have my phone, but no luck. I would just have to commit it to memory.

Duncan stepped forward and raised his arms in a call for silence. He got it. It continued. As a non-speaking celebrant, he was unable to break it. For a ghastly moment, I wondered whether the coronation would be held through the medium of interpretive dance. Then Duncan shot me a helpless look and I realised it was again down to me.

"Friends, Scots, countrypersons," I shouted. "His venerability has taken a vow of silence, but he wants me to thank you all for coming here today and let you know that it looks as if it's going to stay dry."

A cheer went up at this. I looked across at Duncan, who nodded graciously, and smiled beneficently on the assembled throng.

"Since there's nothing to hear from up here, I wonder if I could ask the lads from the abbey to sing a wee song or two to accompany the ceremony?"

The abbot nodded to the phalanx, and they started up some quite jaunty polyphony, appropriate to the festive atmosphere.

Meanwhile, up on the Moot Hill, Macbeth and Gruoch were kneeling in front of Duncan, who had his back to the audience. The sisters stood behind them in a protective semi-circle, resulting in the future royals being shielded from public view.

"This is awful," said Duncan. "A coronation without crowns. What are we going to do?"

"I told you not to worry," I soothed him. "I've got them right here. Mo, I'll pass them to you, you pass them to Mina, Mina passes them to Ina and Ina passes them to the king."

"I won't be king for much longer," chuckled Duncan. "And then it's FREEDOM!"

"Thanks for the reassurance," said Macbeth gloomily.

"Stop moaning," said Gruoch. "You want to be king, remember."

"I do, do I?" said Macbeth. "Not as much as you want to be queen."

We could definitely do without a domestic.

"Listen," I said, "I'm not just a fool, I'm a fool from the future. And I can tell you that you two are going to be brilliant. Everyone's going to love you, the country's going to be in great shape, and you really are going to go on that holiday to France and Italy. So let's get you crowned, okay?"

Macbeth and Gruoch looked at each other apologetically, and the next thing they were giving each other a great big kiss. I decided that they did make a good team.

I opened my pouch, took out the two party hats, unfolded them and handed them to Mo. With a wonderful sense of the theatrical, she held them aloft, the gold foil on the cardboard glinting in the sunlight, and the populace roared their approval, completely drowning out the polyphony.

The crowns passed from Mo to Mina to Ina to Duncan, who expertly placed them on the now royal heads. He led Macbeth and Gruoch to the Stone of Destiny, and they nimbly jumped up on it, the highest point on the Moot Hill, waving to the crowds below and receiving thunderous applause in return.

"Now what?" said Macbeth out of the corner of his mouth to Duncan.

Duncan put his folded hands in front of his face as though in prayer, so that the crowd couldn't see he was talking. "When I did it, we just went back to the abbey for mead and bannocks, and left the crowds to their own devices," he said. "But this lot are so excited that I think they need something more."

"But what?" asked Macbeth.

"Leave it to me," I said. "You two stay up there and just smile and wave."

I turned to the crowd.

"The king and queen have decreed this a day of joy and laughter. What better way to mark it than with a few jokes?"

There were immediate cries of "knock knock" and "oink oink".

"A new dawn for Scotland and new jokes for the Scots," I proclaimed. "Please bid a warm welcome to MacBhàis, brother to the king and brother-in-law to the queen."

At the foot of the Moot Hill, Macdeath, stationed beside the coffin, looked at me in mingled disbelief and anticipation.

"Come on up," I said.

Encouraged by the pall bearers, he sprinted up the hill to stand beside me.

"You really think I'm ready?" he whispered.

"More than ready," I whispered back. "I'll start and we'll take it from there." Raising my voice, I told the crowd, "I knew a thane with one leg called Macduff."

I nodded to Macdeath, who shouted, "What was his other leg called?"

Amid the eruption of hilarity, I whispered, "Now the wolfhound."

"My wolfhound has no nose!" yelled Macdeath.

"How does it smell?" I asked.

"Terrible!" he bellowed.

People were laughing so hard that they were falling over, and the trees were no longer capable of holding their branches upright, but were leaning on them for support.

I nudged Macdeath. "I say," I said.

He took a step forward. "I say, I say, I say!"

"He says, he says, he says!" responded the crowd.

"Why did the vassal get a bag of gold from the king? Because he was out standing in his field. I say, I say, I say!"

"He says, he says, he says!"

"What do you call a bee that can't make up its mind? A maybe. I say, I say, I say!"

"He says, he says, he says!"

Gradually, it dawned on Macdeath that he was on his own. He

was the eleventh-century equivalent of the kid learning to ride a bike whose mum was no longer holding on to it. He shot me a quick grin but, trouper that he was, he didn't miss a beat or a punchline.

It was quite tiring for Macbeth and Gruoch to keep standing on the Stone of Destiny, especially as it wasn't that big. The crowd was so engrossed in the jokes that the duo could step down unnoticed, and then climb down the Moot Hill along with the sisters, Duncan and myself.

"He's great, isn't he?" Macbeth asked me with his shy smile. "I know I'm biased, but I think he's even better than you."

I felt I had done all of the groundwork, teaching the thanes and servants how to respond to interactive comedy, but Macdeath was Macbeth's brother, so I just said, "He's very good."

Gruoch fixed her husband with a steely look. "We're not having two fools, if that's what you're angling for. One's more than enough."

"There could be a vacancy sooner you think," I said. "I'm not going to be around for ever."

"I'm sorry to hear that," said Gruoch sympathetically before edging away and adding, "It's not the plague, is it?"

"I'm in perfect health," I said. "It's just that I'm from another time, and I expect to be taken back there shortly." I hoped that was true. Miss Blaine might have been sending me useful items via the pouch, but there had been no direct communication. If my return depended on the successful completion of my mission, I could be here long enough, since I no longer had any idea what my mission was.

"I should get back to the pall bearers," said Duncan. "I'm sure Birnam Wood and the accompanying thanes will want to head off fairly soon."

"We'll come and see you as soon as we can," Gruoch assured him, giving him a hug. "And if you keep the wig and the monk's cassock, you can come back here whenever you like and nobody will know. Just remember not to talk to anyone on the way."

Duncan nodded, beaming. "That's a great idea."

He bade us all farewell and went to join the trees.

I felt slightly melancholy, which didn't fit with the celebratory mood, so I decided to go for a walk on my own. I switched to unobtrusive mode so that I could pass through the crowds, and was soon well away from the party atmosphere. And then I sensed I wasn't on my own. I stopped and looked around, but could see nobody.

"Who's there?" I called sharply but there was no answer. I set off again, still with the uncomfortable feeling of being stalked, like a game of cat and mouse.

"Frank," I said, "I know you're there."

The black cat with the white spot on his chest emerged from the undergrowth.

"I was hoping to have a word," he said.

I sat down. "If you want me to apologise again for soaking you, I will," I said wearily. "But honestly, it wasn't intentional."

"I've come to apologise to you," he said. "This is the first chance I've had to talk to you on your own. I knew all about Duncan's plan to fake his own death, and when you turned up, I thought you had come to stop it. That was why I lured you into the waste disposal tunnel." He shook himself disgustedly. "Horrible place. And I'm sorry for attacking you when you attacked Gruoch. I didn't realise you thought you were protecting Duncan."

"Apology accepted," I said, stroking his head. "And I should probably thank you. When Macbeth was trying to demonstrate how he murdered Duncan, he was so incompetent that he might have inadvertently stabbed me to death. When you knocked him off balance, I presume that was deliberate?"

"Absolutely," he said. "I was suspicious of you, but that didn't mean I was happy to see you get killed."

"In that case, I'll definitely thank you," I said. "But if you knew Gruoch wasn't a murderer, why didn't you tell me it wasn't true when Mo said she was? And why didn't you try to get the sisters reconciled?"

Frank pondered this. "When I was at the castle, I went along with what Gruoch said, and when I was in the witches' cavern, I went along with what they said. It just seemed easier that way."

You would never get a dog thinking like that. But I recognised that it wasn't just Frank who had got things wrong.

"I have no idea any more why I'm here," I confided. "I thought protecting Duncan was my mission, so that he wouldn't be murdered in Glamis, but would die in battle fighting Macbeth near Elgin."

"Why on earth would he fight Macbeth?" asked Frank. "They're friends."

"I don't know," I said. "Nothing makes sense. I've no idea what's fact and what's fiction."

"In the end, truth will out," he said in a comforting tone.

I recognised the line. "That's from *The Merchant of Venice*, isn't it?"

Frank nodded, surprised.

"I've noticed that you keep quoting Shakespeare," I said.

He arched his back angrily.

"Quoting Shakespeare? I've never quoted that poser in my life. A self-publicist like that doesn't need any more help from me."

"But you're saying lines from his plays," I said.

"*His* plays?"

Frank's fur was standing on end now and, for a moment, I thought he was going to go for me with his claws again. And then I saw him relax again.

"Ah, I understand your confusion," he said. "You don't understand how theatre works, but don't worry, that's not your fault. We can't all be members of the cognoscenti."

I was about to inform him that I was a season ticket holder in all of the Edinburgh theatres, and had seen Sir Ian McKellen and Sir Patrick Stewart in *Waiting for Godot* at the King's, when he went on, "Shakespeare insists on getting his name on the playbills because he's the director of the King's Men theatre company, but that doesn't mean he actually writes the plays. It's an easy mistake for someone like you to make."

I wasn't impressed by being talked down to in this way, especially not by a cat. "I'm perfectly aware of the difference between the director and the playwright, thank you," I said. "And if Shakespeare isn't writing the plays, who is?"

"I am," said Frank.

I was about to make a quip about how difficult it must be to hold a quill in his paw when I remembered that he wasn't a cat back in seventeenth-century London. He was a lawyer, a statesman, a natural philosopher and apparently a playwright as well. And he was always in debt.

Suddenly I realised what had been staring me in the face, although it would have stared me in the face more obviously if he hadn't looked like a cat.

"You're not Frank," I blurted out. "I know who you are – you're Sir Francis Bacon."

"Honestly, I prefer Frank," he said. "But you're not from my time. How have you heard of me?"

I was beyond excited to be in the presence of England's lord chancellor, even if he currently looked like a big black cat with a white spot on its chest.

"You're famous," I said breathlessly. "Four centuries on, we're all still talking about you. The scientific method you developed, having a hypothesis and then collecting empirical evidence, and seeing whether it corroborates your theory or not – that's been the foundation of scientific research."

Frank's ears twitched forward and he purred loudly.

"Your essays," I said. "Beautifully written. Very thought-provoking. Then there's your legal work, where you've been an inspiration as a real reformer. And," I said reverently, "when you were talking about your library, I thought you were just a dilettante. But now that I know who you are, I can tell you that your cataloguing system is genius."

His purring stopped and he looked at me as though he was waiting for something.

"What's the matter?" I said. "Are you hungry? I don't have any cat food. Couldn't you just go out and catch a m…" I was horrified when I realised what I had been about to say. "Couldn't you just go to the kitchen and find some nice vegetables?" I concluded.

Frank's ears folded back and his tail began thumping on the ground, a sure sign of an aggrieved cat.

"You haven't mentioned my plays," he said. "I put my heart and soul into those scripts. Are you telling me they're not famous?"

"They're incredibly famous," I babbled. "I was saving the best till last. Every one a winner. *The Taming of the Shrew*, *Richard II*, *Romeo and Juliet*, *The Tempest*…"

Too late, I realised my mistake.

"I've never written a play called *The Tempest*," he said in a puzzled voice.

"You will, Frank, you will," I said. And then it struck me that if he stayed in eleventh-century Scotland, he wouldn't.

"You have to go back," I said. "You've not only got more plays to write, but you're going to become lord chancellor."

He gave a heartfelt sigh. "That would be nice. I'd like to go back, but really, I can't. Not with all my debts. If you want to live comfortably in London, you need money. Lots of it."

"The situation hasn't improved any over the years," I said. "But couldn't you borrow some? No, don't tell me. Neither a borrower nor a lender be."

"I like that," Frank exclaimed. "Nice turn of phrase. Can I use it?"

"Be my guest," I said.

"You know," he said thoughtfully, "there's a character in one of my plays that that line would be perfect for. He's pompous, he's self-important, he likes giving advice – I can really hear him saying it. I could add a speech with that in it, and a few more aphorisms. But you've really confused me, telling me I should go back to London. I'd like to be lord chancellor, but I don't want to be arrested for debt. And then there's Mo. I just don't know what to do. Should I stay or should I go? I feel really indecisive."

"That sounds like one of your characters as well," I said. "In the same play, if I'm not mistaken."

He stared at me. "What are you talking about?"

"*Hamlet*," I said. "Polonius is the character that you can give the aphorisms to. And the eponymous Prince of Denmark is indecisive."

"No he's not," said Frank. "It starts with him discovering his uncle has murdered his father, so then he kills his uncle. It's one of my shorter plays."

"Have you thought about revamping it a bit?" I said. "I'm sure the groundlings would prefer something longer. They like to get their money's worth. Have him taking a while to work out what his uncle's done, and then he can lay a trap to prove his uncle's guilt. Pad it out by having him think a lot in soliloquies."

"You're good at this," said Frank admiringly. "Have you written a lot of plays?"

"I wrote a pantomime with a couple of friends in sixth year," I said. "But honestly, nothing in the same league as you."

I became aware of a figure trudging towards us. Mo.

"I don't want her to know I've been talking about going back," said Frank urgently. "I haven't decided. I might stay here. Don't say anything."

He disappeared into the undergrowth just before Mo reached me.

"Do you mind if I join you?" she said. "I was finding all the laughing and cheering and celebrating a bit much."

"What's the matter?" I asked.

She sighed. "Everything seems to be working out for everyone. Duncan's off to his croft, Gruoch and Macbeth are running the place, Ina's a makar, Mina's a scriever, and Macbeth's brother's got every thane in the country begging him to be their fool. And I've no idea what I'm going to do."

"You're a witch," I said. "You can do anything."

"No I can't," she said. "I can't make Heml— Frank turn back into a person because he doesn't want me to. And I don't understand why he doesn't want me to."

"It's a pretty good life, being a cat," I said.

"But it must be so limiting," she said. "Those few seconds when I saw him – I could tell how clever he was. If it was me, I would want to be back in the world, doing experiments, contributing to the world's store of knowledge, making a difference."

She couldn't have spoken more passionately if she had been a Blainer.

"You've answered your own question about what you're going to do," I said. "And never forget, you'll always be a witch. You can combine that with anything."

Frank had misjudged me, but I had also misjudged him when I thought he was part of the murder plot. Then, I had been determined to keep him and Mo apart, and never to let him find out her skill as an alchemist.

"Could you show me that spell again, where you turn thin air into gold?" I asked casually.

There was a rustling in the undergrowth and I was aware that we had Frank's attention.

"Of course," said Mo. "It's easy." A sweep of her hand, and there was a gold goblet lying on the ground.

Frank rushed forward and seized it in his teeth. I realised he was checking whether it was real gold or not.

"Heml— Frank!" said Mo, going slightly pink. "Where did you come from?"

"How did she do that?" Frank demanded. "Ask her how she did that."

Given that Mo was such a talented witch, it felt odd that I was the only person who could speak to Frank and interpret for him. But then she didn't share our experience of the animal world.

"He wants to know how you did that," I said.

"I just think gold," she said, sweeping her hand again. Another goblet appeared on the grass.

"Is he impressed?" she ventured.

"This could keep me out of the debtors' prison," he said

excitedly. "I could go back to London and be lord chancellor and rewrite *Hamlet* and write *The Tempest* and develop my library cataloguing system. I could do it with Mo by my side, if she would consent to be my … consort."

I shot him a suspicious look.

"My life's companion," he elaborated. "Would she consider coming to London with me? If not, I'll stay here."

This was serious. A library cataloguing system was at stake.

"He's very impressed indeed," I told Mo. "He comes from the seventeenth century, which is six hundred years in the future. That would be exciting, wouldn't it, having access to the white heat of technology? You could be involved in ground-breaking research if you agreed to move to London with Frank. He's asking if you would go as his companion – his life's companion, not anything unsavoury—"

I hadn't even finished when she said, "Yes!" and lifted Frank up so that she could kiss him on the nose. And then she was no longer kissing a cat's nose but a future lord chancellor's nose, and then they were kissing one another's lips and I was coughing loudly to alert them to my presence before things went too far.

Eleven

We were back in Glamis Castle, the porter once again at his post, checking everyone through the new spyhole. The thanes had all returned to their thanedoms, and in the great dining hall, it was just family and me.

Mo and Frank had the place of honour next to the king and queen. Mo, still dressed in her pink frock, and Frank, in the standard thane's outfit of dark woollen tunic and trousers, explained that they had wanted to mark the royal coronation in a special way and so they had got engaged. All of the family members were thrilled, so I tried to maintain a cheerful expression. But I was in danger of giving way to despair. With Duncan's safe departure to Iona, I had no idea what my mission was, and if I couldn't accomplish it, what was to become of me? I focused on my abdomen in the hope of feeling a twinge that would signal I was on the way home, but nothing was happening.

Gruoch and Macbeth were eagerly planning their continental trip, poring over a map that I'd tried to explain was less than accurate. Mo was conjuring up an entire gold dinner service as a belated wedding present. Macdeath was trying out new jokes on the serving staff, several of whom were laughing so much that they were in danger of dropping their trays. Ina was busy experimenting with a new rhyme scheme Frank had taught her, although when I referred to it as a Shakespearean sonnet, he got quite tetchy. He was now sitting with Mina, explaining public demand when it came to prose, while she made notes on sheets of vellum.

"You've got to make it interesting," he said. "Nobody wants to read about boring ordinary lives. Look at King Macbeth. A lovely man, but if you wrote about him the way he really is, nobody would be interested. But we're writers – we can turn anybody into anything, it's verbal alchemy."

Verbal alchemy, Mina wrote.

"I've started working on something myself," said Frank. "It's going to have all of you in it – well, not King Macbeth's brother because he's just like a bigger, hairier King Macbeth. But even the porter's going to be in it, and Birnam Wood, and there's going to be a ghost, and apparitions."

"That sounds really complicated," said Mina.

"It's a bit advanced for you at this stage. Remember I've been writing plays for years," said Frank.

"I don't think I could ever write a play," said Mina. "It's all the dialogue. I think I'm better with description."

"That's great, go with that," said Frank. "Just don't get bogged down with factual detail. Always ask yourself the 'what ifs'. What if King Macbeth killed Queen Gruoch's first husband? What if he killed King Duncan in a violent battle near Elgin?"

"Excuse me," I said. "I was the one who mentioned that."

"And always keep your ears open for interesting snippets of conversation that you can use," Frank told Mina.

I was beginning to see where the historical misinformation was going to come from. Another thing to mention in my monograph. And then I asked myself who was going to believe it if I wrote about Sir Francis Bacon being a cat, and King Duncan wearing a Jimmy wig while faking his own death, and Gruoch, granddaughter of Kenneth III, having three weird sisters? And how was I ever going to write it, if Miss Blaine had abandoned me here?

Without warning, a sudden violent spasm overtook me, and I doubled up.

"Are you all right?" exclaimed Frank, dashing to catch me before I fell.

"What's the matter?" cried Mo, running over and grabbing my arm.

"I'm ... fine," I gulped before I was caught up in an icy cold vortex, my stomach churning as century after century whirled by. Mo and Frank were still hanging on to me. Despite the discomfort, I was still *compos mentis* enough to think of trying to drop them off at the seventeenth century. But I couldn't be sure of getting the date right, and another thought suddenly reappeared and was now preoccupying me. Had the kettle in the library kitchenette switched itself off, or had it set the library ablaze?

If the latter, I would be pilloried as "Book Burner McMonagle" and stripped of my librarian qualifications. I would be a social pariah. Nobody would talk to me, not even the Waitrose checkout staff. I would have to move. Perhaps I could go to the seventeenth century with Mo and Frank.

With a lurch, the three of us landed at Miss Blaine's feet. We were in the library kitchenette, and her hand was at the kettle.

"I wondered where you'd disappeared to," the Founder said grumpily. "I waited, but eventually since nothing was happening, I came through to make my own tea. I've just this minute switched on the kettle."

It was a great relief to see Miss Blaine, as cantankerous as ever, not burned to a crisp. I had switched the kettle on myself just as I was caught up in my mission, and I was relieved to find it had switched itself off. I hauled myself to my feet and surreptitiously ran a hand down it: it was still warm. That suggested I was returning to the library fairly soon after leaving it.

Mo and Frank edged past me so that they were out of the Founder's direct line of vision. They were still in their eleventh-century clothes, but I was relieved to find my hodden silver replaced by my normal librarian's outfit.

"Let me make the tea, Miss Blaine," I said. "You go and have a seat and I'll bring it through."

"But where did you get to?" she asked irritably.

This was worryingly forgetful of her. But now that I knew she was a hundred years older than I had estimated, I supposed she was entitled to the odd lapse of memory.

"I've been on a mission," I said, slowly and fairly loudly in case her hearing was going as well.

"No need to shout," she said. "And did you find the book you were looking for?"

"Not a library mission, Miss Blaine. I've been on a mission to the eleventh century. I met Macbeth, King of Scots."

"Yes, we were just speaking about him," she said. "But you mean you've been off on your mission and this is you back? How many days have you been away?"

She had made it very clear on my very first mission that I was allowed a maximum of a calendar week.

"I'm not sure," I said. "It involved a lot of night working, so the days merged into one another, but it's definitely not as many as seven."

Miss Blaine took a pocket watch out of her pocket, peered at it, shook it, held it up to her ear and shook it again.

"No, it's no use. I didn't realise you'd gone, so I didn't set the timer."

"But Miss Blaine, you must have known," I said, which earned me a ferocious glare. I quailed, but was determined to say my piece. "There was an awful bit where I was trying to contact you, but I couldn't get through. But then I realised you were all right when I found you had sent me the compostable bags."

"Compostable bags?" she echoed disbelievingly. "You think I would send you compostable bags?"

"I needed them, and they were there in my pouch," I said. "You're the only person I can think of who would send them."

"You think I have nothing better to do than to micro-manage my girls' missions?" she demanded. "In that case, I would be as well, nay better, to undertake the missions myself. You are provided with the relevant necessities. I do not occupy myself with the hows and whys."

"Sorry, Miss Blaine," I said.

"As for your failure to contact me, I am not surprised. There has been the most raucous singing from downstairs, small children obsessed with wheels and buses. I could scarcely hear myself think, let alone hear what anyone else might be trying to say to me."

She turned to study Mo and Frank, who were still wedged at the back of the kitchenette, not daring to speak since they recognised the voice of authority.

"Are these some friends who've come back with you?" she asked me.

"Yes, but they're actually heading for the seventeenth century."

"And you didn't think to let them off on the way here? Now they'll have to go all the way back. Sometimes I think you don't have the sense you were born with."

"Sorry, Miss Blaine," I said. In a bid to appease her, I said, "Mo here is a wise woman."

"Certainly wise when compared to you," Miss Blaine remarked. "I take it you've assisted all of the wise women?"

Of course. At last my mission made sense. This was why Miss Blaine had sent me. Nothing to do with preventing kings being murdered, but assisting wise women. A much worthier cause.

"Everything's fine, Miss Blaine," I assured her. "Just let me get the tea."

"Very well." She crossed the corridor and went back into the meeting room.

"That's your sorceress?" breathed Mo. "She's magnificent."

It wasn't quite the word I would have used.

I reckoned we all needed some tea, and was searching for my pouch with the Earl Grey and Darjeeling blend when I realised I was back in my ordinary clothes. I retrieved the tea caddy and set a tray with more cups and saucers.

Mo observed everything closely and was particularly fascinated by the kettle.

"What a very small cauldron," she said. "And it's a very odd shape."

She was equally enthralled by the teapot, which I gave her to carry while I took the tray, and we crossed the corridor to the meeting room.

"In there," I said, too burdened with the tray to wrestle with the handle.

"Frank, get the door," said Mo, and he obeyed with gratifying alacrity, Mo's man now.

It was lucky that he stood back to let us into the room first, since *The Complete Works of William Shakespeare* was still sitting on the table. I quickly put the tray on top of it before he spotted it, behaviour I would normally deplore, but necessary for Frank's peace of mind.

Once we were all settled with tea and Bourbon biscuits, I thought I should give my report.

"I successfully rescued three wise women, including Mo here, from a toxic work environment," I told Miss Blaine.

"I encouraged them to expand their career horizons, and one is now specialising in poetry, while another is a historian," I said. "Mo has an encyclopaedic knowledge of traditional herbal remedies, and she wants to extend her expertise in this area, so she's moving to the seventeenth century to pick up on innovative research in astronomy, chemistry and natural philosophy. Then she'll blend everything for the benefit of society."

"Admirable," said the Founder. "Given the disadvantage of not having a Blaine education, it is important to begin slowly, then consolidate."

She smiled benignly at Mo. "Once you've mastered the seventeenth century, you can consider moving on to the twentieth century for string theory and biomedical engineering."

"Thanks, but I'm staying in the seventeenth century," said Mo, stroking Frank's arm.

"And the gentleman?" enquired Miss Blaine distrustfully.

"Frank is a friend of Mo's, a man of letters, a lawyer, a statesman and a natural philosopher."

Mo beamed proudly and squeezed his hand.

"Jack of all trades, master of none, I dare say," Miss Blaine sniffed loudly.

"At one point, the wise women's manager turned me into a mouse, and Frank saved my bacon," I told her.

Miss Blaine sniffed even more loudly. "I expect my girls to save their own bacon, and not to be reliant on some man."

"I was actually a cat at the time," said Frank mildly.

"Nevertheless," said Miss Blaine.

"They've both been very helpful in terms of the mission," I said. "I wonder if you might be able to take them to around 1606?"

I could see the date register with the Founder. Any moment now, she would remark that that was the year *Macbeth* was first performed. And then she would give her views on *Macbeth*.

"Frank has met Mr Shakespeare and has a very low opinion of him," I said. "He describes him as a strutting player, whose conceit lies in his hamstring, as well as a poser and self publicist."

Miss Blaine favoured him with a smile. "I see you are an excellent judge of character, young man."

"I like to think so," said Frank.

"Time travelling can be tricky for the inexperienced," she said. "Would you like me to deliver you to your destination?"

"That would be really kind of you," said Mo with enthusiasm. "I can't wait to get started on my scientific studies."

Miss Blaine bestowed an even brighter smile on her. "Very well. Let us go. If you two young people would stand here…"

They stood arm in arm, Mo in her pink frock, Frank in his thane's outfit. I imagined they would stand just like this on their wedding day, Mo in her pink frock, Frank in a fur-trimmed damask and velvet doublet, the sleeves slashed to reveal a silk shirt, set off with a massive lace ruff, and a high felt hat trimmed with an ostrich feather.

Miss Blaine's magic needed no candles, mirrors or snap of the fingers. "Off we go," she said.

An instant later, they were gone, and all I could hear was a faint cry of "Goodbye, fool" from at least a century's distance.

I lifted the tray off the *Complete Works*. We had a number of volumes of Shakespeare's plays, and a number of copies of *Macbeth*.

Frank was going to write a play, a work of fiction, in order to ingratiate himself with James VI and I. But there were some people who would take it as fact. And there were some people who would take historical accounts of Macbeth and his wife Gruoch as fact. I was the only person who knew the true story.

I pulled a notepad towards me and began copying out the words written by Miss Blaine: "The story, characters and incidents portrayed herein are fictitious. No identification with actual persons (living or deceased), places and buildings is intended or should be inferred."

I would put disclaimers in every volume of Shakespeare including *Macbeth*. If they fell out, I would replace them. And I would put them in all of the Scottish history books as well.

Someone had left a *What's On* brochure for the Edinburgh theatres on the table, the cover emblazoned with a photo of the forthcoming production of *Macbeth*. Frank hadn't written it purely to ingratiate himself with the king – with ghosts, powerful women, murder and mayhem, he wanted to enthrall audiences, including the demanding groundlings. And he had succeeded. I went off to book my ticket.

Acknowledgements

I am profoundly grateful to all of the following, without whom Shona's mission might never have been accomplished:

Sara Hunt and all at Saraband, especially editor Ali Moore;
Iain Matheson;
Al Guthrie;
Mòrag Anna NicNèill;
Yvonne Morley-Chisholm;
Arthur Cormack and Blair Douglas;
Catherine Simpson;
Marion Todd;
Dame Muriel Spark;
William Shakespeare;
Graham Greene, supporter of Dame Muriel, for his short story "A Shocking Accident";
and Alistair, who makes me as happy as a shoe.

The Author

Olga Wojtas was born and brought up in Edinburgh where she attended James Gillespie's High School – the model for Marcia Blaine School for Girls, which appears in Muriel Spark's *The Prime of Miss Jean Brodie*. Like Dame Muriel herself, Olga was encouraged to write by an inspirational English teacher there – in Olga's case, Iona M. Cameron. Unlike her heroine, Olga has a deep respect for Dame Muriel's work and is a committee member of the Muriel Spark Society. She is also current President of the Edinburgh Writers' Club. A former Scriever of the Federation of Writers Scotland, Olga won a Scottish Book Trust New Writers Award and has had more than forty short stories published in magazines and anthologies.